WHAT ELSE
BUT HOME

WHAT ELSE
BUT HOME

A NOVEL

SHARON ROLENS

BRIDGE WORKS PUBLISHING COMPANY

Bridgehampton, New York

Published by Bridge Works Publishing Company, Bridgehampton, New
York, an imprint of The Rowman & Littlefield Publishing Group.

Distributed in the United States by National Book Network, Lanham,
Maryland. For descriptions of this and other Bridge Works books, visit the
National Book Network website at www.nbnbooks.com.

FIRST EDITION

The characters and events in this book are fictitious. Any similarity to actual
persons, living or dead, is coincidental and not intended by the author.

Library of Congress Cataloging-in-Publication Data

Rolens, Sharon, 1932-
    What else but home : a novel / Sharon Rolens.— 1st ed.
        p. cm.
Sequel to: Worthy's town.
    ISBN 1-882593-75-8 (cloth: alk. paper)
    1. Journalists—Fiction. 2. City and town life—Fiction. 3. Fathers
and sons—Fiction. 4. Birthfathers—Fiction. 5. Ex-prisoners—Fiction.
6. Evangelists—Fiction. 7. Illinois—Fiction. I. Title.

    PS3568.O53328W47 2003
    813'.54—dc21
                                    2003006671
10   9   8   7   6   5   4   3   2   1

♾™ The paper used in this publication meets the minimum requirements of
American National Standard for Information Sciences—Permanence of
Paper for Printed Library Materials, ANSI/NISO Z39.48–1992.
Manufactured in the United States of America.

For my sons and daughters, Patrick Brannan, Terrie Gay, Michael Brannan, and Jennifer Wallis. For my sister, Bev Jones Gover. And again, for Darwin.

Home is the place where,
When you have to go there,
They have to take you in.

—*Robert Frost,*
"The Death of the Hired Man"

WHAT ELSE
BUT HOME

ONE

Drayton R. Hunt reached into his pocket and took out his watch. He had been a free man for two hours. Although he should have been overjoyed, he felt only bitterness. He rolled and lit a cigarette, and filled his lungs with soothing nicotine. The farm fields speeding past the train window didn't look familiar. It had been night when he made the trip in the opposite direction, handcuffed to a sweating county deputy. Three god-damned years locked away for something I never done, Drayton thought. He recognized the irony, having spent his life committing crimes without serving any time behind bars. But the day he faced a jury of farmers, accused of smothering an old woman, his luck ran out.

Slouching back in the seat, he lit another cigarette and closed his eyes. He had a long train ride ahead of him.

Earlier that morning, Drayton Hunt had walked out of the state penitentiary with twenty-five dollars in his hip pocket and an ill-fitting blue suit, courtesy of the Illinois penal system, hanging on his tall, thin frame. At age forty-seven, his dark hair had no gray except a scattering above his ears. He had not developed the characteristic paunch of middle age, and he carried himself as if he had something to be proud of. Leaving the heavy iron gates behind for good (next time he would be smarter), he hitched a ride to the Chicago & Alton train depot with a guard just getting off work and bought a one-way ticket home, a decision he hoped he wouldn't regret. He was drawn back to Old Kane, Illinois, as if the village were a woman opening her warm thighs to him.

And there was his son, born to a teenage girl, who refused to acknowledge him as his father. Drayton hoped to bring about a reconciliation and end twenty-three years of estrangement.

Drayton woke with a start when the conductor called, "Old Kane!" Gathering his few belongings, he hurried down the steep steps and headed toward Coal Hollow—a three-mile walk. He wanted to be at his mother's before dark.

Leaving the streets of Old Kane behind, he walked along the winding gravel road breathing in the clean, country smells. Prison had an odor all its own: stale cigarette smoke, cooked cabbage and onions, sex between desperate men. Drayton was sure he'd spend the rest of his life trying to forget that stench.

It might as well have been yesterday that he traveled this road; nothing had changed during his years away. Radious Biesemeyer's Jersey milk cows still grazed lazily in the pasture, and crows fussed at him from their perch atop the humming telephone wires. At Prough's Corner, he stopped alongside the dense hedgerow and broke off several branches of bittersweet entwined in the brush. Every autumn when he was a boy his mother, Mae, had sent him to gather bittersweet to decorate the kitchen table. He could still picture the look on her face as she carefully arranged the sprigs of burnt-orange berries in a vase and stood back to admire her handiwork, hands on her ample hips, head cocked to one side, as if she were studying a fine French painting.

Two miles further down the road, Mae Hunt's house came into view. Drayton shivered. He stopped by the mailbox and took in the familiar surroundings, his home since he was a boy. The small white house needed paint, and the front steps were pulling away from the porch as if to distance themselves from the rundown dwelling. The outhouse was overgrown with tiger lilies, the faded orange blossoms already dried in anticipation of winter. Suddenly Drayton was overcome with hunger for a home-cooked meal of fried chicken and mashed sweet potatoes, fresh-hulled garden peas—food he had not tasted since he last sat at his mother's table.

Taking a deep breath, he pushed the front door open and stepped inside the house. It was cold as a crypt. The sound of his footsteps bounced off the papered walls like a hard-rubber ball. Cobwebs hung from the ceiling in lacy folds, and dust bunnies and mouse droppings hid together in the corners. Drayton glanced around the tiny kitchen. Crusted dishes on the dry sink told of his mother's last meal.

When the mail carrier had found Mae Hunt lying on the kitchen floor a hot July day two years before, she had been dead a week. No one was willing to put the house in order, even after it was fumigated. Shortly before Mae's death,

Drayton's sister ran away with another woman's husband, and Franklin Linder, the undertaker, was unable to find her to make funeral arrangements. His request to the warden of the state penitentiary that Drayton be allowed to come home long enough to tend to family affairs was denied. Doing his best, Undertaker Linder put Mae Hunt in a plain pine box, wearing a cast-off dress of his wife's, and buried her in a potter's grave at Jalappa Cemetery.

Drayton continued exploring his mother's house, the floors strewn with twigs and grass dropped by nesting birds and pilfering squirrels, the windows unwashed, dust everywhere an inch thick. She had been proud of her home—tastefully furnished, meticulously clean. Every Saturday morning she got down on her hands and knees and scrubbed the pine floors until they were white. Then she carefully removed each little-girl figurine from the mahogany curio to dust and put back until the next week. She would not be happy to see the shambles her house had become.

Drayton opened the door of his sister's small room and looked at the neatly made bed where he had taught the nine-year-old girl what pleasures men want. And though painful, he looked inside his mother's room at the rumpled bed where she allowed men to satisfy their lust in ways their wives would not tolerate. Mae Hunt was born knowing the pleasures men want. As a young mother with no husband and no education, she had provided for her two children the only way she knew, by unfolding her legs to any man with folding money. Though she warned her children to stay out of sight when she was working, Drayton would always peer around the corner of the house to catch a glimpse of each man. Early on, he understood his mother's profession.

There was one man, Drayton called him the "banker," who came more often than the others. Judging from the way his mother's face would light up when he knocked at the door, he was her favorite. Sometimes after he left she'd be wearing a new trinket—golden eardrops or a strand of colorful beads.

The banker drove a 1911 Oldsmobile Limited touring car, maroon with navy blue fenders. The wheels had fancy wood spokes. It was the most beautiful motorcar Drayton had seen, and was the beginning of his lifelong love of cars. Someday I'll have me such a motorcar, he promised himself. Drayton wondered whether the banker had a snooty wife and spoiled kids who rode in the car anytime they wanted to.

"Take care of your mama, son," the banker always said, ruffling Drayton's dark hair and handing him a dime. Drayton liked to imagine that this man was his father, but he would never know for sure. When he was old enough to fully understand the intimacy of adults, Drayton doubted whether even his mother knew.

Only now, decades later, had Drayton come to terms with the secret world of Mae Hunt's bedroom. What more could a mother do than sacrifice her own body for her children—like Jesus did for His children, as the prison chaplain had preached. Drayton was sorry his mother had not lived to see him a free man again. He arranged the bouquet of bittersweet in a white vase on her dressing table and closed the door to her room.

After putting his bag in his bedroom and opening the windows to air out three years of must, Drayton went to see how his own motorcar had fared during his absence. The sagging shed that served as a garage would not survive a stiff breeze, he thought with dismay.

The 1924 Moon was covered with his mother's "flower garden" quilt, placed there the day the sheriff had taken him to jail to await trial. Carefully Drayton lifted the cover from his Moon, as if the dusty quilt might fall to pieces like Granny's short piecrust. The car had weathered the years better than he hoped. In a rare show of compassion, Judge Jurnikan had allowed him time to put his car on wood blocks and prepare it for the neglect ahead. Drayton walked around the car, modeled after a Rolls Royce, and studied its sleek lines. In spite of its years, it was still the most luxurious car around Old Kane.

Although he had little appetite, Drayton went in search of food; he had not eaten since his final breakfast in prison that morning. The pantry shelves held rock-hard sacks of sugar and wormy flour, canned goods (some bulging from spoiled contents), an unopened bag of Eight O'Clock coffee.

"This is one hell of a homecoming, Mama," he said out loud, as if his words would make his mother appear and life would be as it once was.

Drayton sat alone in the darkening kitchen, lit by a single bulb that hung above the table, and ate from a can of pork and beans. The beans tasted a little off, but they filled his stomach. Swallowing the last forkful and washing it down with sulphury well water, he made a promise to himself: "As God is my witness, I'm through living like a goddamned bum!"

The next morning, Drayton was up early. It would take a month of mornings to break the habit of rising before daylight. He hadn't slept well on the soft mattress, accustomed as he had been for three years to a hard prison bed. And he missed the sounds of the other inmates throughout the night—the swearing, the sobbing.

He found overalls and a faded blue work shirt in the closet and dressed quickly. The room was cold for September. He hoped there was enough wood already cut to take the chill off the house. Before winter he would have to lay in a supply of kindling and seasoned oak logs. After three years of sitting, he would welcome the hard work.

Though Drayton didn't plan to wear his drab prison release suit again, he hung it in the closet and put his underwear and socks in a drawer. (His mother had always liked an orderly house.) He threw away his prison shoes, a size too small. He had blisters on both feet from yesterday's walk.

Drayton laid his Bible on top of the bureau, alongside his comb and cigarette papers. The imitation leather Bible had been a parting gift from Chaplain Davenport. "Good luck to God's newest fisher of men, L. Davenport," was the neatly written inscription. Drayton thought back to the days leading up to his first meeting with the dedicated chaplain.

When the prison guard escorted Drayton down the long corridor to his cell, men already behind bars hooted and shouted insults, or made loud sucking noises to entice the newcomer to look their way.

"Come 'ere, honey, I got something big and juicy for you!"

"Suck it yourself!" Drayton said. The guard laughed. Drayton had heard stories about men locked away from women. No matter what, he would never become some tattooed bully's whore.

Drayton would not forget the sound of the cell door clanging shut. Exhausted, angry at the way life treated him, he fell on top of the cot and tried to sleep, but it was no use. The lumpy mattress was stiff with urine and jism, and something skittered across the floor, a mouse or a rat. He thought of his beloved Moon motorcar rusting away in the shed. He had never known such despair.

During his first few days of imprisonment, Drayton sat in his tiny cell smoking one Lucky Strike after another, seldom eating, sitting alone in the courtyard during the exercise period. He could not afford to attract attention to himself—the new vulnerable guy on the cell block who didn't know the score.

As a boy, Drayton acquired the reputation of a bully—the only way the poor, homely son of Mae Hunt could survive. This truth he knew instinctively at a young age, coming to him as naturally as language.

Growing up lonely taught Drayton that he couldn't depend on anyone but himself, even if it meant getting into trouble. The first day of school at Green Summit he made sure he was caught smoking behind the coal shed, and he swore loudly and often, even at the teacher who boxed his ears until they bled. The other boys went home filled with admiration for the tough little kid who wasn't afraid of breaking the rules, embellishing the story as if he were a folk hero. He continued to play the role of a bully so well that no one in Old Kane had believed he could be innocent of murder. He paid for that reputation with three years of his life.

But the state penitentiary was a world away from the small county jail where Drayton spent time before and during his trial. Around Old Kane his notoriety as a bully served him well; generally, people stayed out of his way. Some even respected him in a perverse way. But here in the big prison he was small as a minnow swimming in the ocean, trying to avoid the bigger fish who would eat him alive. Drayton would have to get his bluff in at the first opportunity, or he would be used in ways he didn't want to think about.

That opportunity was not long in presenting itself. His fourth day in the pen, he was standing in line for his noon meal when someone shoved him aside and took his place. Drayton was tempted to ignore the incident—he was in no hurry to eat the unappetizing food—but he sensed that unless he made a stand his life would be unbearable for the next three years. He spun around, ready to assert himself, and looked down at a short, muscular man with a shaved head. Drayton almost laughed; the man looked like Popeye. All that was lacking was a corncob pipe clenched in his broken teeth.

"I guess you didn't notice you're standing in my place, pal," Drayton said, his voice even but firm.

"I noticed," the man said. He didn't budge.

"Hey, you little shit, move aside or we can settle this later when there's no guards around to protect your fat ass!" At that moment, Drayton acted every bit a seasoned prisoner.

"I'm so scared! Whadya do, steal some little old lady's pocketbook?" The inmates within hearing distance laughed, causing the guards to glance in their direction.

"Listen, Popeye, or is it Olive Oyl? I'm in here for reasons you don't need to know, but bashing your pea brain in wouldn't even make a ripple after what I already done." Without waiting for a response, Drayton picked up his food tray and found a seat at the nearest table. The prisoners already eating didn't look up from their bowls, but the man sitting across from him was eager to talk and possibly get on Drayton's good side.

"That was something back there," he said, "putting Mick in his place the way you done."

"That peewee? He don't scare me!" Drayton cautiously tasted the lukewarm, watery soup.

"Mick may not look like much, but he runs his cell block. Just watch your nuts, he's never without a knife, and he's got a couple of guards in his pocket."

"Thanks for the warning."

For the remainder of his sentence, Drayton would manage to stay out of Mick's way. There was always someone younger and afraid to fight back. But Drayton slept lightly, ready to defend himself should a guard decide to let Mick and his pals inside his cell for a little nighttime fun.

Although Drayton had made many bad choices in his life, he was not dumb. He was determined to leave prison better off than when he came in, but the way was not yet clear. The only certainty in his misery was that he couldn't afford any more mistakes.

Early on his first Sunday morning, several guards entered the cell block, banging on the bars. "Up and at 'em! Time for you jokers to get your weekly dose of religion!"

Drayton had no interest in singing hymns and listening to some self-righteous preacher tell him what a sinner he was. "I think I'll pass," he said to the guard who was unlocking his cell door.

"Think again, pal," the guard said. "Church is one of them things you have to do every Sunday. So wash your ugly face and get it out here!"

"But what about breakfast—?"

"You'll have to make do with dry bread crumbs and weak grape juice."

Drayton's only prior church experience had been at the Holy Roller revivals held each year in Woolenweber's back pasture, a mile west of Old Kane. On a hot summer night he and a handful of other teenage boys would slip into the back of the big tent, eager to watch the show. As the music grew louder and the preacher more agitated, adolescent girls danced themselves into a frenzy, rolling wildly in the grass as the Holy Spirit entered their sweaty virgin bodies. Excited from their religious awakening, the girls ran into the woods where they eagerly shared their new-found spirituality with the nearest horny boy.

Drayton listened halfheartedly to the prison chaplain, an ordinary-looking man with a soiled clergyman's collar too big for his scrawny neck. But during the service, Drayton became aware of the respect the prisoners showed the chaplain. He spoke in plain words about Jesus. Each man listened attentively, as if the words of hope and love were coming from Jesus Himself. Even to Drayton, who was naturally suspicious of men's motives, the chaplain's message hit home. Drayton began to believe the words were directed at him. By the time the benediction was pronounced, he had a plan.

The next day Drayton asked permission to speak to Chaplain Davenport. A guard escorted him to the chaplain's office and waited outside the door, standing at attention—arms at his sides, eyes straight ahead—as if he were guarding the king of England.

The office was small and sparsely furnished: a cluttered desk and two straight-backed chairs, shelves stacked with manuals on religion, a picture of a woebegone Jesus sitting on a hillside pondering what He knew was to come. There was no window. Even *this* room reeks of down-on-their-luck men, Drayton thought, knowing he was one of them.

The diminutive chaplain rose from his desk and shook Drayton's hand, indicating he could sit. "What can I do for you, son?"

Drayton held himself straight in the chair and looked the chaplain steadily in the eye, hoping to show confidence he didn't feel. His usual stance would not work with this man.

"It's like this, Chaplain," Drayton said. "I'm a forty-seven-year-old man who's did some bad things in my life. It's time I done a turnabout face, I ain't getting any younger. I'm asking for help in studying the Bible so when I get out of jail I can make up for the wrongs I've did. And maybe wind up with some stars in my heavenly crown," he added with a nervous laugh. His hands gripped the seat of the chair as if he were riding a roundabout at the county fair.

Chaplain Davenport sighed. How many times had he heard that story since beginning his chaplaincy ten years before? It was not unusual for a man to "get religion" in prison, though the chaplain was skeptical of jailhouse conversions. He focused on Drayton's long, thin face and dark eyes, and wondered what crime had brought him to this maximum-security prison. But he stayed by his personal resolve not to ask. Even a prisoner deserved privacy. "When did you first hear the summons, Brother Hunt?"

"I've been hearing words in my head since I come here last week, Chaplain, how I'm a sinner and how Jesus wants fallen men like me to stand up for Him and do good works." Drayton shifted on the hard chair.

"When are you being released?"

"Not till 1948, so you can see there's time to learn the Bible backwards and forwards." Drayton relaxed a little, his long legs sprawled out in front of him, ankles crossed. He resisted the urge to reach for the lone cigarette that he was saving for his evening smoke.

The man seems sincere, the chaplain thought, although he had been conned in the past. "If you're serious, Brother Hunt, we can begin reading the Scriptures together and see how it goes from there."

"There's a hitch right off," Drayton said. "I'm poor as piss when it comes to reading anything outside of the weekly newspaper. I've never read a real book."

"How far did you go in school?"

"Not far enough. I got fed up with the older boys saying bad things about my mama, so after third grade I quit. Later on I seen the folly of what I done, but by then it was too late."

"If you don't mind my asking, why did the boys speak ill of your mother?"

"She didn't have a job in the grocery store or ball bat factory like the other mothers. She entertained gentleman callers, if you catch my drift. But she always seen to it that me and my sister had nice clothes and plenty of food. She was as good a mother as any town woman." With her black marcelled hair and rouged cheeks, Mae Hunt had been the most beautiful woman around Old Kane to her son.

Chaplain Davenport was touched by Drayton's love for his mother, something he seldom saw in his work. More often, prisoners blamed their mothers for their own failures. "I'll help you with the reading, and we can work on your grammar. How's your writing?"

"I mostly print. My hand ain't the best."

"A man needs to know how to write well, both in content and script." The chaplain was growing eager for the challenge of teaching again, his first love before God had intruded Himself into his life. Most inmates read only action comics—Superman or Batman. "I'll give you some easy books to start with, and we'll gradually get to the Scriptures." He reached high up on a shelf and took down *Huckleberry Finn.* "This is a classic by Mark Twain that you would have read if you'd stayed in school." He brushed dust from the jacket and handed the book to Drayton. "If you don't understand all the words, I'll help you."

By his next meeting with Chaplain Davenport, Drayton had read *Huckleberry Finn* twice—intrigued by a world he hadn't known existed. In spite of the disparity of their ages, he felt some kinship with Huck, who also had grown up without a father. During the weeks to come, he read every book by Twain that the chaplain gave him, including *Tom Sawyer* and *The Prince and the Pauper*, until Chaplain Davenport determined he read well enough to advance to the Bible.

After a month, Drayton was allowed to help with the Sunday worship services, passing out hymn sheets and communion grape juice. On the day of his release from prison, a few weeks early for exemplary behavior, he knew the Scriptures as well as he knew every crack in his cell walls.

Now, in September 1948, Drayton Hunt was home at last, ready to begin a new life in Old Kane. Chaplain Davenport had expressed confidence that his protégé was a changed man. Drayton wasn't so sure.

TWO

At Cappy Giberson's first sight of the old family farmhouse, time took a step back. The two-story house looked the same—the red tiles had faded only a little—but the yard was overgrown with smartweed and lamb's-quarter, and the scalloped picket fence needed a fresh coat of white paint. Ma would never have tolerated such neglect when she was alive, Cappy thought. He turned into the long dirt lane, taking care not to stumble over the deep ruts.

It had been three years since Cappy left Old Kane to study journalism at North Central College in Naperville. Though North Central was not as well-known as some other Illinois colleges, Cappy had liked the look of the place when he came across the catalog. And he would still be in Illinois among students primarily from the Midwest. Cappy's first glimpse of the campus told him he'd made a good decision. He wandered from Old Main, built in 1870, with its ornate steeple; to Carnegie Hall, which housed the library; and to impressive Merner Fieldhouse.

As he watched his fellow students bustling to their first classes, he realized that the population of North Central College was more than twice that of all of Old Kane.

Because of the cost of travel, he had not made trips home as the other students had, working through the holidays, even Christmas, to supplement his scholarship. After the graduation ceremony, he had stuck around as the rest of the class of '48 dispersed, working through the summer, and now, three months later, with his hard-earned diploma in hand, he was home—not to stay, but to begin looking for a job in the newspaper world and to spend some time with Worthy Giberson, the man he considered his father.

Except for Worthy, who had helped raise him from a newborn, the people who previously comprised "home" were no longer there to welcome him. Cappy hoped he could adjust to the long, lazy days here after three busy years. At least it would only be for a short time.

Worthy had been waiting on the front stoop since noon, squinting for a glimpse of his tall, lanky son. Last week the mail carrier had brought a postcard that read, "Dear Pa. I'm coming home. Slaughter the fatted calf!" In anticipation of Cappy's visit, Worthy had aired out the boy's room, dusted the bureau top, and dropped a plump old hen in the cast-iron pot for supper. Woman's work don't get easier, he had lamented earlier in the day as he scrubbed the kitchen linoleum with Willa's frayed rag mop. "But you know I do the best I can, Willa," he said aloud. Worthy had more conversations with Willa since her death in 1944 than during their forty-three-year marriage.

When he saw Cappy turn into the lane, Worthy started out to meet him.

Cappy was struck by the change in his father. His walk was slower, his shoulders had a stoop, and most disturbing of all, his overalls appeared a size too large.

"Cap! I'm right glad to see you!" Worthy grinned and awkwardly shook the boy's hand. "You take after your ma more every day, with that blond hair and all," he said. "Though she had them pretty blue eyes, not brown like yours. Dammit, boy, if you get any skinnier, them blue jeans will fall down around your knees! My work's cut out for me, fattening you up."

"Your cooking will do the job in no time," Cappy said.

"And I can see just by looking at you that you've got a head full of learning," said Worthy, continuing his appraisal. "While we're eating our supper you can pass on what them fancy professors taught you. The high points will do."

Cappy followed the elder Giberson inside the farmhouse that hadn't changed since he was a boy: ivory lace curtains at the parlor windows, hand-hooked rugs scattered about the bleached pine floors, the old melodeon that Willa had despised (but kept) since she was a girl, forced by her mother to spend hours practicing scales and hymns on the troublesome instrument. Without trying, Cappy could have found his way around the rooms blindfolded, a game he played when he was small until Willa put a stop to it. "It's tempting fate to pretend blindness," she warned, shaking her finger in his face. "If being blind is so much fun, God might just give you the gift of it!" On the chance God actually existed—though Cappy saw little evidence, based on a long list of unanswered prayers—he had reluctantly given up the game.

"I'll lift lids while you take your grip upstairs," Worthy said. He stirred the thick chicken stew and turned the gas on under the percolator.

Cappy climbed the steep, narrow steps to his old room and tossed his worn suitcase on top of the "wedding ring" quilt that Willa had pieced and quilted for her hope chest. "It's too pretty to use," she had often said, taking it out of the chest long enough to admire her own fine needlework, touching the soft fabric to her face. One day Cappy came home from school and found it covering his own bed.

Cappy glanced at the orange and blue school banners tacked to the wall; a photograph of himself and Beany Ozbun, his best friend, their arms around each other; and the crystal radio set he had painstakingly built, sitting quiet now on his bedside table. As a boy, he had listened every night to the crackly music coming from faraway St. Louis, the only station he could hear, and then only when atmospheric conditions were right.

But Cappy's prized possession was the letter from Asbury P. Wollums, editor of the *Democrat-Republican Patriot*, announcing that he had won the essay contest: "What I Learned in Eight Years of School." Winning that contest had been the impetus for his career in journalism.

"Soup's on!" Worthy called from the kitchen.

While Worthy cut up the steaming chicken and dropped fat, dense dumplings into the bubbling broth, Cappy set the table with Willa's everyday dishes. She had faithfully gone to dish night at the Old Kane Picture Show until she collected a set of the colorful plates and cups. He handled the crockery with care, as if it were fine Haviland china from Paris, France. The aroma of home-cooked food brought back memories Cappy could almost touch. He sat at his usual place wishing that Willa and his wandering brother, Tick, were sitting across from him, waiting for him to pass the chicken and dumplings.

As he tasted the hot, rich food, Cappy addressed Worthy's earlier remark. "My professors taught me a lot, primarily that I didn't know the first thing about writing."

"Why, that ain't so, Cap, you was a born natural at writing down stories. I'd take what them puffed-up professors said with a grain of salt." Suspicious of educated men, Worthy was reluctant to acknowledge that Cappy had joined that elite group. "Just don't let that flimsy piece of paper go to your head. School can't teach a man all he needs to know in this life. The most of it comes from having plain old horse sense."

"But my professors were right, I was green as a gourd. I didn't know shit about writing."

"Hell, being green ain't exactly a crime."

"I'd think you'd be proud I got through college in three years," Cappy said. "I worked my tail off for that 'flimsy' piece of paper."

Smarting from Cappy's words, Worthy passed a plate piled high with store-bought bread, an extravagance Willa would not have indulged. Worthy took a piece of the soft white bread and buttered it. He moved to a safer topic.

"Sometimes my mouth fairly waters for a piece of Willa's soda bread. It had some body your teeth could sink into. Eating store bread is like eating dandelion fluff. She baked her last loaf the day she fell with that stroke up on MacElroy Hill. I tried making some once, but I had to guess at the ingredients, so it turned out hard and flat as them big round rocks in the creek bed. The trouble is she never wrote down her receipt, kept it somewheres in her head and that's where it'll stay throughout eternity. Dig in while the food's hot, Cap. I hope you wasn't expecting fancy."

"This is the best food I've had in three years," said Cappy, already refilling his plate. "Think I'll swing by Jalappa Cemetery tomorrow," he said between bites.

"I figured you would. I stop by every now and then myself and drop off some wildflowers or cut the grass. Chastity was a great one for wildflowers, and you know how Willa was a stickler for keeping the grass cut.

"Willa was a fine wife," he continued, "and your little mama was as fine a daughter as a man could want. In spite of how things turned out," he added, with an old sadness that never left him. For years he couldn't speak his daughter's name, so painful was the memory of her short life. He easily recalled the day Chastity had died, hours after giving birth to Cappy, and how naturally Willa had put her grandson to her breast to raise as her own. Caught somewhere in the past, Worthy finished his supper before resuming the conversation. "Well, that'll do till something better comes along," he said, as he pushed back from the table and patted his full stomach. He stacked the plates and cups, and carried them to the sink to soak in a pan of soapy water.

"Getting back to Jalappa Cemetery," Worthy said, drying his hands, "I sometimes give Beany Ozbun's grave a hit and miss with the mower, his own daddy don't seem to get around to it. Since Beany passed, poor old Lafe has went downhill like he was on sled runners. He don't weigh a hundred pounds sopping wet. It's a pity how Beany come through the war unscratched, only to be struck down right here in Old Kane the very night he got home."

Cappy would never forget the last time he and Beany were together. They had been sitting in the car after the

March of Dimes dance, Beany still in his army uniform, discussing their plans for his ten-day furlough. Beany had been among the initial group of Old Kane boys drafted. If life had worked out the way it was supposed to, Beany would have graduated from college along with Cappy, and tonight they would be sitting in Mundy's Cafe eating hamburger sandwiches and planning the next phase of their future. But the "best laid schemes o' mice an' men gang aft a-gley," as Robert Burns said—a fitting phrase Cappy remembered from his freshman literature class.

After supper, Cappy and Worthy went to the front stoop to watch the sun go down and catch up on the news. Worthy lit his pipe while Cappy nudged a sluggish dung beetle with the toe of his shoe. In Worthy's presence, Cappy felt like a ten-year-old boy. He wondered whether that was the way with all adult children. Except for the lowing of Biesemeyer's Jersey cows in a neighboring pasture and an occasional hoot owl, the September evening was still. Whippoorwills that come with summer twilight had given up their plaintive calls by mid-August, not to return until another muggy Illinois summer. A family of bats, hanging beneath the eaves, was waking up and taking off like Piper Cubs at a county air show.

"How's your health?" Cappy said, trying to sound casual. "You look a little thinner."

"I may be shrinking some, most old men do, but I've got a full head of hair and my own teeth. I can't ask for more than that."

"What do you do with your time?" Cappy said. "And are you getting enough to eat?"

"I eat a fair amount of food, but I sure get tired of my own cooking," Worthy said. "And I'm as busy as I want to be. You know I rented my best ground to St. Peters and his boys, so about all I have to worry with is feeding enough laying hens to keep eggs on the breakfast table. And me and Bum Hetzel keep ourselves busy pulling bluegill out of Macoupin Creek. They ain't fit to eat, so we toss 'em back so we can have the fun of catching 'em again. Them fish spend as much time in the air as in the water. When I go to town, I still get deviled by the gang at Finice Darr's Garage for being a 'gentleman farmer,' but they're only wishing it was them instead of me."

"Just make sure you don't get too thin."

"I'll keep that in mind." Worthy was amused and touched by Cappy's concern. They sat in silence for a while.

"Cap, I hate to spoil your coming home, but there's something I need to bring up." Worthy's voice had turned serious. "Drayton Hunt's due out of the pen. Think you can handle that?"

Cappy's whole body tensed, as if he were facing a physical threat. "What's there to handle? I'll just stay the hell out of his way. You're sure he's coming back to Old Kane?"

"He's got his fancy car here, and his mama's house. I expect he'll show up, but that's not saying he'll stay. It ain't like he's got friends or family waiting to welcome him home."

"How can he show his face in town? Does he expect Old Kane's forgotten all he's done? It didn't come up in his trial, but I know he caused Beany's death."

"That's over and done with. Put it behind you and move on," Worthy said, advice that he himself could not follow.

"I hope to hell he's learned something in jail," Cappy went on, his voice bitter. "I don't want him going around telling everybody he's my father. And what if I've inherited his mean streak? Or his reckless way with women?"

"There's your real worry, ain't it, him being your real pa?" Worthy said. "But that can't harm you unless you let it. Prison can change a man. Maybe he's done claiming you're his boy," Worthy said. "And I can't see any of Drayton Hunt's traits in you."

The two men were quiet, Worthy puffing on his pipe, Cappy listening to the familiar night sounds and trying to put Drayton Hunt out of his thoughts.

"What do you suppose ever happened to Tick?" Cappy knew Worthy couldn't answer the question, but speaking Tick's name seemed to bring his brother near. "I sure miss him. I wonder if he's still speaking in tongues."

When Cappy was small, he had followed his older brother from morning till night through the woods and across pastures, asking one question after another, with Tick supplying whatever answer he could fabricate. Enticed to leave Old Kane by the Reverend Art Gimmy, Tick had abandoned his family in favor of God, believing it was his destiny. The last time Cappy had seen his brother was four years ago at a tent revival in Hardin, a small town on the banks of the Illinois River. As they shared a few minutes alone, Tick had promised to stay in touch, but as Cappy suspected at the time, there had been no word.

"Sometimes I wonder how my first offsprings would've turned out if they'd lived," Worthy said.

"You had other kids? What happened to them?" Cappy asked, hearing this surprising story for the first time.

"Willa miscarried twice, boys they was. We never talked about it, there wasn't no use. As for Tick, I've give up on ever seeing the boy, Cap." Worthy's voice dropped to a whisper. "You'd do well to do likewise." Talking of his thirty-three-year-old son always caused Worthy to grow uncommonly quiet, as if speaking reverently of the dead.

Cappy interrupted the silence. "This is off the subject, but have you ever thought about moving to Carrollton? There's a show with a different picture every night, and a bowling alley and a couple of good cafés. Maybe you and Bum could move in together and neither one of you would be lonesome."

Worthy laughed. "Just because me and Bum is old cocks from way back when, that ain't to say we could share a roost. Before long we'd be fighting like we was man and wife." Worthy formed a series of smoke rings and blew them into the heavy evening air. They took their time disappearing, as if to linger and listen to the conversation.

"And there's no doctor here since Doc Potter died," Cappy went on. "What if you get sick?"

"Then I expect I'll die, too. Let it rest, Cappy. When a man gets to my stage in life it's hard to pull up stakes. I've come this far and I aim to see it through till me or the last dog dies—whichever comes first. Besides, me and Bum has got several seasons of bluegill fishing left in us."

Cappy could never win an argument with Worthy.

"I don't know what's playing, Pa, but how about the two of us taking in a movie tonight?"

"I ain't up for no show, Cap. Pictures ain't the same since Willa passed, and somewheres along the way I lost my liking for crowds. But that ain't to say you can't go. There's gas aplenty in the old heap to get you there and back."

"Your old Chevy still runs? I thought you'd quit driving it."

"I did. I had drove all my life till some big shot come along and said I needed a damned driving license. Well I showed the bastard! I give up driving the car and dusted off my old Wallis tractor. The road commissioner swears at me, says my tractor's steel cleats tear up his roads, but I say 'Stop your bellyaching, Pete. I ain't breaking the law, and it gives you something to do.'"

Cappy recalled the day Worthy had taken the entire family to buy the secondhand 1926 Chevy, painted egg-yolk yellow by Radious Biesemeyer, the former owner. "That car should be in Ripley's Believe It or Not," Cappy said now. "She runs like a car half her age."

"There's no great secret to it." Worthy filled his pipe with fresh tobacco, tamped it down, and touched a match to it. He drew hard until the fire took hold.

Cappy settled back, his elbows propped against the top step. He knew he was in for one of Worthy's lengthy explanations when a short sentence would have sufficed.

"Here's how it works, Cap. First you give your automobile a female's name and then you treat her like she's all softness and perfume. You never kick her tires or slam her doors, and you never climb inside without saying, 'Flossie, you're looking like you just come out of the factory.' Appreciation and tenderness works with cars and females interchangeable."

"I'll remember that when I get a car of my own," Cappy laughed. "Or a girl," he added.

The sound of frenzied barking came from the nearby woods. "Sounds like St. Peters' hounds has got a coon treed," Worthy said. "I reckon I'm the only farmer in Greene County who's never owned a dog. I figure people make enough noise going through life without having a damned dog to add to it."

"About the movie," Cappy said, "are you sure you won't go? It would be like old times."

"Hell, Cap, there ain't nothing they can picture that I ain't already seen or did myself."

"I don't feel right leaving you by yourself my first night home."

"Think nothing of it, I'm used to being by myself, so you go on and go," Worthy said. "I'll be in bed snoring before you're out the lane."

By the time Cappy paid for his ticket and found a seat in the back row, the second showing had begun. Wisps of cigarette smoke drifted toward the ceiling and mingled with the smell of burnt popcorn. Miss Fenity, who took tickets and sold popcorn, couldn't quite get the hang of the new popcorn machine.

Cappy hadn't remembered the theater's being so small. After his eyes adjusted to the dark, he counted six other patrons. They all left noisily when the newsreel ended. He sat through a Popeye cartoon, laughing at the colorful antics as if seeing them for the first time. And then the main feature began, *The Razor's Edge*, starring Tyrone Power, an old picture but one Cappy had missed. In college, money had been too scarce for movies. He settled down in the worn seat and propped his feet on the back of the seat in front of him.

About twenty minutes into the movie, the projector shut down and the ceiling lights came on. A break in the film, Cappy thought. He couldn't remember a time when the film hadn't broken at least once. Angry customers would stomp their feet and whistle until the picture resumed.

Taking advantage of the film break, the projectionist would snip a frame from the film, splice the severed ends together, and restart the movie. Hidden in Cappy's underwear drawer in a tin box were a dozen such frames of film a former projectionist had sold for a nickel each. Cappy's favorite, which cost a dime, showed Susan Hayward's left nipple as she danced and twirled in a 1940s musical.

Cappy could hear the reels being rattled into their cans to be sent to the next town. "That's all there is, pal!" the projectionist called down from the booth.

"But the picture just started."

"It started and it stopped."

"But I came expecting to see the whole thing!"

"Then you should of come to the early show like everybody else. It went all the way from start to finish."

"But I paid thirty-five cents for a ticket." Cappy knew this was another argument he wouldn't win.

"Sorry, buster, I can't run the whole picture for one customer."

There's no place like Old Kane, Cappy thought. He cranked the Chevy to life and drove the dusty back roads home.

THREE

Since leaving Old Kane in 1939 to follow the Reverend Art Gimmy into the world of tent revivals and free-will offerings, Tick Giberson, known around the evangelistic circuit as Billy Dupré, had returned home only once—to pay his respects to his mother after her stroke. It was not a time he liked to remember. Worthy had been disappointed in him because he couldn't heal Willa, but Tick knew he could never live up to Worthy's expectations, no matter how hard he tried. He would always come after Cappy in his father's affections, and even after his sister Chastity, though she had been dead for as many years as Cappy was old.

"Pa's upset enough without me adding to it" had been Tick's rationale for staying away from Old Kane, words he spoke to Cappy when he showed up unexpectedly at a revival looking for material for a newspaper article. Cappy angrily challenged Tick about how the revival business was "bilking money from people in return for fakery."

"It's not bilking money," Tick argued. "We just tell people how good they'll feel emptying their pockets for Jesus." Tick would not forget Cappy's hateful words.

"And what makes you think there's a God in the first place?" Cappy continued, his voice louder. "Ma was a believer, and look what God let happen to her! You ought to give up traipsing around the state acting foolish, and come home and help Pa with the farming."

Tick hadn't seen Cappy since that night.

When he wasn't preaching, Tick's job was to keep Reverend Art happy by showing unlimited energy and enthusiasm in the pulpit, and in the elder evangelist's bed. Both tasks had become increasingly difficult. Reverend Art grew crankier and more demanding with each sunrise, taking out his petty grievances on Tick, blaming him when the take from the offering plate was small ("You need to turn up the charm!" he'd shout, gesturing wildly), or turning sullen and refusing to speak for no apparent reason. Tick preferred the silence, which usually meant he was allowed to go to sleep without having to satisfy Reverend Art's lust.

One evening, as Tick was getting ready for a revival meeting in Harrison, a hamlet in downstate Illinois, he found the January 28, 1944, issue of the *Democrat-Republican Patriot* lining a dresser drawer in the roadside cabin. He took it with him to the outhouse to make the time go faster. Prominently placed on the front page of the Carrollton weekly newspaper was the notice of Willa Giberson's death. The obituary, written by Cappy, took an entire column, as if Willa had been the mayor's wife or a St. Louis socialite. Tick's eyes watered when he saw his own name listed as her son, for he had not been much of a son the past few years. If only I'd visited more, he thought, maybe she'd still be alive. He tore out the obituary to carry inside his Bible and used the rest of the newspaper for necessary business.

That evening as the two evangelists were dressing in their white suits for the opening night of the Harrison revival, Reverend Art said, "You seem down in the mouth, Billy. Make sure you don't carry what's bothering you into the meeting. God won't abide a gloomy evangelist."

"Ma died. I'm feeling sorry I wasn't home when it happened." His eyes suddenly filled with tears.

"Get a hold of yourself, Billy, we all lose our mothers. Start praying to God for strength to get through tonight's meeting. If the first night goes well, word will spread, and there won't be an empty seat the rest of the week. If you start feeling sorry for yourself, close your eyes and thank God that He took your mother to live in heaven. Now hurry up. You know I like to get to the tent early and size up the audience."

"But what if God *didn't* take Ma to heaven?" Tick went on. "What if God's a fairy tale like my brother Cappy says?" Tick had never felt such despair.

Reverend Art glared hard at Tick, as if he had confessed to a crime.

"Now listen to me," Reverend Art said, shaking Tick by his shoulders as if he were a wayward child. "I've spent the past five years turning you into Billy Dupré so you can save souls for God. You owe it to me and God to keep your personal problems to yourself." But he quickly reconsidered. "Maybe it's not your fault, Billy. Maybe Satan has come into your heart and is trying to push God out. Quick! Get on your knees and tell God you're sorry for doubting Him!"

"Maybe it's Cappy who's wrong," he said to himself, as he dropped to his knees and prayed.

An hour later, the identically dressed evangelists, carrying matching white Bibles, marched down the center aisle of the revival tent to the rousing "Onward Christian Soldiers." They took their places on the platform, Reverend Art in a chair, Billy Dupré in front of the microphone. From the moment Billy Dupré entered the tent, the capacity crowd was hypnotized by the handsome young evangelist as if he were a movie idol: his platinum hair, the hint of rouge on his cheeks, his white, capped teeth. Every man, woman, and child was ready to believe every word that Billy Dupré said.

"Welcome to the house of the Lord!" Billy shouted. He smiled and spread his arms toward the people, indicating a group hug. "Reverend Art Gimmy and me are here to push Satan out of your hearts so there's room for God. Just tonight Satan tried to get into *my* heart, but I prayed and now Satan's gone. So let's all lift our voices and sing God's praises, and don't forget to drop your dollars in the offering basket. After the message, when the organist plays 'Almost Persuaded,' I want all you sinners to walk down the aisle and Reverend Art and me will get on our knees with you and pray for your salvation." He began speaking in tongues: "Oolyadin Chriso Tumz—" A few people waved their arms, trying to mimic the strange words. During the prolonged invitation, fifteen sinners went forward and accepted Jesus as their personal savior.

Back in the cabin, Reverend Art was ecstatic. "Your praying must of done the trick," he said. "Just look at all these dollar bills!" He tossed them into the air. "This calls for a celebration." He rummaged through his suitcase and brought out a pint of whiskey. "God doesn't approve of drink," he said, "except on special occasions." He filled two small paper cups.

"Let's not wear our pajamas tonight," Reverend Art said. He laughed and began to undress seductively, dropping his clothes on the floor.

Tick sighed and climbed into the narrow bed. Tolerating Reverend Art's sour tongue was the hardest part of following God.

On a hot, sticky summer day four years later, Tick walked into a roadside cabin in Round Knob, Illinois, and found Reverend Art sprawled face down on the floor. Tick backed out the door and ran for help, but he had seen enough death to know the evangelist was past helping. The man of God lay in a puddle of his own blood, mixed with bits of plaster of Paris that had once been a statue of Jesus. When the statue had come into contact with Art Gimmy's head, Jesus had crumbled like a piece of brick cheese, but not before a sharp edge on the base had slashed a gaping hole in the evangelist's head, causing him to bleed to death. The coroner arrived with his camera and investigative tools and set to work examining the fatal wound, and what remained of the murder weapon—abandoned in a dark, dusty corner like a new convert's good intentions.

At the coroner's inquest, the cause of death was determined to have been a blow to the head inflicted by a jealous deacon after he had found Reverend Art in a compromising position with the boy song leader. When questioned, the distraught deacon had tearfully confessed, insisting he'd been driven insane by the devil. After brief deliberation, the coroner's jury unanimously agreed the poor man was no match for the devil (who was?), and strongly admonished the remorseful deacon to go forth and sin no more.

Alone for the first time in his life, Tick sat on the edge of the bed considering what to do next. When he was growing up on the farm, Worthy had discouraged him from making decisions except about when the old cow's bag was empty and he could stop tugging the rubbery teats. And Reverend Art had forbidden him to do anything without prior approval. But now he was on his own, a frightening prospect for a thirty-three-year-old evangelist with a fourth-grade education.

Tick had no money of his own. Reverend Art had faithfully deposited their revival offerings in a bank under his own name, making the money available only to himself. He was, as he frequently pointed out, paying for Tick's food and clothes and sharing his own bed. "Be thankful, it's more than I had when I was your age," Reverend Art would say, dropping a few coins in Tick's open hand.

Not so long ago, Tick had believed God would provide. ("God looks after His lambs," Reverend Art preached.) But God hadn't looked after Reverend Art, Tick thought, recognizing the contradiction between what Reverend Art had preached and reality. The few times that Tick had challenged the older man about a Bible verse, Reverend Art had flown into a rage. Tick always backed down. He recalled the last time, a week before Reverend Art was murdered:

"The Bible said all the people on earth drowned, except Noah and his family," Tick had said. "So where'd the new people come from?"

"God supplied mates for Noah's children."

"You mean he made another Adam and Eve?"

"Something like that." Art Gimmy did not like being cornered.

"But it must of took a lot of years for people to cover the earth again," Tick said. "I think the Bible made a mistake."

That was all it took. Reverend Art became furious, pounding the Bible with his fist, the veins in his neck bulging. "There are no mistakes in this Holy Book!" he shouted, waving the Bible in the air. "You'd better pray that God doesn't strike you down for being a heretic!"

"I'll pray right now." Tick dropped to his knees and looked toward heaven, praying for forgiveness.

After a sleepless night, Tick made a bold decision. He tossed his white Bible and white preaching suit in the trash barrel outside the cabin door and set fire to the contents. Watching the flames consume his past, he felt free, as if he had been released from a nine-year prison sentence. About to set out on his journey home, carrying a shabby suitcase of socks and underwear, Tick knew he was officially on his own, especially if God had seen him dispose of his white suit and white Bible.

On a warm September morning in 1948, Tick Giberson left Billy Dupré, who could speak God's own mysterious language, in the tiny town of Round Knob, Illinois, and began walking north toward Old Kane—a trip of two hundred miles. He hoped Worthy would let him come home.

FOUR

Cappy was awakened by a heavy pounding on the bedroom door. He opened his eyes and groaned; it was still dark. Covering his head with a pillow, he worked his way deep under the covers in search of another hour's sleep.

"Get up, Cap, it's five o'clock and past!" Worthy called from the hallway. He pounded again. "You're sleeping your life away, and your eggs is getting colder by the minute!"

"I'm up, Pa!" Even the rooster's not up at this hour, Cappy grumbled as he dragged himself out of bed and put on yesterday's clothes. At college, he had been in the habit of showering every morning along with the other boys, but here on the farm Worthy frowned at the frivolous use of well water except on Saturday night.

Rubbing sleep from his eyes, Cappy walked into the familiar kitchen to find Worthy bustling about like the woman of the house. The Silvertone table radio was tuned to *Pappy Cheshire and His Gang,* a daily wakeup program of hillbilly music broadcast from St. Louis.

"I've come to be a right fair cook," Worthy said, as he set fluffy scrambled eggs and fresh side meat on the table. "It's surprising what a man can do when he has to. But I like to never got used to this damned gas stove. Nothing would do Willa, bless her heart, but what she had to have a stove with burners on the top and the oven down below."

"It didn't take me long to learn what I had to do when I got to college," Cappy said. "Change my way of talking. More than one professor told me I'd starve to death if I wrote the way I talked."

"Damned if I see anything wrong with your talk." Worthy jumped to Cappy's defense, as he had always done since taking his daughter's illegitimate son to raise as his own. He poured coffee into heavy white mugs and joined Cappy at the round oak table.

Before they could begin eating, a truck rattled up the lane and bucked to a stop in front of the house. Worthy didn't bother looking out the window. "Unless I miss my guess, that's Bum's old trap. The man can smell coffee boiling a mile off."

Bum Hetzel, Worthy's boyhood friend, limped through the back door without knocking. Because of a broken leg that hadn't set correctly, he was left with a "bum" leg, hence his nickname. With Worthy being a foot taller than Bum, they were known among their friends as Big Shot and Little Shot. Bum stopped short when he saw Cappy. "Well, I'll be damned if it ain't the prodigal son come home to roost!" He patted Cappy's head as if he were still a child and pulled a chair up to the table. "When did you roll into town?"

"Late yesterday afternoon," Cappy said.

"You here for good or passing through?"

"That depends on where I can find a job."

"Farmers is always on the lookout for a strong back, but if it's newspaper reporting you're thinking to do, Old Kane is slim pickings."

"I know. I'll probably have to go as far as Alton or St. Louis," Cappy said, "but I've got to start paying back money I borrowed for school. My sheepskin didn't come cheap."

"There's drawbacks to everything in life, even to getting smart," Worthy said. He turned to Bum. "I can scramble up a couple more of my famous eggs."

"I've already et, but I could stand a cup of that crankcase oil you pass off for coffee." Worthy set a steaming cup in front of him. Bum took a cautious sip and grimaced. "A man could wind up in jail serving coffee this bad!" He poured a small amount into the saucer and blew on it, then put the saucer to his lips. Abruptly, without finishing his coffee, he stood up. "Well, time I was heading back."

"Do you happen to recall what brought you by?" Worthy asked. Bum was becoming more forgetful every day—hardening of the arteries, Worthy assumed, a fate that befell most men over the age of seventy.

"I expect it'll come to me by the time I reach Prough's Corner," Bum laughed. He turned to Worthy. "I'll be over Friday night." Bum hadn't missed a Friday night game of rummy with Worthy since Willa Giberson had suffered the stroke four years before.

"Hell, that ain't exactly front-page news," Worthy said.

Cappy rinsed and dried his cup and plate and set them back in the cupboard. "Main Street was sure hopping yesterday," he said. "It looks like everybody in Old Kane is driving a new car."

"Except yours truly," Worthy said. "I ain't about to jump on that fool's bandwagon. If you ask me, the country's heading for another monumental fall, but everybody's so busy raking in the money and spending it they don't give what's ahead a thought. Turk Mowrey even bought his wife a machine that washes the dishes, but I won't begrudge how the man throws away his money. Poor old Turk, he's got them cataracks in both eyes. It's pitiful hearing him go on about how every day's cloudy, and nobody's got the heart to tell him the sun's shining bright."

Cappy wandered around the kitchen opening cabinets and drawers, reacquainting himself with home, though he knew he'd find nothing moved from the time Willa decided where things in her kitchen belonged.

Because of the Sears, Roebuck catalog, a farm woman could have a kitchen as up-to-date as her city cousin's. Willa's kitchen was no exception: a floor of inlaid linoleum squares, a gas refrigerator, a sink with two faucets—one for cold, and one for hot (when the water heater worked), and to take the chill from a dark winter morning, a small gas stove in one corner. Cappy noticed that the kitchen wasn't spotless the way Willa had kept it, but Worthy did his best.

"Anything going on around town?" Cappy said, knowing that Worthy kept up with the latest gossip.

"There's plenty. You'd think Old Kane was Chicago. You knowed about Pick Richards selling his grocery store to some big shot from Jerseyville who turned it into an eating place—I wrote you that in a letter—but it's too fancy for Old Kane. Most folks still go to Mundy's Cafe where they ain't hampered by checkered tablecloths and dim lights. The last straw come when the new owner posted a sign in the front window that said *No Loitering!* And you know how me and Bum is famous for our loitering," he laughed, then turned serious. "But no joke. The last I heard, Pick's turned into a feeble old geezer, and some days he don't even bother getting out of bed except to set on the slop jar. A man who gives up work needs something to fall back on, even if it's only bluegill fishing."

"You know, I never once tasted a bluegill," Cappy said. "Ma said she wouldn't cook one unless we were down to our last string bean."

"Willa was a smart woman. When I was too young to know better, I tried to choke one down. My own ma used to fry 'em up when Pa was unlucky enough to catch any. I had a mouthful of fishy-tasting bones that I spit out quick. Even the barn cats backed off from them bones. But if you ain't obliged to eat one, bluegills make for fine fishing."

"I sure need a haircut," Cappy said, running a hand through his unruly blond hair. "I suppose Old Man Sipes is still butchering hair?"

"You missed out by a month. Seems he nicked the ears of several customers as his hands had got shaky from drink and age, so he decided it was time to hang up his striped apron and straight razor before he done serious harm. Them was his words, but I think he got tired of dealing with all that dandruff. You might give Myrna's Beauty Shoppe a try. She's cutting men's hair these days, but I expect it ain't easy getting in. Every woman around Old Kane is sporting one of them fancy cold wave permanents. Willa, bless her heart, always done up her own hair, and was none the worse for it."

Home one day, and Cappy felt he had never left.

After breakfast, Cappy set out for Jalappa Cemetery, cutting across rows of corn stubble and stepping over sagging barbed-wire fences. He breathed in the heady aromas of fresh-cut lespedeza (the final cutting of the long summer season), honey-scented wildflowers, Radious Biesemeyer's hog lot—a lifetime away from the city smells he had lived with the past three years when windy Chicago blew its industrial fumes southeast to the Naperville campus.

As he neared the cemetery, he recalled how often he had walked these two miles to visit his mother's grave. Except for a faded photograph, he had never seen Chastity Giberson, the teenage girl who gave birth to him and promptly died, as if she couldn't stand the sight of him. Reading her name and dates on the small stone, "Chastity Giberson, 1911–25," Cappy felt a connection to her that he experienced at no other time.

When Cappy visited Jalappa Cemetery as a child, he liked to sit on a flat tombstone and listen to the wind soughing in the white pines. He imagined the wind was Chastity's voice whispering to him, telling him to do his arithmetic or wash his hands and face, the way mothers do.

Beany Ozbun was buried not far from the Giberson family plot. His grave was marked with the largest stone his old parents could afford: "Bean Ozbun, 1924–1944." Beany was there because of Drayton Hunt, a fact never proven, but one that Cappy and most of Old Kane believed to be true. Drayton had been found guilty of second-degree murder and sentenced to three years, not for causing Beany's death but for causing Willa's. Because her Kewpie doll was found hanging in Drayton Hunt's car, he had been convicted of her death by smothering based solely on that bit of circumstantial evidence. It was a complicated twist of justice that had not satisfied Cappy.

As he pulled open the rusty gate to the shady old cemetery, Cappy noticed a man standing with one hand resting on the Giberson family stone. In his other hand he held a lighted cigarette, occasionally putting it to his lips, then flicking away the ashes.

Cappy recognized the man. "What the hell are you doing here?" he shouted.

Drayton Hunt turned and looked into the angry face of his son. "I've got as much right to be here as anybody." He dropped his cigarette and ground it into the grass with his heel. "I was on my way to my ma's resting spot when I saw your mama's grave," he said. "I stopped by to pay my respects."

"That's rich! You're the cause of her being here!" Cappy spat out the words, as if he were spitting out spoiled meat.

"That ain't exactly how it went." Drayton reached for another cigarette and touched a match to it. He inhaled. "Maybe someday we can set and talk about your mama. There's things that need saying."

"There's nothing you can say that will change how I feel." Cappy clenched his fists.

"And you can't change how I'm your daddy!" Drayton said. "Have you looked in a mirror? You've got my lanky build, my walk, my brown eyes—"

"My real father is the man who raised me, Worthy Giberson. My name's sure as hell not *Cap Hunt*," Cappy interrupted. Even saying the name caused his stomach to turn. From the look on Drayton's face, Cappy knew he had hit a nerve. But as much as he wanted to deny it, even Cappy could see the resemblance between Drayton Hunt and himself. Their mannerisms were similar—the exaggerated gestures when they talked. Both were six feet tall, and thin. The one striking difference was Cappy's hair, blond like Chastity's.

"Make no mistake, Cap, there'll come a time when we get them things between us said. They've been festering like a carbuncle for twenty-three years. They ain't doing neither one of us a particle of good."

He turned and walked toward the low end of the cemetery, the section that flooded with each year's spring rains. The potter's section. At first he couldn't find Mae Hunt's grave. There was no stone, only a small temporary marker. And when he finally did find it hidden in a clump of pokeweed and prairie grass, it read, "May Hunter." Drayton swore, promising himself that he would buy her a decent stone, maybe have her dug up and moved to a resting place next to the Giberson's fancy plot. Wouldn't that get Worthy's goat! he thought, as if it still mattered.

"But I've got to get my damned mouth under control," Drayton said out loud, as if he were talking to Mae. He knew it wouldn't be easy to stop blurting out his anger; he'd done it all his life. But he came home from prison with two goals: to prove to Old Kane that his religious conversion was genuine and to persuade Cappy to accept him as his biological father. He had a long way to go.

Cap yanked up a cocklebur that had sprouted since Worthy mowed and started home. As he was closing the cemetery gate behind him, he looked back to see Drayton Hunt pulling weeds from his mother's grave.

Walking off his anger, Cappy took the long way home, past Jake Woosley's rundown farm, over Wisdom Hill, past Chief's Gulley, piled with junk cars and Old Kane's throwaways. Before he realized it, he was approaching Bum Hetzel's truck farm. When Bum went out of the hog business, he began growing vegetables to sell in town on Saturdays during the summer and fall. Throughout the winter months, he spent the overcast days listening to the radio or the telephone party line that had grown to include twelve families. Cappy, still seething from his encounter with Drayton Hunt, hoped he could get past the driveway without being seen. "Given the chance, Bum could talk the legs off a centipede," Worthy said of his old friend. Cappy hoped to avoid a lengthy one-sided conversation with Bum.

"Hey! Cap Giberson! When did you get back in town?" called a girl's voice.

Cappy turned to see Oleeta Hetzel, Bum's younger daughter, walking toward the mailbox with a letter in her hand. She was wearing rolled-up blue jeans and a loose plaid shirt, brown and white saddle shoes, and her dark brown hair was long and curled under—a style made popular by Ella Raines in the movies. Her lips were bright red.

"Wow, you look different!" Cappy said.

"I hope so." She smiled to show off her perfect teeth. "I helped in Dr. Vedder's dental office in Carrollton for two summers, and besides paying me, he fixed my teeth. He said my crooked teeth weren't good for his business. They don't protrude anymore. See?" She smiled again.

"They look great. *You* look great."

"So when did you come home?" she repeated.

"A couple of days ago. The professors got tired of my sorry face and booted me out." What a dumb thing to say, he thought, wishing he could retract it, like a misquote in the newspaper. "What about you? Married yet?"

"I'm not the marrying kind," she laughed, "but Ogreeta, she's been married two years now. She lives over in Calhoun County, happy as if she had good sense! I've got another two years left at Blackburn College, but I can't settle on a major so I'm taking this semester off to decide. I don't want to be a nurse or a teacher, that's for sure."

"You should have had a career in mind before you started," Cappy said, a little too smugly. "I've known what I wanted to do since I was fourteen. You've wasted a lot of time."

"Maybe we aren't all as smart as you, Cappy Giberson," she said. "And getting required subjects out of the way has *not* been a waste of time. When I go back I'll be able to concentrate on my major."

Oleeta dropped her letter in the mailbox; Cappy stuck his hands in his pockets. The silence was awkward.

Oleeta spoke first, her mood abruptly changed. She smiled. "I was thinking about that Saturday night on Kid Corner when you tried to kiss me. It must have been ten years ago."

Cappy was surprised she remembered. "I didn't just try, I did *kiss* you. Beany put me up to it. Your mouth was wet."

"That didn't keep you from kissing me again. But then you stopped going to Kid Corner with the rest of us."

"I got busy with my job at the newspaper."

"You got busy with Min Wollums, you mean. Everybody was talking about it, how you were cozy with a thirty-five-year-old married woman. Your boss, no less."

"She was a nice lady," Cappy said. "Time for me to head home," he added quickly, afraid she'd say more about Min. "My dinner may get tossed to the barn cats if I'm late, and I've got some letters to write.

"To some girl you left behind at college?"

"I didn't have time for girls."

"I have a boyfriend at Blackburn," she offered. "David Carr. He's a city boy."

Another prolonged silence.

"Well, I really do have to start for home," Cappy said.

She touched his arm, as if to detain him.

He blushed. "Pa expects me home at straight-up noon. But I'm not leaving Old Kane until I find a job. We'll have plenty of other times to talk."

"What if *I'm* too busy? You aren't the only person with important things to do." She turned in a huff and started toward the house.

What did I do to cause that? he wondered. Nevertheless, he walked the rest of the way home with a light step.

"I ran into Oleeta Hetzel today," Cappy told Worthy that evening as they sat on the front stoop. He didn't mention Drayton Hunt.

"Me and Bum always wondered why the two of you never hooked up. I can see why knobby-kneed Ogreeta didn't catch your fancy, but little Oleeta was cute as a ladybug, and still is. She can be damned aggravating when she wants to, though. When she was nothing more'n a tyke she like to drove Bum crazy trying to find him a wife. He'd come in from the fields for supper never knowing what unattached female he'd find setting on the davenport with a white pocketbook in her lap. Oleeta's got a headstrong streak. She'll make some man's life a misery if he don't put his foot down on the wedding night."

"I saw some of that temper this morning, but she is cute." Cappy's thoughts returned to his years at the *Democrat-Republican Patriot*, working for Asbury and Min Wollums. "Back when I was a teenager I couldn't get past Min Wollums's breasts," Cappy said, remembering the taste of them.

"You and every other male in Old Kane," Worthy said. "Willa no doubt kept you on the tittie too long for your own good. But I'll wager that editor lady taught you a thing or two." He elbowed Cappy's ribs as if they were adolescent boys sharing a barn-loft secret.

Cappy stood. "I'm going up to my room, I've got job letters to write. Unless you want to support me from here on out," he added with a grin.

"Better get them letters wrote. I'm done raising offspring."

Cappy took his ancient Smith-Corona typewriter out of its case and set it on a card table. It would take some time to get used to the three-row keyboard again. In school he had used his roommate's typewriter with the standard four rows of keys. Cappy needed a newer typewriter now, along with a reliable car of his own—two reasons for finding a job soon.

Cappy wrote inquiries to all the local newspapers, and to some as far away as St. Louis and Chicago. Too bad Min had left Carrollton, he thought; she could have given him some advice. According to Worthy she had found a new husband, sold the *Patriot*, and moved to California. But Cappy knew he couldn't have gone back to that weekly, gossipy newspaper, or to Min's generous bed, though he was grateful for the education he'd received from both.

That night as Cappy was getting ready for bed, he thought about asking Oleeta to a movie or to go roller-skating at the new outdoor rink in Carrollton. But except for pocket change, the money he had earned during college waiting tables at Al's Diner was gone. Worthy would have given him a loan, but Cappy believed a twenty-three-year-old college graduate couldn't ask his seventy-three-year-old father for date money. He would have to find a way to earn something while he was waiting for that ideal newspaper job.

He turned out the light and pulled the quilt up under his chin, thinking of his conversation with Oleeta. He wondered how it would feel if she were lying here next to him. His only sexual experience had been with Min Wollums. What if he couldn't perform in bed with an inexperienced girl his own age? He had read that even young men couldn't always manage an erection, especially if they were nervous. What if Oleeta laughed at his attempts? With Min, all he had to do was lie back and enjoy her expert hands and tongue. When he finally fell asleep, he dreamed he was standing naked in front of a crowd on Kid Corner. Everyone was laughing, no one louder than Oleeta.

For several days, Oleeta expected to hear from Cappy. Every time she walked past the telephone she looked at it, willing it to ring. She kept her hair curled and lipstick on in case he dropped by unexpectedly. She was surprised at how shy he had seemed. Along with everyone else around Old Kane, she had heard the rumors about Cappy and Min Wollums. Maybe I'm not his type, she lamented, absentmindedly tracing her small breasts with a finger.

Since she was a teenager, Oleeta had harbored a secret ambition to leave Old Kane. She hadn't even told her sister, Ogreeta, who was one year older. When Oleeta was thirteen she had persuaded Chig Mundy to let her work in his cafe, washing dishes and sweeping the floor, and now she was a part-time waitress. While Oleeta's girlfriends were spending their allowance on Tangee lipstick and Evening in Paris perfume, Oleeta was saving her money for college. Although Bum earned an adequate income from farming, he couldn't afford to contribute much to her higher education. Tuition alone was $600 a year. Four years of college would allow her to move away from Old Kane, where the only opportunity for a girl was to marry the boy next door and have his fat babies. Oleeta was determined to have control over her life as well as the lives of those close to her.

At Blackburn College, Oleeta dated David Carr, a nice boy from Alton who was studying to be an English teacher. He was more serious about their relationship than she was. Over summer vacation they wrote frequent letters and talked infrequently on the telephone. Calling long distance was an expense neither could afford. While Oleeta was back on the farm making up her mind about her future, David was still in school, surrounded by girls who admitted they were there solely to find a husband. I'll be back there in January, Oleeta thought, simultaneously wondering whether anything could develop with Cappy in four short months.

FIVE

Except to fetch a can of gasoline from Finice Darr's Garage, where a sullen teenage boy put aside his Superman comic book long enough to fill the five-gallon gas can, Drayton had not risked going into town. He was not ready to face Old Kane.

After several hours of tinkering and a few hard turns of the crank, his car sputtered to life. The engine ran a little rough, but with some loving care and sweet words Drayton knew it would eventually run as smooth as the day it rolled out of the Moon Motor Car factory in 1924. He had spent an entire day traveling to St. Louis on the train to pick up the car, then proudly drove it back to Old Kane. The Moon had cost more than a thousand dollars, but the money was well spent. The luxurious car elevated him in the eyes of his peers as well as their fathers, who drove Plymouth sedans or pickup trucks.

Drayton was skilled with automobiles. And women. Though for the past three years he'd had no contact with either. As he gently polished the Moon with Mae Hunt's best dish towels, he recalled the rainy summer day, twenty-four years before, when he offered Chastity Giberson a ride home in his brand-new Moon. To extend the ride with the thirteen-year-old girl, Drayton had taken a detour through the countryside, ostensibly to show her the wild-flowers. But Chastity wasn't fooled. When he stopped the Moon by the side of the road and put his hands on her breasts, she punched his nose and ran across the wet fields toward home. Drayton, nursing his bleeding nose, was not discouraged. There would be another time.

But living in the past was a luxury Drayton couldn't afford. After buying canned goods and coffee for the pantry, Drayton's prison release money would be gone. But he wasn't ready to dig up his stash of bootlegging profits, buried in a watertight box beneath the lilac bush in his mother's backyard. He couldn't be seen throwing money around and thus raising suspicion that he'd fallen into his old ways.

Drayton was sure that Undertaker Linder, frugal to a fault, would have scoured Mae Hunt's house for hidden cash to pay her burial expenses. But Drayton knew a hiding place Franklin would never have found, one that Drayton had discovered when he was a ten-year-old looking for movie money.

Feeling like that wayward boy again, though any money he found now legitimately belonged to him, Drayton unscrewed the decorative pineapple on the headboard of his mother's bed. Rolled tight, secured with a thick rubber band, was a wad of bills. His heart pounded as he began to count. One hundred and seventy-six dollars, all that remained of the bootleg money he had given his mother.

"This'll do," he said out loud, pocketing the cash. "Now, to make myself look respectable. Thanks for not spending it all, Mama!"

Drayton rummaged through his closet for clothes to fit his new image and found some gray wool trousers and a white button-down shirt hanging in the back—clothes his mother bought that he had refused to be seen in. But his zoot suit days were over. He slipped on the unfashionable shirt and pants smelling faintly of Mae Hunt's mothballs and frowned at his reflection. A stranger, wearing an old man's garb, frowned back at him. He leaned close to the bureau mirror and examined his face. Maybe he would grow a beard to hide his acne scars, though women never seemed put off by his pitted face in the old days. Apprehensive about what lay ahead, he slicked his hair down with Brylcreem and drove to town. Since he had thrown away the remainder of the stale food in Mae Hunt's pantry and the Sears catalog in the outhouse was used up except for the index, his first business in Old Kane was to replenish the household necessities.

After Pick Richards sold his grocery store, a retired cobbler named Sorphus Peak opened a small grocery store in the building where the dry goods store had been. Sorphus was arranging canned goods on the shelf when the tinkling brass bell on the front door announced a customer.

Drayton hesitated at the door, smoothed his hair again, then warily approached the store owner. "How's life treating you, Sorphus?"

"Fair to middling." Sorphus looked up from his work and adjusted the bifocals that slid down his nose. "I'll be damned if it ain't Drayton Hunt in the flesh! Just so's you know, Hunt, I don't give credit like poor old Pick. No cash, no carrying out the door." He glanced at Drayton's scuffed shoes, a habit from his cobbler's days.

It took all of Drayton's strength of will to keep from swearing in the old man's face. "I wasn't wanting credit," he said evenly. He took a scrap of paper from his pocket and dropped it on the counter. "Here's what I'm in need of. I'll be back as soon as my business with the Baptist preacher's done with."

"Don't tell me you got religion in the pokey!" Sorphus laughed loudly, ending in a fit of coughing.

Drayton jammed his fists deep in his pockets. "I lost three years of my life, but I found Jesus."

As Drayton walked out the door, Sorphus muttered under his breath, "Jesus sure as hell has his work cut out for him."

"Son of a bitch," Drayton said as he climbed into his Moon and roared down Main Street. Much as he thirsted for a cold beer, he would stay away from Oettle's Tavern. I sure as hell hope I can stick to my guns, he thought. Drayton Hunt knew he was facing the greatest challenge of his life.

Reverend Marcus Smith was at his desk working on Sunday's sermon when Drayton knocked at the door of his study. The conscientious minister put a lot of work into each sermon, though he believed most of what he said went over the heads of his congregation. "Come in," he said, looking up at the stranger who had the shadow of a beard. Except for beard-growing contests at county fairs, facial hair was uncommon.

Drayton entered the sunny room, a puzzled expression on his face. "I come looking for Brother Beams. Is he around?"

"Brother Beams retired last spring. I'm his replacement, the Reverend Marcus Smith." He stood and held out his hand, his smile practiced. He was short, about five feet, with a full head of black hair, pale blue eyes behind thick rimless glasses, his high-pitched voice a monotone. He wore the usual clergyman's collar.

Drayton was caught off guard. With Brother Beams he knew who he would be dealing with—a devout simpleton. But this man, despite his bookish appearance, had a look about him that was intimidating. Nevertheless, Drayton was determined to speak his rehearsed piece.

"I'm Drayton R. Hunt, you may of heard my name bandied about. The past three years I've been in jail, but I'm out now and I guarantee I ain't—I'm not the same man they locked up." Drayton was trying hard to improve his grammar.

"I don't recall hearing your name, but I've had a lot of names to learn in the past five months." He studied Drayton carefully, the dark steady eyes, the set of his jaw. Although Marcus Smith prided himself on being a good judge of character, he felt he would withhold judgment of this man until he had more evidence.

Anticipating the next question, Drayton said, "In case you're wondering why I was in jail, I was railroaded. I don't want to go into the whole story, but I'll just say I wasn't guilty of what everybody said I was."

"Have a seat, Mr. Hunt. What can I do for you?" Marcus Smith leaned back in his chair.

His confidence returning, Drayton looked the minister in the eye; his hand rested lightly on his Bible for support. "Chaplain Davenport at the prison taught me the Scriptures. I can quote Scriptures with the best of 'em, but I don't always know their true meaning. Some of them sound downright foolish. That's why I need some help, to make sense out of the words."

"First of all, Mr. Hunt, there's certainly nothing in the Bible that's 'foolish.' You simply misinterpreted what you read. Are you a member of this church?"

"No, but I can remedy that problem pretty damned quick. Sorry that word slipped out, Brother Smith. That's one of the things I need to work on, cleaning up my language. Chaplain Davenport told me that more than once," Drayton laughed nervously. "I've almost broke myself of saying 'ain't' except when I get provoked." He fidgeted in his chair, wishing for a Lucky Strike.

"So, you want to become a Baptist?" Marcus Smith believed there was generally something hidden in a man's first words that would come out in later conversations.

"That's what I'm hoping for," Drayton said. "But you may be rode out of town on a rail if you let me in. I ain't exactly well-liked around here, but like I said before, I ain't—I'm not—the same man who got locked up."

"And I'm not the same man who drove into Old Kane five months ago," the minister said to put his visitor at ease. "Change is inevitable, Mr. Hunt, and usually desired." Reverend Marcus Smith was not convinced of Drayton's sincerity, but he would give the man a chance. "I can meet with you once a week to study the Bible, and when you feel ready, and if you choose to, you can come to Sunday worship."

Drayton laughed out loud. "The day I walk in the front door, the rest of your flock will run out the back!"

"You underestimate my Christian congregation, Mr. Hunt. They understand how it is to be a lost sinner who's finally seen the light. So if you're here Friday afternoon at two, we can begin reading together. Today I'll assign a chapter for you to study and on Friday we can discuss what it means to you." He thumbed through the thin pages of his worn Bible, searching for a particular passage. "Let's begin here, the book of Esther." He wrote the name on a piece of paper and handed it to Drayton.

Drayton squinted at the writing. He had rejected reading glasses, offered free in prison, believing that they weakened a man's masculine image. "I can't figure how a book about some woman would apply to me." Drayton was disappointed that Brother Smith couldn't see that for himself. "Can't I start off reading about a man? Maybe one who changed himself like I'm doing?"

"Once you begin reading, you'll understand why I chose the book of Esther. It's about politics in high places, and how one person changed the future of a whole race of people. You see, Esther was a Jew who married King Ahasuerus, and she used her powers of persuasion to convince him to spare her people. It shows what a strong personality can do. Even when it's a woman," he added with a smile.

"I ain't convinced, but I'll give your Esther a try. Speaking of politics, what do you think about this little man running for president? He looks like some kind of dandy to me, strutting around in those round eyeglasses."

"Harry Truman's a decent, hardworking man." Marcus spoke as if he knew him personally. "Before he went into politics, he failed at every job he had, but he wouldn't give up. He's a good example to follow. And of course he's already the vice president," he added.

"If you think he's the man for the president's job, Brother Smith, maybe I'll give him my vote."

Marcus didn't tell Drayton that as a felon he might not be allowed to vote. "Then I'll see you Friday afternoon at two?" He stood up, assuming their meeting was finished.

"I'll be here." But Drayton made no move to leave. "There's something that's been in my craw since I was twenty-three years old, something I done that turned out bad. I was to blame for somebody dying. I didn't mean to cause it, but I done—did it just the same."

"We Baptists don't believe in confession," Marcus Smith said, "but if it will make you feel better, go ahead." He settled back in his chair to hear what more Drayton Hunt had to say.

"I need to get the deed off my chest before we go any farther down this muddy road."

Marcus listened carefully, tapping his pencil against the desk, as Drayton told of his brief sexual encounter with Chastity Giberson in the haymow and the subsequent birth of Cappy. "What happened to the bastard boy?" Marcus said.

"He's been off at some fancy college learning to be a newspaper writer," Drayton said. "Worthy and Willa Giberson, the girl's folks, they raised him from a baby. They done all they could to set him against me. I tried to give the boy a dime once, and you should of heard the ruckus Worthy raised." That long-ago day in Pick's Grocery Store, when Worthy had humiliated him in front of a store full of men, was still vivid in Drayton's mind.

Marcus was beginning to recall pieces of the story, but the Gibersons didn't attend church so he didn't know them personally. "You said you caused someone to die?"

"There's where the story turns sour," Drayton said, wishing for a shot of home brew. "If I hadn't showed up at Worthy Giberson's barn that morning, Worthy's girl and me wouldn't have laid together and she wouldn't of died from it. But that ain't—isn't all. Cappy had a friend named Beany Ozbun. Sure as I'm setting here, I killed him. Me and him got in a fight over Cappy—you see, Beany was a queer and I told him to stay the hell away from Cappy or else."

Marcus Smith nodded in agreement. "You were wise, Mr. Hunt. We have to protect our sons from such a sin against God. The Bible says, 'If a man also lie with mankind, as he lieth with a woman, both of them have committed an abomination.'"

"Anyhow, after the scuffle I hauled him to Chief's Gulley and thinking he was only knocked out, I left him laying in a snowdrift and I drove off."

"What did you think would happen when you left him there?"

"I wasn't thinking clear. I figured he'd get up, brush the snow off, and walk home. But I must of hit him harder than I thought, or else he hit his head when he fell. All I know is the queer bastard died on me."

Marcus winced at Drayton's account. He hadn't expected such a grisly and complicated story. "So you went to jail for killing your son's friend?"

"Not exactly. The jury said I smothered Willa Giberson, Chastity Giberson's mama, who was the same as dead already from a stroke. I never done that deed—hell, I'm no brute. But somewhere down the road I just give up defending myself, figuring I had only got what was coming to me, even if it was for the wrong reason."

Drayton Hunt seemed genuinely remorseful, Marcus Smith thought, but as a Baptist minister and not a Catholic priest, he couldn't simply say, "Do this penance and all is forgiven." Besides, he believed a man should work hard for God's forgiveness. "Everyone has regrets, Mr. Hunt. The best any of us can do is promise ourselves that we won't repeat our mistakes. You've spent time in prison, and now you're out. It's a new start."

Drayton reached across the desk. Marcus Smith's hand was smooth as a woman's, but his grip was a man's, strong as a vise. "I've chose a different road, Brother Smith, and you're a witness to my first step."

"I'll see you Friday afternoon, Mr. Hunt. And from now on, I would appreciate if you would call me 'Reverend' Smith." After his years at a Southern Baptist seminary, he had earned the respectful title of "reverend."

"Well now, he's the most interesting person I've met in Old Kane," Marcus Smith said to himself in the wake of Drayton Hunt. "Something tells me I'd better keep my eye on him, as well as on my wallet." He wrote the time of their next appointment on his calendar and went back to preparing Sunday's sermon.

Drayton picked up his grocery order and drove home, going over his meeting with the Baptist minister. A self-righteous little son of a bitch if ever I seen one, Drayton thought, looking down his nose at me the way he did. But as much as Drayton disliked the idea of associating with Reverend Marcus Smith, he needed the man's help.

Drayton hoped his new path in life would allow for slipping into the bushes now and then. Maybe that dishwater blonde's still waitressing at Mundy's Cafe, he thought. He was aching for a woman.

As he was getting ready for bed, Drayton heard a scratching at the kitchen door. Probably that damned possum that's been nosing around, he thought. He opened the door to find a stray dog, mangy, part shepherd, whimpering for a handout. Her legs trembled and she was so weak she could barely hold her head up. She licked Drayton's shoe.

Drayton had never liked dogs. "Either they're under-foot begging for a handout or they're sniffing your crotch," he claimed. He kicked the stray's nose with the toe of his boot and closed the door. But when a few minutes later he opened the door again, she was still there. "Hell, you might as well come on in, dog, there's room in this house for one more outcast." As she cowered at his feet, he examined her closely for ticks. He noticed her teats were enlarged. Drayton suspected that her newborn litter had already been drowned in some farmer's watering trough.

Drayton shared the last of his milk with the dog and turned out the kitchen lights. In the morning, the dog was curled up at the foot of his bed. He reached down and stroked her head. "It's nice to have something else in the house that breathes," he admitted to the dog.

Six

H eard from any of them editors yet? It's been near three weeks since you come home," Worthy said as he watched Cappy stroll aimlessly from room to room, stopping now to pull a curtain aside and stare out the window at a squirrel busily hiding acorns.

"Every editor who took the trouble to answer said they hire only writers with four years of college and two years of journalism experience, no exceptions," Cappy said. "Much as I'd like to, I can't argue with them. Why would anyone hire me when they can hire a journalist who saw the big war up close and reported on it?" He recalled how many times he tried to enlist but was rejected because he lived on a farm.

"But didn't you tell 'em about working at the *Democrat-Republican Patriot?*" Worthy said.

"They only count work after graduation."

"But what about that award you won for writing of Drayton Hunt's trial?"

"Same thing, it doesn't count."

"You'll turn into a cabbage plant if you set here every day watching dust pile up," Worthy said. If only the boy had studied something useful, Worthy thought, like heifer breeding. But anymore, young people don't listen to their elders. Not that I was any different, he thought, remembering the daily disputes with his own father over everything from how short to cut the lespedeza to the time of day.

"Maybe I'll write a book," Cappy joked. "I could write about Old Kane and how it's got everything a big city offers, just not in plain sight."

"In my lifetime alone I've heard stories enough to fill up ten books," Worthy said. "Some I even made up myself. If you was to go that route, Cap, writing a book, your old room is yours for as long as it takes." He pondered the idea. "How long do you suppose it would take? Writing a full-size book?"

"I don't know, but getting a book published would be harder than getting a newspaper job. Besides, I haven't experienced enough to write a book."

But Worthy was a practical man. "Have you give any thought to doing regular work till a newspaper job comes along?" he said. "Finice Darr's looking for a hand."

"You mean pumping gas?" Cappy said incredulously.

"There's worse jobs. Dirt washes off, you know." Worthy recalled the long, hard days walking behind a plow, the sweaty horse's coarse tail flicking giant flies from its rump and his own face. A bite from a horsefly was worse than a bee sting.

"I'll be back around five," Cappy told Worthy, as he put on a light jacket and started toward the door.

"Going to Jalappa Cemetery again, are you?" Worthy's tone was accusatory.

"I've got some thinking to do."

"Seems to me you're spending way too much time setting amongst the damned tombstones thinking," Worthy said. "It ain't healthy."

"But *you* go there too," Cappy said.

"I go there and I do my business and I come home. I sure as hell don't set there listening for ghosts. Maybe you'd ought to get yourself a live friend."

"Who do you suggest? Shag Kallal and his pigs? All my old friends from school left Old Kane and haven't come back. I'm going." Cappy let the door slam shut behind him.

"Go right ahead!" Worthy shouted through the door. There's times I don't think that boy will ever grow up, he thought.

Cappy knew Worthy could never understand. Jalappa Cemetery was the one place where he could sit quietly with few sounds to disturb him except woodpeckers or chattering squirrels. Some of his best ideas came to him as he sat near Chastity and the other dead Gibersons letting his imagination run free. Beany, who'd played the piano, had told him that songwriters who sit alone, away from the sound of music, heard notes. Cappy, away from other people's conversations, heard words.

Cappy was amassing a stack of rejections. When a letter came from the *St. Louis Post-Dispatch*, he dropped it on top of the pile without bothering to open it. It was several days before he read the letter:

Dear Cap Giberson: Thank you for your inquiry. I'm sorry to say we are not currently hiring journalists. However, we will consider work submitted on a freelance basis. If this interests you, we would be happy to look at samples of your writing, and if we use anything you send, you will be paid the standard rate of eight cents per word. We are especially interested in human interest stories for the Sunday edition. Sincerely, Joe Bray, Editor.

Being published in the *St. Louis Post-Dispatch*, even as a freelance writer, would look impressive on a résumé, Cappy thought. Now all he needed was an idea. He rolled a fresh sheet of paper into the typewriter and stared at the blank page until midnight.

The days were noticeably shorter. Soon it would be too cold to sit on the front stoop, but Cappy and Worthy were slow to give in to the autumn chill. They slipped on light jackets and took their respective places. A coyote howled and an owl hooted back, as if they spoke the same language. Worthy touched a match to his pipe and sucked hard until the tobacco began to glow.

"I had an interesting letter from the editor of the *Post-Dispatch*," Cappy said.

"A job offer?"

"Sort of. It's a chance to do freelance work."

"When I was young there wasn't such a thing as part-time work," Worthy scoffed. "How can a man work part-time when he has to live full-time? One thing's for damned sure, you'll never hear of a farmer plowing or planting a field partway."

"It's getting a foot in the door." Cappy knew he was being drawn into one more argument he wouldn't win.

"A man's got to get more than a foot in the door if he expects to get ahead in this world," Worthy said, raising his voice. But in spite of his disparaging words, Worthy was interested. "If you was to do it, what would you write about?"

"I have a few ideas, but I don't want to tell them yet so they'll be fresh when I sit down at the typewriter." In truth, he had no ideas. "Anybody new moved to town?" Cappy said, moving to a less controversial subject. "Maybe a buxom girl or two?"

"No girls that I know of, but there's a new preacher at the Baptist Church. He come to town after Brother Beams retired. He looks to be somewhere in his late forties. He didn't bring a wife along so I figure she must be dead. Baptist preachers don't hold with divorce."

"Maybe he's a bachelor," Cappy said.

"That ain't likely," Worthy said. "Generally, the first thing a preacher does is find a wife. It's expected. Even Brother Beams found hisself a round little woman from Haypress."

"Reverend Art Gimmy didn't have a wife," Cappy said.

"Don't remind me of that bastard, sweet-talking Tick away from home like he done." Worthy pounded the step with his fist. "We'd all been better off if he'd never set foot in Old Kane."

"Tick thought he was doing a good thing," Cappy said in defense of his brother. "He said it was the only way he'd amount to anything."

"Change the tune," Worthy said. He relit his pipe. "Is that the telephone ringing?"

"I'll get it," Cappy said.

"If it's for me, tell 'em I'm on a slow boat to China," Worthy grumbled, still angry at the mention of the Reverend Art Gimmy.

The phone rang a dozen times before Cappy answered. Several people on the "W" side of the party line had already picked up their receivers to listen in.

"Hi, Cappy. It's Oleeta. I didn't think anybody was home, it took so long."

"Pa and I are having our evening talk on the porch. It's a ritual."

"Oh . . . I hate to bother you, but I was wondering if you could come over some night and look at something I'm writing."

"You're writing?"

"It's nothing much, but one of my professors suggested we should keep a journal, and I wanted to ask what you thought of mine so far."

"Journals are generally private," Cappy said.

"There's nothing that secret," she laughed. "I thought maybe you could give me some pointers about my sentence structure."

"I guess I can look at it," Cappy said, reluctant to judge another person's writing, especially Oleeta's. "But you have to agree not to get offended if I say something needs rewriting." He had found that writers, including himself, were sensitive to criticism.

"I agree. Can you come this Friday night? I'll make supper. My pa and yours always get together on Fridays, so we won't be interrupted."

Cappy hesitated. "I guess I can do that."

"Then I'll see you Friday at six."

"Who was that on the phone?" Worthy said, when Cappy returned to the stoop.

"Oleeta."

"What did she want?

"She wants me to critique her writing."

Worthy laughed and shook his head. "Sounds to me like the little lady's throwing out a net."

"It's not like that. She has a boyfriend at school. She knows I'm a writer, and she wants my opinion of her journal."

"You just keep thinking that if you want to," Worthy said, chuckling.

"If you're right about her 'throwing out a net', she's wasting her time," Cappy said. "I can't get involved with any girl when I don't have enough money to buy her a movie ticket or a bag of popcorn."

"I could probably scare up a couple dollars," Worthy offered. Over the years he had been concerned that Cappy showed so little interest in girls his own age. He didn't count Cappy's involvement with Min Wollums, a passing stage with an older woman that most boys go through if they're lucky.

"No thanks, I'll work something out. Who would have thought I couldn't find a job after graduating from college?"

They sat and listened to the few remaining night sounds of autumn—crickets and an occasional fox scream.

"Looks to be a long, cold winter," Worthy said.

"All Illinois winters are long and cold."

"But some's worse than others. There's been winters in my lifetime where a body couldn't get to town for weeks, even on the back of a horse."

"What makes you think this will be one of those?"

"Woolly-worms, they're crossing the road one right after the other as fast as they can inch along," Worthy said. "There's no more reliable forecaster of a bad winter than a horde of woolly-worms crossing the road. Of course it only counts if they're crossing the north-south roads. If you see a white one, look out, Mabel! We're in for a winter of blizzards."

Cappy laughed. "I wonder where that story came from?"

"There's some things we have to take on face value and not question." Worthy had great respect for folklore, which he found generally to be true if you didn't look too close.

"Speaking of roads," Worthy continued, "the state's tearing up the hard road this side of Carrollton to put in a new bridge. You'd ought to see the mess. Finice Darr is hauling away chunks of concrete as fast as it's broke up, says he's going to build a house out of it. It may not turn out pleasing to the eye, but it'll be stout as hell."

"At least he won't be bothered by termites," Cappy grinned, falling in with the elder Giberson's logic.

A sudden gust of wind from the north caused both men to pull up their jacket collars, but neither made a move to go inside, sensing these times together were numbered.

Friday night, while Worthy was out of the house feeding the chickens, Cappy took a quick wash pan bath (which used only a little precious well water) and put on a clean plaid shirt and blue jeans. He borrowed Worthy's old yellow Chevy and drove to Oleeta's. He parked in front of the house and combed his hair again. Even though he'd applied extra Brylcreem to his coarse blond hair, it went in all directions. He walked up to the door, rubbing his sweaty hands on his jeans.

Oleeta met him at the door, her long hair in an updo, a frilly apron around her tiny waist. "Come on in the kitchen while I finish up," she said, smiling. Cappy was amused that she had gone to so much trouble to present this domestic scene. He recalled Worthy's warning.

"Supper's ready," she said. "I hope you like tuna casserole. Sorphus was out of tuna fish so I had to substitute sardines. Sorphus said we'd never notice the difference."

"After school cafeteria food, I can eat just about anything," he said.

"Pa always did the cooking until Ogreeta and I were old enough to take over," she said, filling glasses with water. Bum had been a widower since Oleeta was born. "Go ahead and sit at the table while I take the casserole out of the oven."

"It smells great," he said.

Cappy waited politely until Oleeta joined him. She filled his plate with the steaming food and passed a slice of bread and a saucer of butter. She watched as he took a big bite, waiting for his reaction.

"Mmm. This is—very good, Oleeta." He drank a full glass of water. "Really very good. Could I have some more water, please?"

"Are you sure you like it?" she asked, an expectant look on her face.

"Who wouldn't?" He forced a smile.

"I'm so glad. It's my specialty. Wait till you see what I made for dessert," she said. "Now, tell me about school."

"I had to work like a dog to get through in three years," Cappy said, moving the sardines around on his plate. "You should have seen me wait tables. I was the fastest Al's Diner ever had. After graduation I stayed on a few weeks until Al could find a replacement."

"At Blackburn College everybody works at the school," Oleeta said, "even if they don't need the money. It's a pretty good system, you can't tell the rich from the poor. My job was in the laundry washing sheets and towels."

"That wouldn't have left much time for a social life."

"It wasn't any different from working at an outside job."

"But why would a rich kid go there and do menial work when he didn't have to? That doesn't make sense."

Oleeta didn't respond, not wanting to argue so early into the evening. "Are you ready for a second helping of my casserole?"

"I still have plenty, thanks." His stomach was queasy from the oily sardines. "The thing is, I'm trying to cut back since I came home."

"You're sure you don't want more?"

"I'm positive."

"Then let's go on in the front room for dessert and coffee. I'll clear the table later. Sorry we don't have a television set, but we can listen to the radio."

"What did you say you made for dessert?" Cappy said. He hoped his stomach settled down soon, or he would have to make a quick exit.

"Chocolate cake. I didn't have enough chocolate for the icing, so I iced it with peanut butter and grape jelly mixed together."

Cappy's stomach growled. "Maybe I'd better skip dessert, it sounds a little rich. But I'll have coffee."

They sat on the davenport, sipping coffee and laughing together at *Fibber McGee and Molly,* now in its thirteenth year on the radio. In this episode, Fibber was frantically looking for his golf clubs. "Did you look in the hall closet, dearie?" Molly said. The studio audience began to laugh in anticipation of the running gag which they knew would follow. "I'll look there now," Fibber said. "Make sure you stand out of the way, dearie," Molly said. "Don't worry," Fibber said, "I cleaned out the closet just the other day." He opened the closet door and items began noisily falling out; the last item was a bell. "Heavens to Betsy, McGee—"

When the program ended, Cappy looked at his watch. "Pa's old car might turn into a mushmelon if I'm out too late. But we haven't looked at your journal."

"There'll be another time," she said, touching his arm. "Maybe we can see a movie together."

"I don't have money right now for movies. You'll have to wait until I find a job." The edge in his voice was slight, but it didn't get past Oleeta.

"And what exactly would I be waiting for?"

"Maybe a movie isn't a good idea," Cappy said, angry and embarrassed that she couldn't understand. "I have a lot of things hanging over me that need settling. I'm not ready for dating."

"Who said anything about dating? You know I have a boyfriend at school. You'd better leave." Oleeta stood up.

"Fine! And thanks for the supper!" He let the door slam shut behind him.

"Don't mention it!" she called after him through the closed door. Furious, she threw his coffee cup across the room; it shattered as it hit the wall and the coffee spilled across the linoleum. After sweeping up the pieces of the broken cup and dumping them in the trash barrel, she went to her room and started filling out papers to return to Blackburn College for winter quarter.

Oleeta was accustomed to having her own way. That wouldn't change because of Cappy Giberson. The disastrous supper brought back the memory of another supper, fourteen years before, that had gone awry.

In 1932, if brothers or sisters were nearly the same age, it was customary in country schools to hold the firstborn back so the siblings could start school together, easing the burden on the overworked teacher by requiring her to teach one less grade. Ogreeta, older than Oleeta by one year, was held back, setting a pattern that dogged her days, while Oleeta forged ahead with confidence. It was Oleeta who packed their lunch buckets every morning with minced ham sandwiches and Hostess pies. And it was Oleeta who saw to it that her own long, thick curls were neatly brushed, and Ogreeta's thin braids were in place before they went out the door to school.

Taking control was second nature for Oleeta. Bum attributed her strong will to not having a stern mother to chase her with a fly swatter or pinch her arm when she got out of line.

Then one day Oleeta decided to fix Bum's life.

As she was nearing her eighth birthday, Oleeta looked around the school and realized that she and Ogreeta were the only children without a set of parents. Taking a long hard look at her teacher, Miss Coonrod, a slender young woman who smelled of Ivory soap, Oleeta decided on a plan to complete the set.

"Miss Coonrod," Oleeta said at first recess, "Pa says to ask you over Saturday night to eat."

"Why, how nice of your father," she said, smoothing her wispy hair. A newcomer to Old Kane, she had never met Bum, but she knew the Hetzel girls had no mother. "Shall I bring something for the meal?"

"No, he'll do the cooking hisself."

"Himself, Oleeta."

After school, Oleeta confronted Bum. "Pa, any chance you might boil up a hen for Saturday night?"

"You know I never go to all that trouble unless your uncle Rube's dropping by." Bum had a foreboding. Oleeta was up to something.

"It's Miss Coonrod that's dropping by!" Ogreeta blurted out. "Oleeta asked her!"

"Jesus, what possessed you to do such a thing? I can't cook for no woman the caliber of Miss Coonrod!"

Nevertheless, by five o'clock Saturday morning, a fat Rhode Island Red hen, freshly killed and dressed, was floating in a pot of hot salty water, along with two yellow onions and a whole turnip.

As suppertime grew near, the girls eagerly watched out the window for their guest. "Here she comes!" they shouted when her car turned into the lane. They ran and hid, leaving Bum to let Miss Coonrod in.

In spite of his initial objection, Bum was looking forward to the evening. He licked his fingers and ran them through his thin gray hair before opening the door.

Miss Coonrod, wearing a powder blue skirt and a white blouse with an artificial red rose pinned at the collar, looked prim and proper as a schoolteacher should. She carried a white pocketbook that matched her high-heeled pumps, and a powder blue sweater was draped casually around her slim shoulders. Her brown hair was pulled back in a smooth, tight bun, and imitation pearl earrings were clipped to her tiny ears. The faint scent of lilac surrounded her. Bum's eyes nearly popped out. Oleeta and Ogreeta, watching from the next room, exchanged glances.

"Do come in, Miss Coonrod," Bum said, regaining his composure. "I hope you held back on eating today so's you'll have room to fill up on my famous boiled chicken."

Miss Coonrod looked for a place to put her pocketbook and sweater, but every chair was piled with clothes or newspapers. She decided not to let her belongings out of her sight.

Proud of his cooking ability, Bum ladled two drumsticks and a dipper of thin broth onto Miss Coonrod's plate. "These legs is fresh," he said. "Just this morning they was strutting around the chicken yard."

Miss Coonrod quickly put a handkerchief to her mouth. "Mr. Hetzel, I appreciate all the work you've done," she said, staring at the gray legs (she thought she saw one move), "but I never eat chicken on Saturdays. Perhaps I'll just have some coffee."

Miss Coonrod was the first of many marriage candidates that Bum's daughters paraded before him. No unmarried woman who was ambulatory had been excluded. Oleeta was unstoppable, with Ogreeta her willing accomplice.

Finally Bum had enough. "Hasn't it come to you girls yet that a wife ain't in the cards for me? I've had my turn at marrying, but from now on—and I'm talking direct at you, Oleeta—let me die a peaceful bachelor!"

"But what's wrong with you marrying again?" Oleeta longed for a grown woman in the house who could clean, wash the clothes, and cook delicious meals.

"Let's just say marrying again ain't in the cards," Bum said. "I was fifty-one years of age and your ma not far behind before persuading her to marry me. When she got that mothering-bee in her bonnet I told her she was too old for childbearing, and I was right, it turned out. She come through bearing your sister, but having a second baby so soon after proved to be the last straw. You wasn't more than a month old when your ma come down with a case of the dropsy she never got over. She swelled up like a balloon. The doc said she was weak from birthing you and that let the dropsy take hold."

So Oleeta gave up her search for a new mother and focused her attention on her own future. Now that Cappy Giberson had returned to Old Kane, she broadened her focus to include him.

SEVEN

After leaving Round Knob, Illinois, Tick ambled along the shoulder of Highway 24 hoping for a ride, but the cars sped by so fast he hardly had time to stick out his thumb and grin before they were out of sight. So he left the highway and strolled along the dusty country roads where he felt more at home. The only person he saw all morning was the mail carrier, who stopped long enough to say he couldn't give him a lift. His car was full of Sears winter catalogs and boxes of day-old chickens peeping like mad. It's too early for those chicks, Tick thought, they'll not last the winter. From habit, Tick considered blessing the mail carrier in tongues but quickly thought better of it, lest the carrier think he was a foreigner. Besides, he was through giving blessings.

By noon Tick's stomach was growling. Except for some dried-up berries growing along the side of the road, he hadn't eaten since yesterday noon. At the next little town he was prepared to spend the last of his money on a hamburger sandwich; his mouth watered in anticipation.

Maybe he would offer to wash dishes in exchange for the hamburger and save his coins, for he would undoubtedly be hungry the next day. Had he stayed on the main highway, he lamented, he would have come to a town by now and his belly would already be full.

As he turned a corner, he saw a small unpainted building ahead with a red gas pump in front. The roof of the building advertised "Drink Coca-Cola" and pictured a girl holding a frosty bottle to her cherry-red lips. There were a couple of chairs on the porch. A woman was sitting in one, her eyes closed. She was not young, but her henna-rinsed hair was tightly braided as if she were a first grader whose mother had just combed her hair for school.

As Tick approached her, she jumped awake. Generally, people who stopped at her business were driving a car. She hoped this bedraggled young man wasn't there to rob her—it wouldn't be the first time. She looked him over. He hadn't shaved recently, and his clothes were wrinkled from sleeping in them, she guessed. His dyed-blond hair needed retouching and made his heavy, dark eyebrows look out of place. She wondered how long he had been on the road. "What can I do for you, fella?"

"I was hoping this was a cafe, but I can see it ain't," Tick said. "How far to a place that can sell me a hamburger sandwich?" He would have liked to sit in the other chair and rest his feet, but he didn't want to appear rude.

She made a quick judgment. "Funny thing, I was just getting ready to fry a hamburger for my own dinner. You're welcome to share what I've got." She stood up and reached for his hand. In spite of her age, which Tick guessed to be forty or so, her hand was soft as silk.

"I'd be proud to, ma'am."

"But you have to promise not to call me 'ma'am.' My name's Clover. I know, it's a dumb name, but Mama said a clover patch was where I got my start so that's what she named me. And what's your name, honey?"

"I go by 'Tick.' I give up another name I had, but I'd just as soon not speak it. I didn't have good luck using that name."

"Then I'll call you Tick," she said. "Follow me inside, Tick, and I'll get that hamburger on. I've got a hot plate in the backroom where I do my cooking, and a cot for sleeping. All the comforts of home!" she laughed. "Did anyone ever tell you that you resemble Van Johnson in the movies?"

She looks ten years younger when she smiles, Tick thought. Almost pretty.

Tick looked around the small store. There were deep shelves stocked with all kinds of items for cars, racks of magazines, and postal cards, and glass cases of candy bars and cheap, gaudy jewelry. The floor was bare wood, swept as clean as if it were in someone's kitchen. A ceiling fan was turned low, clicking with each revolution, its blades gently stirring the stale air. It was unseasonably hot for an Illinois September day. The aroma of the sizzling hamburger made Tick's stomach hurt from hunger.

"It's ready!" Clover called from the backroom. She had opened a sack of potato chips and a jar of bread-and-butter pickles, and set out a can of cold beans, and for dessert a package of Twinkies to share. A feast, Tick thought. He ate hungrily and politely licked his fingers when he finished. "How much will all this cost me?" he asked. He'd been so busy eating he had forgotten that everything comes with a price. "Could I maybe trade some work for this fine dinner?"

"What can you do?"

"About anything, but there's some things I won't do, even if I can."

"I might be able to come up with something," Clover said. "You've never said where you're headed. My guess is you're not out sightseeing."

"Home is where I'm going, but I've got a lot of things to think about so I'm taking my time. I hope to be there before the first snowflake falls on my head."

"How about if you stay here with me for a while, help pump gas, ready the place for winter, things like that?"

"Well, those aren't on my not-to-do list." Now that he was making his own decisions, he had to be cautious.

"I've only got one bed," Clover said, tentatively. "Is that a problem?"

"Not for me, it ain't. But I have to tell you, Miss Clover, I never slept in a bed with a woman, only a man. I didn't exactly want to, I've always liked the looks of women best, but this preacher I worked for said God wanted me to warm his bed. It wasn't altogether unpleasurable, but I'm tired of dealing with peters that ain't my own."

That night, Clover heated two cans of chicken noodle soup and set a box of saltines on the table. When she and Tick were finished eating, she cleared the table and then pulled aside a curtain to reveal the cot where she slept. "Honey, you just sit there on the bed and watch," she said, as she began to undress. "Have you seen a naked woman?"

"Only in an eight-pager," he said, watching Clover's every move, "and they was cartoons."

Clover let her shirt and slacks drop to the floor. She unhooked her brassiere and slipped out of her lacy underpants. She spread her legs slightly. "As you can see I don't have a peter, but I've got something better. Now, you take off your clothes and let me see what you've got."

By the time Tick's underwear lay on the floor next to Clover's, he had a full erection. The last two years with Reverend Art, he couldn't get hard.

"Lie on your back, honey," Clover said, "and let me show you how to love a woman." She guided his mouth to her small breasts, moaning softly as she coaxed his hand over her body. She taught him the ways to love a woman, the special places she needed to be touched, words he could whisper that would make her ache for him.

Afterwards, perspiring as if it were July, he said, "Did I do it right?"

"Honey, you're a natural." She stroked his penis until it grew hard again.

Tick was happy with Clover, though he recognized she was exchanging room and board for the use of his body. Not so different from Reverend Art, he thought, except Clover didn't require him to change his name or wear a white suit or speak in tongues.

Being with Clover was the brightest time of Tick's life so far. When they weren't lying on her cot taking turns pleasing each other, they sat on the front porch counting red cars that drove by—two points for a red car with white sidewalls, three points if a red car stopped for gasoline. Tick would have been content to stay with Clover, but a stronger emotion was drawing him home—his longing to reunite with Worthy and Cappy and to make up for his years away. Some nights, when he couldn't fall asleep, he pictured arriving home. Worthy and Cappy would be waiting at the front door ready to shake his hand and welcome him, no questions asked. But other nights, they would refuse to let him in, pretending they didn't remember him. After I get home I'll start helping Pa farm, Tick thought, and me and Cappy can walk through the pastures together, just the way we did when he was little. And then they'll be glad I'm home.

One morning Tick looked at the wall calendar and knew it was time to go: September 21, the first day of autumn. He'd been with Clover three weeks. "If I ever get back this way, I'll sure stop and see you," he said, hugging Clover one last time.

"Don't you go forgetting me." She sighed, watching Tick walk away from her. She hoped home would be all he expected it to be.

EIGHT

Drayton was early for his first meeting with Reverend Marcus Smith. He had read and reread the assigned Scriptures, coming away with admiration for Esther and what she managed to bring about, right under the long nose of King Ahasuerus. She had a quality Drayton had admired in the past, that special talent for putting something over on an unsuspecting fool. Gripping his Bible for moral support, as if he were about to battle Satan, Drayton smoothed his new beard and knocked on the door of the church study.

"Come in, Mr. Hunt," Marcus Smith said. "You're on time. I like punctuality in a man."

"It's easy when you don't have a wife hanging on to your shirttail," Drayton laughed cautiously. Light conversation didn't come easy.

"My thinking exactly."

Drayton took the chair opposite the minister. "So, how is it you're a single man? Preachers generally have a wife, dead or alive."

"Maybe I haven't found the right person, but I can ask the same of you, Mr. Hunt."

"In my younger days I wasn't looking to settle down, and now I'm too old. Who would want a broken-down relic like me?"

"You might be surprised," Marcus Smith said. He touched Drayton's arm briefly, as if brushing away a fly. "With that dark beard and slim body, you're quite an attractive middle-aged man. But let's get started. Now that you've read Esther's story, what do you think of the lady?"

The two men spent the rest of the hour discussing the book of Esther and how it might apply in today's world.

"Is this a true story?" Drayton said at the end of the hour. "Chaplain Davenport said that some Bible stories are made up, like nursery rhymes, and were told to make a point. If I read a story, I want to know what's true and what isn't."

"Every word in the Bible is true, Mr. Hunt. Every single word."

Drayton doubted that claim, being naturally a skeptic of what other men presented as fact. "I studied the whole book of Esther," Drayton said, "not just what you told me to study, and I could just as well of been reading what goes on in the newspapers today. The queen quit spreading her legs in the king's bed, so he booted her out and got himself a willing younger woman who had her eye on being the new queen."

"That's a crass way of putting it," Marcus said, "but keep in mind that God planned the whole thing so that ultimately the Jews would not be destroyed."

"A lot of time would of been saved if God hadn't made the first queen so damned stubborn about her married duty. Then Esther could of stayed with her own people and not had to meddle in men's affairs."

"Mr. Hunt, it's good to question what's in the newspaper or on the radio," Marcus said, "but you'll never understand the Scriptures if you waste time wondering whether they're true. You came to me for help because I'm an expert, so let me do my job. Next I want you to read the book of Ruth," Marcus said. "It tells the story of a woman who longs to go home—much as you did." He stood up and firmly grasped Drayton's hand. "An enjoyable session, Mr. Hunt. Will I be seeing you next Friday?"

"I'll come again, but don't expect me to set here like a bump and not ask questions. It ain't—it's not in my nature to believe everything I'm told."

"Fair enough," Marcus Smith said.

Feeling suddenly hungry, though it was only three in the afternoon, Drayton parked in front of Mundy's Cafe. The jukebox blared "Open the Door, Richard." The front window that looked out on Main Street hadn't been washed since Chig bought the business. A half dozen booths sat along one wall, and several small round tables were placed at random. In the back of the room were four pool tables. In the evenings, men waited in line for a turn to show off their skill with a cue. Today, except for two men reading newspapers and smoking nickel cigars, the cafe was empty.

Chig Mundy was vigorously sweeping the pine floor, fogging the air with dust devils. He wasn't happy to see Drayton Hunt. He still recalled a summer day years before, when Drayton, dissatisfied with a meal he had at the cafe, had sneaked back late Saturday night and unplugged the ice cream freezer and food cooler. Monday morning, when Chig opened up for business, he found the ice cream melted and the meat spoiled. Knowing he couldn't prove Drayton Hunt was guilty, he hadn't bothered to report the incident to the sheriff.

Drayton chose the counter stool nearest the coffeepot and glanced at the grease-stained menu. As he suspected, there were no new items. Chig had offered the same menu since he opened the cafe ten years before: a daily plate lunch of fried pork steak smothered in greasy brown gravy and a side of mashed potatoes, or hamburger steak and red beans, smothered in gravy left from the pork steak day. In the winter he offered chili with beans, and hamburger sandwiches were always available.

June Plummer, the full-time waitress, was off sick and Oleeta was filling in. "Good morning," she said pleasantly, her manner with every customer.

Drayton took special notice of Oleeta's short skirt and shapely legs. While most girls were now wearing longer skirts, Chig required his waitresses to wear short uniforms, recognizing that most of his customers were men and boys. "You're Bum Hetzel's girl, aren't you?" Drayton said. "You've growed up real nice."

She didn't acknowledge the compliment.

"Where's that other waitress?"

"She's home sick today. Do you know June?"

"We've talked a couple of times when I come in for coffee. Do you know if she's got a man friend?"

"We don't ask each other's business," Oleeta said. "What can I get for you?"

"Well, right now I'll settle for a cheeseburger. But maybe when you get off work I can drive you home in my Moon."

When she was a teenager, Oleeta had refused the same offer. Drayton had always liked young girls. "No thanks, I have a way home." She tried to sound friendly, but she didn't like Drayton Hunt. "Coffee? I just made a fresh pot."

"If you made it with your dainty little hands, I'll just try me a cup."

Prison didn't change him, Oleeta thought as she poured his coffee.

While Drayton was waiting for his sandwich, Cappy walked in. When he noticed Drayton at the counter, he hesitated briefly and started back out the door.

"Hold up, Cap!" Drayton called out. "How about you and me having a cheeseburger together? I'm paying."

"Not if I was starving." Cappy said, not trying to hide his hatred.

"Suit yourself," Drayton said, "but being as you're here, maybe we can set and have a word. There's things between us that needs to be settled."

"You settled Chastity Giberson's future, and you settled Beany Ozbun's future. That's all your settling I can tolerate!" Cappy shouted. The men put down their newspapers and looked his way, then went back to their reading.

"In the Bible it says there'll come a time when the sheep lays down with the lion. Maybe that'll be you and me."

"I don't believe for a minute that you've changed for the better," Cappy said.

"Believe what you will or not, but I got out of jail a changed man." He turned to Oleeta. "Never mind the cheeseburger, girlie." He left a nickel by his untasted cup of coffee. "And give my regards to June."

Oleeta picked up the nickel and dropped it into her pocket. "What do you suppose he wanted to talk about?" She asked Cappy when Drayton was gone.

"Something I didn't want to discuss with him. Or you," he added. "Why is everybody so interested in my business!"

"You don't need to yell, I'm not deaf! Cappy Giberson, you're impossible!" She turned abruptly and walked into the kitchen, the swinging door banging against the wall.

After leaving Mundy's Cafe, Drayton thought about this latest run-in with Cappy. Nothing he tried made a difference. "Maybe it's too soon," he said out loud as he drove past Prough's Corner. He would wait until he proved to Cappy, and to Old Kane, that he wasn't trying to present himself as something he wasn't. The course he had set, with Chaplain Davenport's help, had crooks and turns, and the chaplain said he should expect temporary setbacks. "Just ask God's help when things get too rough," Chaplain Davenport had said. But Drayton, who had grown up self-reliant, was slow to ask for help, even from God. He saw it as a weakness. And he had nagging doubts about whether there was a caring God who listened.

Oleeta was busy mixing ground beef with stale bread for hamburgers when June arrived for the afternoon and evening shift. "Hi, I'm back," she said. "I'm not any better, but I need the money." She sneezed several times.

Oleeta hung her apron on a nail and pulled the black snood from her hair. "Somebody was asking about you," she said.

"Who was it?" June took a lipstick from her pocket and dabbed at her dry lips. Her black hair was pulled back in an old-fashioned bun.

"Drayton Hunt. When did you get to know him anyway? He was in jail when you moved to Old Kane."

"He's been in for coffee," June said. "He came expecting to find the waitress who worked here before me. They went out some. I feel sorry for the man. I must be the only person in Old Kane who'll give him a decent word."

"It's his own fault. June, it's not my business, but are you sure you want that man for a friend?"

"Maybe he deserves another chance. Besides, I think he's kinda cute with that beard and all. I thought it would be bristly, like steel wool, but it's soft as down. I asked him once if I could feel of it," she added.

"Just be careful," Oleeta said.

NINE

S ince the evening Worthy mentioned the Baptist minister, Cappy had been thinking about interviewing him. Seldom did anyone move to Old Kane who didn't have relatives already living there, and Cappy wondered why this man had chosen this particular village. Cappy dropped in unannounced and found the minister sitting at his desk in the church study, reading.

"Reverend Smith? My name's Cappy Giberson." He extended his hand. "Can you spare a few minutes for an article I'm writing?"

Marcus recognized Cappy's name. "I heard you were a writer." He looks like a high school boy, Marcus thought.

"I have a diploma that says I am, but my pockets have nothing to show for it. Maybe that'll change if the *Post-Dispatch* publishes an article about you and your ministry."

Marcus Smith did not like talking about himself, but a favorable account of his work at the Old Kane Baptist Church might entice new members, maybe even some disgruntled Methodists. Offerings were not what they should be to maintain the church building and pay his salary. His predecessor, Brother Beams, had lowered his own salary during a financial crisis, a move Marcus Smith intended to avoid. He turned down the corner of a page in the book to mark his place and set it aside. It was a new book entitled *The Protestant Era.* Serious about his career, Reverend Marcus Smith kept up to date on the latest religious writings. "Just what do you want to know about me, young man?"

Cappy opened his notebook and uncapped his pen. "First of all, how did you happen to come to Old Kane?"

"The State Baptist Association keeps a list of churches needing a pastor, and when Brother Beams retired, Old Kane went on the list. I had been at my former church in Murphysboro, Illinois, for ten years, which was far too long."

"Oh? Why's that?"

"A pastor gets complacent, and that rubs off on his congregation. After a few years, it's impossible to get anything new past the old deacons and conservative trustees."

"Have you studied at a seminary?"

"Of course. I'm certain I have more credentials than any minister who's ever pastored this church." Marcus was proud of his education.

"With all those credentials, why didn't you look for a bigger church, one that pays more money?"

"Young man, there's more to pastoring than money, and I resent the implication that any man of God would concern himself with the salary." Marcus pounded his desk as if he were in the pulpit pounding home God's message. "It's my belief that I was chosen for the Old Kane Baptist Church by God Himself." He did not add that sometimes he woke up in the night wondering why he was stuck in this godforsaken place.

"My brother's a traveling preacher," Cappy said. "He claims he heard the summons at a revival, and the following week he started preaching. Why does God require some men to go to school, and some not?"

"Being mortals, it wouldn't be appropriate to understand God's reasoning."

Joe Bray's readers would yawn through this interview, Cappy thought, wondering how he could make it interesting. "Brother Beams preached against dancing, playing cards, and movies. How do you feel about those things?"

"Sins, every one of them. I hope I won't encounter such sins here in Old Kane."

"Does the Bible say they're sins?" Cappy knew the answer to this question, but he wanted to hear what Marcus Smith had to say.

"Not in exact words. There weren't any movies when the Bible was written, but a true Christian can see what's between the words and lines. A true Christian knows right from wrong and won't stray from the path of righteousness."

Cappy hadn't expected a sermon.

"I read that the Methodist Church no longer considers movies and dancing to be sins. What do you think about that?"

Marcus Smith laughed heartily. "Young man, what I think is that Satan sneaked into the hearts of those Methodist leaders. But at least if they continue soft-soaping sin, Heaven will be less crowded without all those misguided Methodists."

Marcus Smith stood up to indicate the interview was over, but Cappy remained seated.

"One more thing before I leave," Cappy said. "Can you think of anything that might grab the reader? Don't be offended, but what you've given me so far could be every minister's story."

For several minutes the reverend stood looking out of the window. Then he turned back to Cappy. "There *is* something about myself that I've never told, but maybe it's time. I'm confident enough now to reveal my past. Reading about my early life might help someone else who believes he's on the wrong path. You see, I came to the Baptist religion by the back door."

Suddenly interested, Cappy turned to a clean page in his notebook.

Marcus sighed. "I didn't start out life as a Baptist, my parents were Amish. I spent my young years in that large Amish community up north in Arthur. I dressed like all the other boys—dark pants and jacket, always a hat—and went to Sunday meeting where I sat obediently on the hard benches listening to the elders, studied my school lessons at home by lamplight, and rode into town once a week in a buggy. When I saw non-Amish families riding in cars, and kids not wearing black uniforms and hats, I looked at them as odd. It never occurred to me that *I* was different. Until I was about fifteen, I never even wondered what was over the hill in the next county."

Marcus Smith had all of Cappy's attention. He wrote as fast as he could.

"But slowly my curiosity began to grow," Marcus continued. "I knew about advances in technology, and I wondered why I was living the same life my great-grandfather did. And I knew I'd be expected to marry an Amish girl. But I wasn't too concerned until my parents told me I was being paired with Rebecca Schroeder, and we'd be attending the Sunday night singing. Afterward I would be expected to drive her home in the buggy, and the next step was to be 'published'—engaged, in other words. You have no idea how repugnant that was. Girls were a mystery with their long skirts and secretive ways and I had no interest in solving the mystery. That was the day I decided to leave the Amish faith. I was fifteen."

"Did you pack your clothes and slip away at night?" Cappy said hopefully.

"That's exactly the way it happened. I walked into town and took a bus to Missouri. I knew my parents would be worried, so I sent them a letter as soon as I got settled. They didn't write back for several months, and they made it clear they would never get over their disappointment in me. There's a Scripture that says 'Train up a child in the way he should go; and when he is old, he will not depart from it.' They still can't forgive me for proving that Scripture wrong."

"Did you go directly to a Baptist seminary?"

"I didn't have money for school, so I worked two years as a belt boy at the International Shoe Company in St. Louis. Then a man I met at the shoe factory invited me to his church, which happened to be Baptist. The minister was a young fellow, not much older than I was, and his passionate words led me to join his church. That's when I decided the pulpit was my vocation."

"That's an impressive story," Cappy said, putting away his pen and notebook. "The *Post* readers will love it."

As the two men shook hands, Marcus Smith noticed the resemblance between Cappy and Drayton Hunt—their build and their casual way of standing. Handsome boy, he thought.

Before he finished the article about Marcus Smith, Cappy wanted to hear him preach. So Sunday morning, he put on his suit and necktie and drove in to Old Kane. By the time he arrived at the church, the street was already crowded with Chevrolet sedans and two-ton trucks, but he found an empty parking place around the corner on Main Street. He could hear the singing a block away: "I come to the garden alone, while the dew is still on the roses." Cappy recalled how Willa always made sure they arrived early to get a back-row seat so she could be the first one out the door after the benediction. (If she hurried, she could avoid Brother Beams's handshake. "His hands are always clammy," she claimed. "Who knows where they've been?") Cappy smiled at the remembrance.

Cappy had brought a notebook that he slipped inside a hymnal so his writing would be less conspicuous. Along with the congregation he sang, "And He walks with me and He talks with me"—the last chorus of "In the Garden." The words came back to him as if he had been singing them every Sunday of his life, but he had not seen the inside of a church since Willa's funeral.

Dressed in a long black robe, Reverend Marcus Smith took his place behind the lectern. To appear taller, he stood on an apple crate. He opened his Bible to a marked page and laid his pocket watch alongside.

A good omen, Cappy thought, as he tried to get comfortable on the folding wood seat.

"Good morning," Marcus Smith said. "It's nice to see so many familiar faces. Remember, you're in the house of the Lord, so let's not have any whispering." After reading a short Scripture, he closed his Bible with a flourish and arranged his notes. He believed a minister should preach from the heart, not a written text. Anyone can *read* a sermon, even the church janitor.

"The topic of my sermon today is Truth," he began. His preaching voice was deeper and more authoritative than his conversational voice. "There are many Truths written about in the Bible, but I will elaborate on only a few. Here's a Truth, now listen closely." He paused for dramatic effect. "Sinners pay dearly for their few moments of pleasure in a pool hall or dance hall, or in the back of Oettle's Tavern holding a deck of cards in their hands and a bottle of beer to their lips. I trust the ladies present today will not be offended if I mention the worst sin of all that husbands partake of once Satan gets them in his grip. Fornication in the bed of a harlot!"

Several women gasped.

"So the Truth of the matter is this. A life of sin guarantees you will spend eternity rotting in the ground, while the virtuous will be lying on a cloud, listening to angels play hymns . . ."

Marcus Smith spoke for another forty minutes and included several pleas for money. A few men had nodded off, waking with a start when their wives elbowed their ribs. During the lengthy invitation, no one went forward to accept Jesus as their Savior. Every person in the congregation of an accountable age already belonged to the church. "What the church needs is a spirited revival to draw in the unsaved," Marcus said to himself.

After the benediction, the reverend stood at the door shaking hands. He smiled broadly when he saw Cappy. "Well, young man, it's a pleasure to see you here." Unlike

Brother Beams's moist hand, Reverend Marcus Smith's hand was dry as dust. "I hope you found some points in my message to include in your article. The world needs all the Truth it can get. Of course I didn't have time this morning to mention all of God's Truths, one of my favorites being how God controls everything that happens in the universe, even little things right here in Old Kane. When you woke up this morning God said, 'Cappy Giberson, put on your suit and necktie and go to church!' And here you are."

"One of my professors said Truth is a matter of perception," Cappy said. He couldn't keep from provoking the self-assured minister.

Marcus Smith frowned. "Well, now, we know college professors are generally heathens, so that in itself means they wouldn't recognize Christian Truth if they saw it." Still bristling, he moved to the next person in line.

After an evening of writing and rewriting, Cappy finished the article about the Reverend Marcus Smith and put it in a large envelope to mail. The *Truth* is, Cappy thought, I hope Joe Bray will publish this and send me a big check.

Two weeks later, Worthy returned from town carrying a copy of Sunday's *St. Louis Post-Dispatch*. "Cap! Get yourself down here!" he shouted up the stairway.

Cappy ran down the steps two at a time. "What's wrong, Pa?"

"You're famous! Take a look at this." Worthy opened the Weekend section of the paper and laid it on the table.

Cappy read the headline and byline out loud: "Old Kane's Amish Connection, by Cap Giberson."

"It looks like you're on your way up," Worthy said, "being published in a big-city newspaper. Your ma would've sure been proud of you. She'd of went straight to the kitchen and mixed up a sour cream cake like it was your birthday."

Cappy read the headline again.

"It ain't the same as having a sour cream cake," Worthy said, "but how about you and me driving to Day's Cafe in Carrollton for a chicken dinner and a piece of cherry pie? My treat."

"That sounds great, Pa. I'll get my coat."

"While you're at it, you'd better bring along a fountain pen," Worthy said. "I expect everybody'll be asking for your autograph!"

TEN

Every Friday since his return to Old Kane four weeks before, Drayton had scoured the help-wanted ads in the local weekly newspapers, but he found no work he was qualified for. Then one day as he was walking along Main Street, he saw a small hand-printed notice posted in the front window of Linder's Undertaking Parlor.

HELP WANTED
MUST BE HANDY WITH SPADE
AND ABLE TO HEFT DEAD WEIGHT
INQUIRE INSIDE

"Why the hell not!" Drayton opened the door and stepped into the shadowy visitation room that reeked of yesterday's sweet funeral flowers.

Hearing the doorbell jingle, Bert Linder emerged from the basement, wiping his damp hands on his stained apron. The odor of strong chemicals surrounded him. He squinted in the semidarkness. "What can I do for you?"

"I come about the job."

Bert walked closer. It took a minute before he recognized the bearded Drayton Hunt. "You're saying *you* want the job?"

"It's not that I want it, but I sure as hell need it. I done my time in jail, and I need somebody who'll give me a chance. I'm not afraid to work."

When the elder Linder retired, Bert had taken over his great-uncle's business. As a boy, Bert loved watching his uncle Franklin at work, delighting as the scalpel sliced into a carotid artery and following the path of the blood as it emptied onto the porcelain table and down the drain. When Bert became an adolescent, Franklin taught the eager boy the entire embalming procedure, and how to apply only enough color to the bloodless face to make the deceased appear blissfully asleep.

Now Bert was desperate for help. He had been unable to find anyone willing to do what the job entailed: picking up the recently deceased, washing bodies, shaving the men's lax faces, scrubbing the preparation room after each use, occasionally helping the grave digger when his rheumatism flared up. If Bert gave Drayton Hunt the job, he would have to make sure the ex-convict stayed out of sight, or bereaved families might feel threatened and take their loved ones to an undertaking establishment in Carrollton or Jerseyville.

Bert frowned to show he was not a pushover. "I can't hire a man who's looking to steal from me, and the pay ain't nothing to brag about. But there's always somebody dying so there's never a lack of work. Dying comes in threes, you know. Have you got a telephone?"

"Phone company says the house is too far off the main line to run the wires."

"That could be a problem. A death call is likely to come in any hour of the day or night. But you could show up every morning at 6:00 A.M. Any call that comes during the nighttime can wait till daylight. It's not like the deceased's condition would get worse!" he laughed, the sound reverberating around the dim room.

Drayton had never heard an undertaker laugh. It sounded unnatural and gave him second thoughts, but he couldn't afford to turn down work.

"Before I make up my mind, there's a test," Bert said. He picked up a pencil and tablet from a table. "Write your name here, as little as you can. Uncle Franklin said never hire anybody who can't write so little you can't read it."

At the ridiculous request, Drayton was ready to turn and walk out the door, but he needed the job. After several attempts, Bert was satisfied with Drayton's minuscule writing. "You're hired."

"You won't be sorry you took me on, and I won't steal from you. Them days is in the past." He reached out to shake Bert's hand to secure the deal but thought better of it.

Since his release from prison, Drayton had been following his resolve to work at an honest job, study the Scriptures with Reverend Smith, and avoid Oettle's Tavern. He had chosen not to renew old friendships and perhaps get himself in trouble, and since he seldom left his house, he was unlikely to make new friends. He wanted to become better acquainted with June Plummer, the waitress at Mundy's Cafe. But she probably has half a dozen men sniffing after her, he thought.

His longing to know Cappy, the only son he would ever have, had intensified since coming home to Old Kane. Surely Cappy's missing his real father, he thought. That's what sons do. At night, somewhere between awake and sleep, Drayton pictured the two of them fishing for carp in Macoupin Creek, skinning a rabbit and keeping a hind foot for luck, discussing the quickest way to remove a girl's underpants.

"What do you intend to do with all this Scripture knowledge?" Marcus Smith said to Drayton during one of their Friday sessions. "You must have something in mind."

Drayton had been expecting the question. "I want to be a preacher. Like you." In spite of his general distrust of men, Drayton had grown to cautiously respect Marcus Smith.

Those were the most unlikely words Marcus had expected to hear. "But I've had years of formal education. Is that what you want? To go to college and seminary and pastor a church?" He tried to imagine Drayton in a theology class with students young enough to be his children.

But Drayton was confident that he would be a natural at preaching, the way some men can play the piano without lessons. Speaking about Jesus from a platform under a big tent couldn't be much different from being the barker at a girlie sideshow, which he had done at county fairs. Both involved standing in front of a crowd and promising a reward to anyone who paid their money and entered in.

"There's preachers who just get the calling and the very next Sunday they start preaching," Drayton said. "So long as I know the Bible I can save souls the same as you. Ain't—isn't that right?"

"You're right, Mr. Hunt, there are Baptist ministers with no special training, only the desire to preach. But they lower the status of the profession."

"But if a man of my age is called to preach," Drayton argued, "God wouldn't want him wasting the years he's got left sitting in school listening to a bunch of professors blowing off."

"Think about what you're saying, Mr. Hunt. Even *you* recognized the need for training when it comes to interpretation of the Bible. Unless I'm mistaken, that's why you're sitting here in my study." He sat silently for a moment. "But I have to be honest, the devout young man who led me to Jesus could barely write his own name. So maybe you should put your future in God's hands and see what happens. And you're absolutely sure this is what you want?"

"Sure as I'm setting here. Then Cappy won't be ashamed of his real daddy."

Well, that explains a lot, Marcus Smith thought. "Have you talked to the young man about your feelings?"

"I would if I could get within a mile of him. One look at me and he's gone like a jackrabbit. You'd think I had the pox. But what if *you* was to step in?" Drayton said, "and maybe suggest a get-together between him and me?"

"But I've only briefly met your son—"

"Brother Beams used to visit folks around the county for no special reason," Drayton said. "Maybe you can drop in on him and Worthy, and bring up how the Bible says that sons and their real fathers ought to get better acquainted."

Marcus Smith laughed. "And just where in the Bible does it say that?"

"Hell, I don't know, you're the one with the fancy Bible schooling. But it must be in there somewhere."

After Drayton left, Marcus Smith sat in his office and pondered the problem. Unfortunately, there was more to being a pastor than preaching two sermons on Sunday and saying grace before a potluck dinner in the church basement. He would give some thought to getting the two men together. Good works on earth would undoubtedly add to his own riches in the hereafter. The Reverend Marcus Smith was always looking for a way to increase his heavenly reward.

Bert Linder paid a pittance, and Drayton needed money to make repairs on his house before it fell down around him. Every time it rained, he had to set pans on the floor in every room to catch the water pouring through the roof. The last heavy rain had left his mother's couch soaked and ruined. Surely no one would notice if he flashed a little cash, he thought.

He carried a spade to the lilac bush behind the house and easily found the tip of the rock that indicated the place, like a grave marker. His pulse raced in anticipation as he began to dig. It had been years since he had seen the leather bag filled with his hard-earned bootleg money.

As a teenage boy, Drayton had taken over his uncle's moonshine business and parlayed it into a lucrative income until the repeal of Prohibition had drastically limited his customers. But even though they could buy liquor legally from a saloon, some men still preferred whiskey made from a home recipe.

Drayton dug until his spade hit the watertight steel box; he lifted it from the hole and brushed away the dirt. The box was heavier than he remembered. With shaky hands, he opened the lid and removed the bag. He untied the leather lace that held the bag closed and dumped out the contents. Small rocks spilled across the ground, rolling like marbles. A few found their way back into the freshly dug hole. Dumbfounded, Drayton stared at the worthless rocks. "Son of a bitch! Somebody must of been looking over my shoulder when I buried my money!"

Then he noticed a small folded paper with DRAYTON printed in bold letters. He held the paper at arm's length and read:

By now you have found your money gone. You can tell the sheriff if you want to, but I will tell him that money belongs to me for the nights you used me like a whore. So this is for all the times you stuck your ugly thing inside me. Your sister.

Drayton opened his hand and let the note fall to the ground, mashing it into the fresh dirt with his heel. "Damned female! It wouldn't of killed her to leave me half of it! When it comes to money a man can't even trust his own flesh and blood."

But as much as he wanted to blame his sister, he wondered if the ultimate blame was his. He had used her in a forbidden way, even though she never once put up a fuss, not even the first time when she bled all over the sheet. "I was a selfish son of a bitch in those days," he said out loud. "I guess she deserved my money." He pushed the rocks back into the hole, shoveled dirt over them, and went to polish his Moon.

The following Friday morning, Reverend Marcus Smith telephoned Cappy and asked if he could stop by his study that afternoon to discuss another article, this time focusing on the history of the church, which was one of the oldest in the state.

"What time?" Cappy said.

"Whenever it's convenient for you, say two o'clock sharp." I hope I'm not making matters worse, Marcus thought. He carried an extra chair into his study and straightened his desk. He was uncharacteristically nervous.

Five minutes before two, Cappy knocked on the study door.

"Come in and have a seat," Marcus said, "either one."

"Someone else is coming?" Cappy said.

"People are always dropping by."

"Specifically, what do you want this article to cover?" Cappy said. "The person responsible for organizing the church or—"

"Looks like I have another guest," Marcus Smith said, as Drayton appeared in the doorway. "Come in and take the empty chair, friend."

Cappy moved to the edge of his chair. "What's going on here?"

"It's a surprise to me, too," Drayton said, "but a good one."

"Men, I'm sorry to have tricked you, but it goes with being a pastor—a harmless ruse when it's in the best interest of parishioners."

"The joke's on you, Brother Smith," Drayton laughed. "Neither one of us fits that bill." He glanced at Cappy, whose face was sober.

Cappy stood up to leave, but Marcus Smith said, "Just a minute before you run off, Cap. This man wants a conversation; it doesn't have to be long. It can be in the form of a debate, and I'll be the moderator. Can't you spare a few minutes?"

Cappy didn't want to seem unreasonable in front of Reverend Smith, and maybe some part of him wanted to hear what Drayton had to say. "Five minutes."

"Are you agreeable?" Marcus said to Drayton.

"We'll have to talk fast to get everything said in five minutes, but it's a start." Drayton wasted a few seconds choosing a topic. "Cap, I've had to watch you grow up from afar, but I've kept track of you, like when you won that contest at the *Democrat-Republican Patriot* and then went to college. But I don't know what you think about, like when you're sitting on a tombstone at Jalappa Cemetery."

Cappy was surprised. He assumed Drayton would want to bring up the twenty-three-year paternity issue. "Since I won that contest, all I've thought about is being a journalist," Cappy said stiffly.

"But you've been setting on tombstones since you were six or so."

"Back then I guess I was wondering why all the kids had mothers except me. But *you'd* know about that," he said, the bitterness still there, itching to come out.

"I had worlds of time to set and think when I was in jail, mostly about getting out," Drayton said, "but now I think about other things. Like reading library books. John Steinbeck writes good because he writes about poor workingmen, and how when life turns against them, they hang in there. Like me," he added. Drayton couldn't help but brag a little about his newfound knowledge of books.

Cappy was surprised again. Who would have pictured Drayton Hunt with an open book in his hands? "Which of Steinbeck's books do you like?" It won't hurt to act interested, Cappy thought.

"So far I've only got through *The Grapes of Wrath*. It's a thick book."

"I read most of his stuff in college," Cappy said. "There are better writers."

"It looks like Worthy never taught you that one-upping your elders isn't polite." Drayton struggled to keep his composure.

Marcus knew it was time to interrupt. "Gentlemen, that's enough for today. Next time you can choose the subject, Cappy. When would you like to talk again?"

"I'll let you know," Cappy said. He was first out the door.

"Nothing ventured, nothing gained," Drayton said. "He's a hard one to get close to."

"So it appears, but I have a feeling that he's no happier with this estrangement than you are. Now, shall we look at the book of Proverbs?"

ELEVEN

Late one afternoon, when Cappy walked into the kitchen, Worthy was not at the cookstove. Cappy felt a sudden fear, recalling Willa's stroke four years ago. What if Worthy had collapsed somewhere? "Pa! Are you all right?" Cappy called out.

Worthy appeared in the doorway, a broad grin on his stubbled face. "Why wouldn't I be!" He was in a jovial mood.

"I don't smell supper cooking. I thought you were sick or something."

"When you get an eyeful of what's setting in the front room, you'll forget all about supper!"

Cappy followed Worthy into the front room, puzzled by the elder Giberson's uncommon mood.

"Well? Ain't she a beauty?" Sitting atop a small table in the corner was a seven-inch Motorola television set in a dark mahogany cabinet. A staticky sound came from the speaker, and a snowy test pattern flickered across the tiny rectangular screen.

"I can't believe it!" Cappy said, as excited as Worthy. "I saw one demonstrated at the university once, but I never thought I'd see one in our house. Is the picture clear?"

"Clear as it'll ever be this far from St. Louis. I worked most all day putting an aerial up on top the roof. If it ain't high enough, you won't get no picture, that's what the salesman at North End Appliance told me. It set me back a whopping two hundred and eight dollars."

"Whatever prompted you buy it?" Cappy said. Generally, Worthy was close with a dollar.

"Funny how that come about. I woke up this morning feeling like I do every morning, kind of stiff and achy, and while I was laying there trying to get up, I got this itch to have the first television set in Greene County. At my age there ain't many things you can be first at. Call it an early Christmas present for you and me—no need waiting till Christmas Day."

And maybe with a television set to watch, Worthy had thought, Cappy won't want to leave home anytime soon. "Something will be starting at six o'clock," Worthy said. "I don't know what it'll be about, but it's bound to be good."

Cappy couldn't remember the last time Worthy had been this enthusiastic.

"According to the salesman there's two hours of watching before the station signs off for the night," Worthy said. "Afterwards we can eat a baloney sandwich." He turned off all the lights. "The salesman said the picture shows up better if the room's dark."

Worthy had arranged two chairs close to the screen. He and Cappy sat quietly for fifteen minutes until the test pattern faded into *The Russ David Show*. The girl singer, Dottye Bennett, sat on the piano bench alongside Russ David as his hands flew up and down the keys. Cappy and Worthy sat transfixed for the next two hours, watching whatever was broadcast on the only channel: *Face the Music, The Dione Lucas Cooking Show,* and finally *Pabst Blue Ribbon Boxing.*

After the "Star Spangled Banner," the test pattern reappeared and Worthy switched off the power. "Wait'll Bum sees it, he'll want one of his own. I wouldn't be surprised if he don't give up piking!"

Friday night when Bum arrived, Worthy had the kitchen chairs in place. He could hardly wait to show off his new purchase and to see Bum's face. However, Bum took one look at the television set and flew into a rage.

"Jesus, Worthy, what have you done! I read all about these damned things in the paper," he said, keeping his distance from the potentially dangerous box. "Before long the whole country will end up sick from them television rays coming into the house."

"For Christ's sake, Bum, you'd take the fun out of a tilt-a-whirl, and you ain't even watched it yet."

"And I ain't about to! I come to play rummy!" Bum started for the door.

"Come on, Bum, don't be a spoilsport. In the first place, if televisions wasn't safe, Uncle Sam would put a stop to the country buying 'em. It won't hurt you to watch at least one picture. If you don't like it, you can leave and we'll forget the whole thing."

Grudgingly, Bum agreed. *Stop Me If You've Heard This One,* where a panel of comedians told jokes, was beginning. Not once did Bum's eyes leave the grainy black-and-white picture, even when it occasionally faded out white or began to roll. When *The Gillette Cavalcade of Sports* ended, Worthy turned off the power and the two men carried their chairs back to the kitchen.

"Worthy, I have to say that was a pleasurable way to spend a Friday night," Bum said, "and my eyes didn't water once. Fact is, Worthy, I've been meaning to start coming by more often, to keep you from being so lonesome. Say on a Monday night. What do you reckon the shows might be on a Monday night?"

"Come by and we'll have a look-see," Worthy said, chuckling to himself.

As word of Worthy's television set spread, a group of town men began showing up at Worthy's house to watch wrestling. Two Saturday nights in a row, Finice Darr picked up Dabs Terpening and Sorphus Peak and drove to Worthy's. Whereas Worthy's Saturday evenings were once tranquil, they now resounded with yells and arguments about the merits of each gaudily costumed wrestler.

"Worthy, you might think about serving a potato chip or a cracker," Finice said during a commercial. "Nothing makes me so hungry as a wrestling match."

"Maybe you could bring your own potato chip," Worthy said, "seeing as how I'm furnishing the house, the television set, and a jug of cider." Some people are never satisfied, he thought.

"These kitchen chairs are hard on my piles," Dab said, squirming to get more comfortable. "A cushion would sure be nice."

"Jesus, now I'm supposed to baby your butt? Next you'll be expecting me to furnish a wet-nurse." Worthy went to the cellar for more cider. "Willa, I sure wish you was here to watch the programs with me, a picture show right in our own front room. And wouldn't Tick be in hog heaven!"

After Pick's Grocery Store sold, Worthy and Bum and others of their generation found Finice Darr's Garage the most friendly place for conversation and camaraderie. Chig Mundy's Cafe, the only other possibility, was noisy with pool players who swore loudly when they missed an easy shot and teenagers who kept the jukebox turned to a deafening level. But on this day, despite the aggravating noise, Worthy was hungry for one of Chig's greasy hamburger sandwiches. A hamburger cooked on Willa's fancy gas stove didn't taste the same. He sat at the far end of the counter and ordered a tomato burger with onion and dill pickle, and black coffee.

All four pool tables were busy with men who worked the late shift at the Western Cartridge Factory in Alton looking for a little relaxation before making the twenty-mile drive. Two spinsters sat in a back booth knitting and sharing gossip, occasionally sipping their coffee and giggling like high school girls as they recalled an incident that took place fifty years before. Worthy was glad no one else was sitting at the counter; he wasn't in the mood for company. Since television had come into his life, he welcomed the times he could sit alone and enjoy the quiet.

"Here's your grub," Chig said as he set the sandwich and coffee in front of Worthy. Chig was never without a cigar in the corner of his mouth.

"Much obliged." Worthy covered his tomato burger with ketchup and was about to take his first bite when Drayton Hunt swaggered in the front door.

"Chig! Where's them pretty waitressing girls at?" Drayton said. He took off his jacket and sat at the opposite end of the counter. "That's why I come here, you know, it sure as hell ain't for the food!" He laughed. "But so long as I'm here, how about a couple of eggs, runny side up, and a thick slab of fried ham. You can start me off with a cup of black coffee, and make sure them cigar ashes don't fall in it," he said.

"Coming right up." Chig never discouraged business, even when the customer was Drayton Hunt.

Drayton tasted his coffee and for the first time noticed Worthy, who was concentrating on his food.

"Well, if it ain't Mr. Worthy Giberson, setting practically in my lap."

"I hope to hell my food don't spoil," Worthy said back. He didn't look up.

"Come on now, Worthy, don't you think we've carried this feud on long enough? Twenty-four years it's been since I met up with that girl of yours. I know you still hate my guts, but her and me produced a fine boy without half trying. Cappy's got her good looks and my superior brains."

His appetite gone, Worthy pushed his food away. "Don't fool yourself, Hunt. Cappy's got Chastity's brains as well as her looks. The only dumb thing she ever done was lay with you. Females ain't particular when it comes to the haymow."

"I don't know who my own daddy was. He could of been most any married man around Old Kane with an itch and no place to scratch it," Drayton retorted. "Come to think of it, he could even be you, Worthy, we're the identical height. You sure you never made a trip to my mama's bed?" He laughed at the look on Worthy's face.

"You son of a bitch, you've not changed an iota!" Worthy jumped up, his fists clenched, and knocked over the stool. "I was all for Cappy burying the past, old grudges don't help either party, but you're still the bastard you always was. Cappy's a decent young man. Stay the hell away from him!"

Drayton realized he had gone too far. "Settle down, Worthy, I couldn't help goading you some, old habits are hard to break, but I'm as proud of that boy as if I'd raised him myself. It galls me to say it, but you done good by him, you and Willa. I learned a lot in jail, mostly about myself, and I come out with a new way of looking at life. I won't steer Cappy wrong. And I'm sorry my joking got out of hand."

Worthy had heard enough. Even though he knew about Drayton Hunt's claim to religion, Worthy didn't believe his conversion was genuine. Leaving his food on the counter, Worthy walked out, muttering under his breath.

Chig tried to call him back to give him his ticket, but he was already out of hearing. "Looks like he et for free," Chig said. "Goddammit."

"Here, give me the ticket." Drayton dug into his pocket and handed Chig enough change for the two meals. "Just don't let Worthy know I done this."

"He wouldn't believe it anyway." Chig dropped the coins in the cash register and put a hamburger on to cook for his own lunch.

Chaplain Davenport preached that a man's good deed means more in God's eyes when he doesn't take credit for it, Drayton said to himself. I hope God's watching. Drayton dropped a nickel in the jukebox and ate his meal with gusto.

He regretted that he had missed out on Cappy's growing-up years when he could have been a strong influence on the boy's life. He suspected he was already ruined by living under the roof of Worthy Giberson, a man he considered "soft." While he was in prison, hoping to make up for those lost years, Drayton had written regularly to Cappy, but there had been no answers. "Sure as I'm setting here, Worthy tore 'em up," he had said to the chaplain. Though it had been three years, Drayton easily recalled the first letter word for word. Even with Chaplain Davenport's help, it had taken him an hour to get it just right.

Dear Cappy, I am not good at writing letters but I hope you will take the time to read this once or twice. I have did some bad things in my life. Your little mama was sweet and I sure did not mean to make her die. I am sorry about your queer friend Beany but I did not mean for him to die either. I also did not mean for Worthy's wife to die but I was no wheres near her at the time. Yours truly, Drayton R. Hunt.

Someday I'll say those words to Cappy's face, Drayton promised himself as he was trying to get to sleep each night. He pictured the scene: He and Cappy would be standing eye to eye, as only father and son can do. Drayton would say, "I'm sorry for doing you harm," and Cappy would say, "Let's forget all that's gone before and be a real family." But when the morning sun edged into his bedroom window and spread lazily across his bed, like spilled fence paint, Drayton Hunt feared he was becoming as soft as Worthy Giberson.

In 1945, when the mail carrier had delivered Drayton's first letter, addressed to Cappy and postmarked from the state penitentiary, Worthy stared at it a few minutes, then dropped it in the trash barrel and tossed in a lighted match—as if he were disposing of a dead shrew. Although curious to see what Drayton Hunt had written to Cappy, Worthy was not the kind of man who would read another's letter. But as the flames touched the edges of the envelope, he abruptly changed his mind. "Willa, I almost forgot your rule of keeping every piece of paper that comes into the house," Worthy said out loud. "I'll just stow this away in the attic for safekeeping." He retrieved the singed envelope and stuffed it, still smoldering, into his pocket. It was the first of many unopened letters Worthy would carry to the attic.

At eight o'clock, the Saturday night wrestling fans knocked on Worthy's front door. Tonight was a championship match between Gorgeous George and the Caped Wonder, and they had made wagers on the outcome.

Worthy opened the door and the men filed in. They went directly to the front room for a good seat.

"Don't bother taking off your coats, fellas, I've got bad news," Worthy said. "The television set's on the blink, probably the picture tube. That's usually the first to go, like a human being's heart." The television was sitting where it always had, but was covered with a hooked rug. Each man respectfully took off his cap and lifted the rug to take one last look. "Sorry to hear about your television," they said. "Funny how it broke so soon after you bought it. Will you be getting it repaired anytime in the near future?"

"Picture tubes are dear," Worthy said, shaking his head. "I'll no doubt have to go back to listening to the radio." He guided the men toward the door. "If and when I get a new tube, I'll give you a holler."

Worthy sighed with relief. "Thank the Lord, that's over," he said to Willa. "It ain't really broke, it's unplugged—only a little white lie. That television set was company at first, but it got to where it was like a relation that come to visit and never left. I sure hope Cappy won't be upset if he don't get to watch it every night." Worthy turned on the radio in time to catch the end of *Twenty Questions*.

TWELVE

Tick was making slow, steady progress on his walk home. It was now the first week of October and he had been on the road five weeks. Still avoiding the main highways, he meandered along the dusty country roads of southern Illinois—stopping at villages and offering to do handyman jobs when he needed to earn a couple of dollars for food. Daylight was growing short and the evenings cool. He shivered in his thin jacket and pulled up the collar, small protection against the nighttime autumn chill. If he expected to be home before the hard winter set in, he needed to pick up his pace.

When a drizzling rain started, he ran ahead to an old barn, arriving just as the drizzle turned into a downpour. He sat on the seat of a rusty corn planter and ate the Twinkies Clover had packed for him. Wishing he were back sharing her small, cozy cot, Tick burrowed into a mound of loose hay and used his folded jacket for a pillow. When he finally fell asleep, he dreamed of Clover's smooth female body and its musky scent, and the statue of

Jesus that smashed Reverend Art's head, and long summer walks across the south pasture with Cappy at his side when he taught the inquisitive boy everything he knew.

Tick woke up stiff from lying in one position all night. The dry, dusty hay caused him to sneeze a dozen times. He stretched to ease the soreness from his muscles and stepped outside the barn to relieve himself under a wild cherry tree. The night sky was beginning to lighten, and he was hungry again. He remembered Worthy's saying, "We'd be rich as Rockefeller if we didn't have to feed our face." Maybe he could find a garden, although vegetables would already have been picked or dug. But surely he could find a potato buried deep that had been missed by the probing potato fork. He picked up his bag and started walking north again.

When he'd walked ten miles down the main blacktop road between Ozark and Energy, a man driving a propane gas truck stopped and rolled down the window. "Need a lift, pal?" He was smoking a cigarette, which Tick thought risky considering his cargo.

"Are you going north?" Tick said.

"Only as far as Energy."

"That'll do," Tick said. He climbed inside the truck and put his suitcase on the seat beside him. With everything he owned stuffed inside the worn bag, he couldn't let it out of his sight.

"Been on the road long?" the driver asked. He wrinkled his nose and cracked his window open.

"Not long enough," Tick said. "I've a far piece to go. Just outside Old Kane is where I live, or where I used to live till I started following Jesus."

"You one of them hell-and-brimstone preachers?" The driver sounded disapproving.

"Not anymore, I ain't. Traipsing around the country-side wore me out for preaching. It got to where I couldn't speak in tongues, so I took that as a sign from God that He was done with me."

"Never met a man who could speak in tongues. Can you say something in tongues? Like, 'Good morning, Pete'?"

"It don't work that way, I have to be in a church or a tent. Besides, the last time I tried, the words wouldn't come out." Tick wished he hadn't brought the matter up. It always caused a stir.

"Oh, come on, give it a try," the driver insisted. He flicked his cigarette out the window and looked hard at Tick. Hitting a stretch of loose gravel, he nearly slid into the ditch.

Tick didn't want to antagonize the man and provoke a fight—bringing God into a conversation could do that. The worst fights he had seen were over whose God was greater. "I'll do the best I can," Tick said. Imagining he was standing on the platform at a tent revival, he closed his eyes and opened his mouth. "Oolyoolyrach ee Prsstll."

The driver laughed happily. "Damn! That beats anything I ever heard! Say it again, brother!"

"Oolyoolyrach ee Prsstll." Tick began to sweat.

"That last part, does that stand for 'Pete'?"

"Yes." Tick was worried about using God's own language to tell a lie. You never knew what God would do if you got Him mad. Cyclones or floods or locusts came to mind. Hoping to steer the driver away from the inflammatory subject (as volatile as his cargo), Tick said, "Think there might be a job in Energy? I'm near out of money."

"Jobs are scarce for somebody passing through town, but the farmer I'm delivering this gas to is looking for help. Know anything about a farm?"

"I growed up on one!"

"Well, here's your chance. Good luck to you, brother." He slowed the large truck to make the turn into the lane. The name on the mailbox read "Beal Wehrly and Sons."

Tick walked to the back door of the two-story farmhouse and knocked. The tiny woman who answered the door didn't look happy. Maybe it's because it's dinnertime, he thought, recalling how last-minute company always upset Willa.

"Mr. Wehrly's in the cow barn," she said, her tone surly. "What do you want?"

"I hear he's looking for a hand, and I've got two good ones!" Tick held up both hands and grinned.

The briefest smile crossed her face, as if she were unaccustomed to smiling and had forgotten how. Tick could tell she had once been pretty, maybe even prettier than Clover, but farm wives get old quicker from being out in the weather too much, he thought.

"Mr. Wehrly will be in soon for his dinner," she said, examining Tick. "You're welcome to stay and eat."

"Thank you, ma'am, I'd be proud."

Tick followed her into the sunny kitchen. The aroma of food was so overpowering he thought he would faint.

"You can wash up there at the sink," she said. She began dishing chicken and dumplings and buttery corn into large white bowls and set a hot apple pie in the center of the table.

Tick recalled the last meal Willa had cooked for him prior to his leaving with Reverend Art Gimmy, and the apple pie she had baked because it was his favorite. "Winesaps make the best pies," she had said that day as he watched her peel the dark red apples. Memories of Willa and growing up caused him to hurt inside as much as hunger did.

As the clock struck twelve, Beal Wehrly, an unshaven, heavyset bear of a man, strode into the kitchen and took his place at the head of the long rectangular table, built to accommodate the large family. "Pass the food, Mother, I'm way behind with my chores." He glanced at Tick, seeming to notice him for the first time. "Who's this setting at my table?"

"Tick Giberson's my name." Tick stood and offered his hand to the farmer, but he was busy buttering his bread. "I hitched a ride with the gas delivery man, and he said you was needing help. But I seen on the mailbox how you've got sons, so maybe you've got all the help you need."

Beal Wehrly scowled. "Sad to say, all them boys turned out to be girls," he said. "Mrs. Wehrly done her best, but she couldn't produce a single boy."

Tick wanted to begin eating but thought he should be polite and wait for his host.

"I reckon I could use some help, but not permanent," Beal said. "I promised work to my newest son-in-law, but it seems he stubbed his toe and can't work. Boys these days are helpless as heifers on skis. When I was young, I broke my arm once and kept on bucking bales like nothing had happened. Go ahead now and dig into that food, boy. You'll need some pep if you expect to keep up with me."

Tick worked alongside the farmer until sundown. "Time for supper," Beal said, as they finished feeding the livestock. "Afterwards you can bed down in the barn, there's a cot that ain't being used. Make sure you're up and in the kitchen by five if you expect to eat."

Tick slept as soundly as if he were in his old featherbed.

THIRTEEN

The Sunday after Cappy's article on Reverend Marcus Smith appeared in the *St. Louis Post-Dispatch*, the Old Kane Baptist Church was packed with visitors who had driven from Jerseyville and Carrollton to hear the newly famous reverend preach. When Marcus saw the crowd, he changed his sermon from "Why Baptists Have the One True God" to "Giving More Than Your Tithe."

Cappy considered interviewing more local people for stories—a step back in his career, but it occupied his time and provided a little income until he could find a full-time job. At least he was writing. And there was always a chance some long-hidden secret would come out of his questioning, as had happened with Reverend Smith.

"Too bad Robert Wadlow ain't around to talk to," Worthy said, as he and Cappy took their places on the front stoop. Worthy filled his pipe and held a match to the fresh tobacco. "Robert Pershing Wadlow, now there'd be a story worth writing. Before I knowed better, I thought he was a fairy tale. Did I ever tell you about the time I seen the boy in person?"

"Not that I remember."

"It was the summer of 1940, you was in your early teens. That particular day, me and Willa was taking in the Greene County Fair, mostly to see the sulky races. Your ma was as keen on seeing them pacers race around the track as I was. Watching 'em you'd think their legs would get tangled, the way they crisscrossed."

"When I was a kid my favorite carnival ride was the RolloPlane," Cappy interrupted. "But I only got to ride it once before Ma found out. She said it would scramble my brains and I'd end up like Burley Walk."

"That ain't likely. Burley Walk's brain troubles was caused by shellshock in the first big war," Worthy said.

"When I was old enough to ride without Ma's permission, I didn't care about doing it."

"Funny how that works, ain't it? Once we can do a thing free and clear, we'd just as soon not. But getting back to the fair, me and Willa was headed for the frozen custard stand when we seen this commotion up ahead. We shoved our way in close and couldn't believe our eyes. There sat Robert Wadlow, the 'Alton Giant' he was called, and he was bouncing a three-year-old girl in the palm of one hand like she was a rag doll. As you can guess, the parents was nervous but proud to be so honored. For years I'd been hearing stories about the giant, but knowing people's bent toward stretching the truth, I was skeptical. After seeing him in person, I can vouch that the stories was true and then some.

"The next thing we know he's handing the girl back to her mother, and then he stands up to his full height, a fraction under nine feet. A growed man barely come up to his belt buckle. Then, real slow, he starts turning in a circle, like a figurine on a music box, so folks could see him from all angles. He acted like he was enjoying hisself. Then he give a big grin and waved and started weaving off through the crowd. Going home, I reckon he was."

"I wish I'd seen him," Cappy said, "but Beany and I were probably trying to slip into the hootchy-kootchy show."

"But I'll tell you this," Worthy continued, "seeing the boy give me food for thought. Did he feel special going through life like he done, or was he mad at being singled out in such a way? It sure as hell made me glad of being an ordinary man. But there's a sad ending to the story. Only a week later I read in the *Alton Evening Telegraph* that he'd passed, some kind of foot infection, and I felt like I'd lost my best friend though I'd only saw him once in my lifetime. I can't explain it, but that's how it was, almost like he was kin. I bet he had a world of stories that never got told."

"Any other ideas?" Cappy said, seeing that he was too late for this story. "I promised Joe Bray at the *Post* that I'd send something in a couple of weeks."

"I hear the mayor's called an emergency town meeting tonight in the back of Darr's Garage. It's likely a false alarm, Old Kane don't have many emergencies, but you can go and see for yourself."

After supper, Cappy borrowed Worthy's Chevy and drove into town. Main Street was as crowded as on Saturday nights. Cappy had to park on Mill Street, two blocks away. Apparently everyone was going to the town meeting. Cappy got the last available seat.

Mayor Varble was speaking. "Now, folks, I contend that every Greene County citizen is entitled to a dog of their choice, either for warding off burglars or being a widow's lap dog. But Cleo Clendenny far oversteps the boundary of prudence. The odor of dogs had sunk so deep into her skin that soap can't reach it. Store owners won't wait on her, and Reverend Smith won't let her inside the church unless she sits near an open window. Anymore, Cliff Cory's afraid to roll down his car window and put mail in her box for fear of losing a hand to a cranky Doberman. Who wants to suggest a way of persuading her to cut down her number of dogs to one, two at the most?"

"We could threaten to put her in jail," someone in the front row suggested.

"That's no good," Sheriff Ridenour said. "She lives outside the town limits, so she's not breaking no law."

"Then hit her with a stiff nuisance fine," someone else said.

"She was left well fixed so she'd pay the fine and keep the dogs."

"Cleo Clendenny's dogs has been around for years," Finice Darr said. "Why are you just now getting around to the problem?"

"Because lately I've been getting on the average two calls every day about them dogs," the sheriff said. "I can't hardly get my sheriff work done for answering the damned phone."

"How about sending out a sharpshooter to pick 'em off one at a time?" a man standing at the back of the room said.

"We're getting too far afield," the sheriff said. "How about if I talk to the woman first and see if she comes around on her own. We might be saving ourselves a world of grief."

"See what you can do," the mayor said. "We'll meet again Thursday night at seven, two days from now."

When Cappy got home, Worthy was waiting up for him. "Well, what was the to-do?"

"It was about Cleo Clendenny. Something about her dogs." Cappy remembered Cleo Clendenny as his Sunday school teacher—a tall, plain young woman who lived alone in Coal Hollow.

"Her and them dogs goes back to the year she was engaged to marry," Worthy said. "But maybe you'd ought to talk to the lady herself. My featherbed's calling me."

The next morning Cappy drove the narrow winding road to Coal Hollow and parked in the driveway of the old Clendenny place.

The Clendenny farmhouse was in shambles: windows broken out, porch steps rotted away, the yard bare of grass. Crushed cans and broken bottles were scattered everywhere. Nearby sat a rundown trailer with an old truck parked in back. Before Cappy could get out of his car, he was met by a woman he assumed to be Cleo Clendenny, though she didn't resemble the young woman he remembered. She looked sixty, but Cappy knew her age to be no more than forty. She wore a crumpled straw hat, and her soiled dress hung loose from her thin body. Even from a distance, he could smell an offensive odor, as if she no longer bathed. Struggling along behind her was an old blind German shepherd, his hind quarters stiff with age, his head down like he was perpetually sniffing a trail.

"Stay right where you are!" Cleo said, her voice sharp. "State your business!" She carried a cocked shotgun at her side.

"It's Cap Giberson, Miss Clendenny. Don't you remember me from Sunday school?"

"Maybe," she said, squinting. "I'm not in the market to buy anything."

"I'm not selling," Cappy said. He opened the car door and cautiously placed one foot on the ground. "But if you have time, I'd like to ask about your dogs."

"Are you looking to take them away?" She raised the shotgun.

"No, I'm writing an article for the *St. Louis Post-Dispatch.* Readers are always interested in dog stories. Can we talk inside your house? It's pretty cold out here."

She thought for a minute. "We can sit in the trailer. That's where I live nowdays."

Cappy followed Cleo into the cramped trailer. It smelled of rotten meat and dog shit. She cleared papers and dirty clothes from a kitchen chair and brushed crumbs from the tabletop so Cappy would have a place to write. She sat in the chair opposite and put the shotgun on the floor close to her feet.

"Are there more dogs than the shepherd I saw?" Cappy asked.

Cleo cackled like an old hen. "There's more."

"Can you tell me their breeds, and how and where you got them?"

"My memory's been slipping, but I'll give it a try. The story goes back to the day after my folks passed on, twenty-three years ago. That was the day I got two shepherd pups from a neighbor. Mutt and Jeff I called them. I'd only had them twenty-four hours when I walked into the kitchen and found Jeff on the floor dead. His lips were pulled away from his teeth like he was grinning at me, an awful sight. Poor Jeff had consumed an entire pan of table scraps my ma had seasoned with rat poison. I buried Jeff under a cottonwood in the backyard. That very afternoon I went back and got another dog so Mutt wouldn't grow up lonesome—like I did," she added. "When I was a girl growing up, I begged for a dog to have as a playmate, but Pa refused to have an animal that didn't pay its own way. I can still hear his voice bellowing at me: 'If it can't be ate, milked, or relieved of its wool, we sure as hell don't need it occupying valuable space.' Pa was a practical man."

Cappy let her ramble on. He made a few notes.

"I had a suitor for a while," she said wistfully. "A nice enough man, Specs Kirbach, works as a deputy sheriff these days. He gave me a female beagle for my twentieth birthday. Then somebody dumped a gunnysack full of newborn pups in my driveway. You should have seen 'em, poor little things, squirming in that sack like starving rats. I had to feed them with eyedroppers. But they all lived. That made ten. My suitor said he'd marry me if I gave up some of the dogs, but of course I couldn't do that, so we went our separate ways. To cheer myself up, I went to the dog pound over in Carrollton and saved six homeless dogs that were next in line to be disposed of—gassed, I expect. Sixteen dogs to care for didn't leave me time to feel sorry for myself. Or to miss Specs."

"How many dogs do you have now?" Cappy began to itch, certain he was being invaded by fleas.

"They won't stand still long enough to be counted, but as near as I can figure, sixty-seven, with more pups on the way. You'd have seen them, but this time of day they're in the house, most of them sleeping."

"Maybe I could take a quick look?"

"Suit yourself. Just don't wake 'em up."

Cleo pushed the door open and Cappy stepped inside. Dogs of all sizes were asleep on the floor and the furniture. Turds piled up in the corners. In the dining room, two Irish setter males were fighting over a beagle in heat.

"I've seen enough, Miss Clendenny," he said, nauseated from the rank odor. "I'll send you a copy of the article if it's printed."

"Anytime you need some dogs of your own, just let me know, Cap."

When he got home from Cleo's, Cappy scrubbed himself with Lifebuoy soap and changed his clothes. He assembled his notes, but he doubted Joe Bray's readers would be interested in an eccentric spinster who liked dogs. "So much for that," he said, tossing his notebook aside.

"Something will turn up twice as good." Worthy always encouraged Cappy's writing. "I'm warming the boiled beef and cabbage left from last night. We can set and eat a bite before our television programs start." Since the town men no longer came on Saturday nights, Worthy had a renewed interest in watching. Only Cappy and Bum knew that the television set was not broken.

"I'm starving," Cappy said. He set the table and dipped two glasses of water from the bucket. The water from the faucets came from the cistern and wasn't suitable for drinking.

"Damn, somebody just drove up," Worthy said. "If I didn't know better, I'd think it was Bum's old Ford pickup, but this ain't Friday night. Go see who it is. Willa always hated when folks dropped in at mealtime."

Cappy was surprised to see Oleeta at the door. "Want to come in?" he said after a moment.

"Well it *is* a little chilly to stand on the porch." She stepped inside the warm kitchen and hung her coat over the back of a chair, as if she intended to stay.

"Have you et?" Worthy said, hoping she had. "There's plenty of beef and cabbage."

"Thanks, I've already had supper. But I can sit and watch the two of you."

Cappy and Worthy hurried self-consciously through their meal. "I'll clear the dishes," Worthy said. "You two can go set in the front room."

"Did you come by for help with your journal?" Cappy said, as they sat together on the davenport.

"I thought maybe we could watch your television set. Pa's always talking about it, and I've never seen one."

"We can watch a program, I guess, but I have to work on my article," Cappy said, wondering why he was so nervous that he was lying.

"You can't take the evening off even when you have company? If I'd known, I wouldn't have wasted gas driving all the way here for nothing."

"There's always the telephone," he said.

"I thought yours was broken since you never call." She jumped up and grabbed her coat. "I've changed my mind about the television. I have a dozen chores waiting at home.

"Well, that was one for the books," Worthy said when he heard Bum's truck roar away. "In my day, you'd never see a girl calling on a boy, the boys done the pursuing, the way nature intended. I couldn't taste my boiled beef and cabbage for her setting there watching every bite I put in my mouth. Damned rude stopping by at mealtime."

"It's not uncommon anymore for girls to take the lead in a relationship," Cappy said, defending Oleeta. "Some girls even pay for dates."

"It's setting a bad example," Worthy said. "Next thing you know, girls will be proposing marriage."

Cappy wondered if Worthy could be right that Oleeta had more than a friendly interest in him. In spite of her bad temper and stubbornness, he was happy at the possibility.

Wednesday night, as Cleo Clendenny slept fitfully in her stifling trailer, dozens of hungry dogs left the farmhouse and gorged on Charlie Shackelford's sheep.

At the next town meeting, filled again to capacity, Charlie was the first to speak. "Them goddamned dogs chased my sheep till they couldn't run no more," he said, his voice breaking. "Once a sheep falls over, it'll never get up on its own. I had to shoot a couple of my best ewes in the head—they was laying in a ditch with their feet up in the air, crying for help. Up to now, them dogs of Cleo's was just a stinking nuisance, but last night changed everything. Us sheep farmers can't afford to lose our livelihood."

Turk Mowrey stood up, hesitant to offer his plan. "I've got an idea, but it's drastic. Once a week I deliver dog food to Cleo, she can't manage all them bags of feed herself. What if I was to quit stocking it? Even if she drove all the way to Carrollton to get feed, she's too frail to unload those fifty-pound bags, and she's too proud to ask for help. Without food, them dogs will die off real quick and our problem will be solved. They probably wolf down a bag every day."

The mayor thought for a minute. "I don't like the smell of it, but this calls for extreme measures. Go ahead and put your plan in action, Turk. We'll meet right here Tuesday night and evaluate our success or failure."

So Turk Mowrey stopped supplying Cleo with dog food. Restless from not having their bellies full, the dogs soon began to fight among themselves. In desperation, Cleo cooked pots of vegetables, but the dogs came down with the runs. As she prepared for bed, Cleo locked the trailer door against her beloved dogs.

At the next meeting, Sorphus Peak spoke first. "Cleo Clendenny ain't bought groceries in two weeks."

"I had a Monkey Ward catalog for her the other day," Cliff Cory said, "and when I slowed down to toss it out, there wasn't a dog in sight."

"Maybe Turk's plan worked," said Mayor Varble. "Who wants to check it out?"

"I'll go," Deputy Sheriff Specs Kirbach said.

The next day around noon, Specs drove up the Clendenny driveway and parked the squad car in front of the farmhouse. He had not been to see Cleo since he had backed out of their wedding. He switched off the engine and sat for a minute, listening to the unnatural quiet. No birds were singing, no dogs growling or yipping. Something's out of kilter, he thought. He walked toward the house calling Cleo's name. The screen door was standing open. He stepped inside.

Bones of small dogs were everywhere. The large dogs were nowhere around. The deputy's stomach began to roll. Covering his nose with a handkerchief, he continued searching the filthy house. He found Cleo in the kitchen lying face down on the faded linoleum. The remaining bits of her torn flesh were alive with flies, and maggots crawled inside a deep wound in her thigh. Her dress was in shreds, exposing her brittle bones. Her starving dogs had done what was necessary to survive. Specs went outside and vomited until his throat was raw.

Deputy Specs Kirbach returned to inform Sheriff Ridenour that the matter of Cleo and her dogs was taken care
of. That night the Clendenny farmhouse and its grisly
contents burned even with the ground. "Although there
was not a cloud in the sky, the fire was determined to have
been an Act of God sent in the form of a well-placed light-
ning bolt," Cappy concluded his article.

Joe Bray didn't print Cappy's story. "It's a little gruesome
for my readers, but it's a good tale. Save it for a book."

Since Joe Bray had chosen not to publish the article on
Cleo Clendenny, Cappy got busy looking for other inter-
views. He thought a good angle would be how the war had
changed Old Kane. He found Harry Vandersand, disgruntled owner of a partially built meat locker, standing
in the middle of Main Street calculating his losses. He was
eager to discuss his bad luck.

"Looks like one of them bombed-out buildings in the
newsreels, don't it?" Harry said, gesturing toward the
brick walls and rubble. "Timing is everything, Cap. I
hadn't no more than got the locker under way when the
war started, putting the kibosh on new buildings that
wasn't part of the war effort. And now Mayor Varble says
I've got to tear it down. An eyesore, he calls it. More good
money chasing after bad. I lost my damned shirt."

"Have you thought about finishing it?" Cappy said.
"Most farmers have given up curing meat and hanging it
in the smokehouse to age. Seems to me they'd like having
a central place like this to keep a side of beef frozen till
they were ready to cook it."

"These days families are buying their own home freez-
ers to put in their basements. Hell, Cappy, I've even got a

Sears Roebuck freezer in *my* basement." He smiled grimly. "No, I won't be finishing the meat locker. Its time has come and gone."

So Vandersand's Meat Locker, obsolete before it had a door to open, would remain permanently abandoned.

Next Cappy drove to Radious Biesemeyer's to see whether the farmer would discuss the loss of his son, Willie, Greene County's first war casualty. Cappy and Willie had not been close friends, but he remembered watching the four Biesemeyer brothers helping Radious paint everything on the farm eggyolk yellow: the house, the corn crib, the outhouse. Willie was barely old enough to hold a paintbrush then.

When his body was brought home for burial, Cappy interviewed the accompanying soldier but didn't disturb the grieving family.

"Come on in the house, Cap," Radious said now. "I'll see if I can scare up some coffee." Cappy followed the elderly farmer up the porch steps and into the old-fashioned kitchen. Radious poured coffee and the two men sat down at the table.

"Say, does that old yellow Chevy Worthy bought off me still run?" Radious said. "I ain't seen it in a coon's age."

"It runs, but Pa doesn't have a license anymore to drive a car, so he goes to town on his tractor."

"A good old car, all right, and a pretty color. But then I'm partial to yellow. Now, why'd you say you stopped by?"

"I'm working on an article for the newspaper about the lingering effects of the war. If it isn't too hard to talk about, how did you and your wife get through Willie's death?"

Radious took a long, slow drink of coffee, gathering his thoughts. "Well, it's the hardest thing we ever undertook. Willie was different from our other boys, kind of special, you might say. He could bake a better pie than his mama could. Chocolate cream was his specialty. If I put my mind to it, I can taste that flaky crust and creamy filling. My wife still misses him helping out in the kitchen. As for getting through his death, there's a trick to everything, Cappy. If you'll look around the house, you'll see pictures of Willie setting on every table and hanging on every wall. There's even pictures in the outhouse and the root cellar. We see more of Willie now than we did when he was alive." Radious smiled briefly, then became solemn again. "Of course, it ain't the same as being able to walk over and touch his shoulder or ruffle his hair when he's setting on the davenport listening to the radio . . . More coffee?"

"I have to be going. Thanks for talking to me," Cappy said. He shook the old farmer's callused hand.

"It's the least I could do after that nice article you wrote about our Willie when he passed. 'Death of a War Hero' you called it. We cut it out of the *Patriot* and put it in a nice wood frame. It's hanging over our bed."

Joe Bray published both of Cappy's articles on war and Old Kane.

FOURTEEN

Since his return to Old Kane, Cappy had been having a recurring nightmare so real and terrifying he would delay going to bed until he couldn't read another page. In the disturbing dream he is about to be hanged on Kid Corner by an angry mob, eager to see him drop through the trapdoor and swing by his neck so they can get back to their coffee and gossip.

"But what did I do?" Cappy asks Mayor Varble.

"Not a goddamned thing!" says the mayor. "That's why we're hanging you!"

"You mean you're hanging me because I didn't do something?"

"That's right as rain! You knew a certain party was innocent of a certain crime and you kept your mouth shut. That much I'm certain of! Now hold still while I loop this noose around your neck."

At that point Cappy generally woke up, sweating like he'd been in a Decoration Day footrace. One night in October, after Mayor Varble tightened the noose, Cappy jumped out of bed, put on his pants and shirt, and went outside to clear his thoughts. He pumped a dipper of water from the well, took a long drink, and splashed what was left on his flushed face.

He sat on the back porch step, shivering in the cold night air. The sky was overcast, hiding the moon and stars that would have brightened the night and perhaps his mood. Maybe coming home had been a mistake, he thought. That's when the nightmares began.

Cappy couldn't discuss his feelings with Worthy; he was too close to be objective. Oleeta would try to be helpful, but he sensed she liked him too much to give an objective opinion. It didn't occur to Cappy that the person he should talk to was Drayton Hunt, the source of his nightly bouts of conscience.

As much as Cappy believed his biological father deserved to be in prison for a lifetime of hurtful acts, Drayton Hunt was innocent of the charge that sent him there. Worthy confessed to Cappy that he was the person who had held a pillow over Willa's face to end her months of suffering. Cappy was having trouble justifying his own part in that misdirection of justice.

Beany was another matter. Had Drayton been convicted of causing Beany's death, he would have spent a lifetime in prison, but there had been no hard evidence to implicate Drayton. At the trial, Cappy had been satisfied to see Drayton sentenced even for the wrong reason. Now, three years later, he was having second thoughts.

In spite of Cappy's vow not to call on Oleeta until he could afford to ask her for a date, Friday night he found himself standing outside of her door. He wasn't sure what kind of reception he'd get. When they had bumped into each other on Main Street, she barely spoke. Now, he ran a comb through his hair and knocked.

Oleeta opened the door a crack.

"Can I come in?" Cappy said.

"I suppose." She opened the door wider. "I was about to have some tea." She got out a second cup and set the teakettle on the stove. "Why are you here?"

"I thought I could help you with your journal." He glanced around the old-fashioned kitchen: the faded linoleum rug, yellow-flowered wallpaper, a sink with a hand pump. He wiped his clammy hands on his blue jeans.

"I haven't had anything to write in it lately and—" She stopped, a smile beginning. It wasn't in Oleeta's nature to stay angry. "Cappy Giberson, don't you know there isn't any journal?"

Cappy laughed out loud. "I suspected that might be the case."

"Let's go in the front room, the seats are softer," Oleeta said. They sat together on the sofa, sipping the strong, hot tea. She handed him an oatmeal cookie from a plate on the coffee table. "I keep telling Pa we need a television set for company, but he says he won't have one in the house. Though he thinks nothing of spending an entire evening watching the one at your house."

Cappy bit into a cookie. It was as hard as a rock. He dipped it in his tea to soften it. "I may as well get to the reason I barged in. There's something on my mind, and I need to talk to somebody."

"You sound serious."

He took another sip of tea and tried to think how to begin. Confiding was not in his nature, a trait he had inherited from Worthy. "A man went to prison for something I knew he hadn't done, and I kept quiet."

"Cappy, that almost makes you an accomplice."

"I know."

"Who was the man?"

"I don't want to say."

"Is he somebody I know?"

"Who he is doesn't matter."

"At least tell me what the crime was."

He hesitated. "The crime was smothering Ma."

"But isn't that why Drayton Hunt went to jail? Because your mama's Kewpie doll was found hanging in his car?"

"You're right but—"

"Everybody knows he's a crook. Pa says Drayton Hunt would steal the shell off a turtle if he could make money on it. And when he was just a boy he went into his uncle's bootlegging business. So why do you think he wasn't guilty?"

Cappy hesitated, not sure how much to tell Oleeta. "Because I know who *was* guilty."

"Then why didn't you just turn *that* man in?" The solution to Cappy's problem seemed simple to Oleeta.

Cappy paused. "Because I couldn't, and I still can't."

"How can I help when you aren't telling me everything?"

"You don't need to know the whole story." Cappy was beginning to be sorry he'd come.

"Since you don't trust me, how can I give an objective opinion?" Oleeta bristled. She picked up the empty teacups and carried them to the kitchen.

Cappy followed. "There's more to the story."

"You're sure I can keep a secret?" She stacked the cups in the sink.

"I can't tell you everything without betraying a trust."

"I guess I overreacted," she said. "I promise to listen and not make judgments." They returned to the sofa.

"I believed Drayton Hunt had something to do with Beany's death," Cappy said, "and that those moronic Woosley twins witnessed what happened but were too scared to say anything. I didn't speak up about my ma's murder. At the time I believed that Hunt belonged in prison, no matter what."

Oleeta touched Cappy's hand. "It must have been difficult these three years, carrying the burden of what you knew."

"Here's my dilemma. Should I confess to the sheriff that I know Drayton Hunt was innocent of smothering Ma, and get it off my conscience? I've been having awful nightmares."

Oleeta thought for a minute. "You wouldn't help anyone by telling what you know. Drayton Hunt served his sentence. He can't get those years back, and the sheriff would insist on your telling him who the guilty person was. He might even reopen the case. Sheriff Ridenour likes nothing better than a long, drawn-out trial. Whatever happened that night at your house, it was for Willa's best."

Oleeta pulled Cappy close to her; he put his head on her shoulder and closed his eyes. Weeks of sleepless nights suddenly caught up with him and he fell asleep.

Worthy was so accustomed to Bum's weekly visits that they had become as necessary as breathing the air around him. Bored with television, the two old friends had returned to their weekly game of rummy. On this particular Friday night Worthy was sitting in the dark, rocking. He didn't get up when he heard Bum come in the back door.

"Jesus, Worthy, I could of tripped and broke my neck in the dark. Are you too tight to pay the electric bill?" He felt for the string and pulled on the dim light.

"The damned electric's been weak," Worthy said. "I might as well go back to using my old Aladdin lamp. But no matter. I do my thinking better if I can't see things to distract me, like the davenport where Willa laid after the stroke. Or pillows in general," he added.

Bum had not seen Worthy so low since Willa died. "What's eating at you, Worthy? Has it got something to do with Cappy? Are you ailing?"

"No, it ain't Cappy, and I'm fit as a seventy-three-year-old man can expect to be. But there's something eating at me all right, treacherous as gangrene."

Bum settled back in the overstuffed chair, knowing he was in for one of Worthy's lengthy dissertations.

"Drayton Hunt, bastard that he is, shouldn't of gone to jail for an act I done. The man was innocent, Bum. I didn't speak up when I had the chance, and now it's come back to haunt me, like Marley's ghost."

"Jesus Christ, Worthy. Drayton Hunt ain't been innocent since the day Mae Hunt birthed him! Seems I recall us having this conversation before. Back then I told you no good could come from owning up to what you done, and I stand by them words. And what about poor Beany Ozbun coming home from the war only to die that very night? Most everybody suspected Hunt had something to do with that, me included. So leave it lay, Worthy."

"I reckon you're right, Bum. At the time I done the deed, I was thinking only about easing Willa's life. Who'd of thought I'd end up feeling sorry for Drayton Hunt?"

Later that night when Bum returned home, Cappy and Oleeta were asleep on the sofa. Well, what have we got here! Bum thought, seeing the two young people, who slept through his noisy entrance. He tiptoed up the stairs, grinning. Wait till Worthy hears about this! he thought. But by morning, Bum had forgotten all about it.

FIFTEEN

Cappy had finished reading the fifth chapter of *The Naked and the Dead,* a novel by a new young writer, Norman Mailer. Since borrowing it from the Carrollton library, he had been caught up in the tense story of World War II. And he's only two years older than I am, Cappy thought, enviously. But reading Mailer's account of the fighting was as close as Cappy wanted to be to the real thing. He put the book aside and was ready to turn off the bedside lamp when the telephone rang. Knowing Worthy had been asleep since sundown, he ran downstairs to pick up the receiver, wondering who was calling at eleven o'clock. Unless it was bad news, no one in Old Kane would risk a call after 8:00 P.M.

"Joe Bray, Cappy. I'll be brief about this, I know how you country people like your shuteye." The editor laughed heartily. "Here's the thing, I'm happy with the work you've been sending, real gut-wrenching stories about the human condition in rural Illinois. Funny stuff, too. Our readers love those homespun tales. Now here's the deal. I'm excited about it and hope you will be, too."

"Does it mean coming to St. Louis?" Cappy didn't trust the old Chevy to get him there and back.

"No, you can handle it right where you are. I got the idea from your story about the unkempt woman with sixty-some dogs. It showed a lot of imagination, and your writing style was right on the mark. I could smell those damned dogs! Do you think you can come up with enough country stories to make a book? I've got a friend in the publishing business who's agreed to look at your manuscript, after I've done some editing, of course. This could be your big chance."

"But even if I wrote a book that got published, there wouldn't be any royalties coming in for months. *If* there were any royalties," Cappy said.

"You let me worry about that, Cappy. If my pal likes what he sees, he can be persuaded to give you an advance. It might not be a lot, but you're living free with your dad. And how much can it cost to live in Old Kane anyway?"

"But I don't know any stories," Cappy insisted.

"Sure you do. You've got stories stored away in your unconscious that you don't even know are there. Just dig deep for those tales you heard as a kid and put up your listening aerial when you get a chance to hear the old-timers reminisce. They love talking about the olden days and how good life was then. Folks in the city will get a kick out of your down-home stories, and the way you people talk. It's like a foreign language to them."

"Don't expect me to make fun of people in Old Kane," Cappy said, feeling he should stand up for his town. "Rural people are as smart as city people, just in different ways."

"Sorry, I didn't mean to poke fun," Joe Bray said, "but it won't hurt to put a little humor in your book."

Cappy's future flashed through his mind, and how he would spend the wealth from his best-selling novel. He would never give up the farm entirely, but he would have a beach house on one of the oceans where he'd be inspired to write classic novels. Movie studios would call for rights to his books, and he would write the screenplays—

"Well, Cappy, what do you say?"

"Let me think about it for a day or two," Cappy said, back in the present.

Cappy spent the entire night watching the shadows of the cottonwood branches do-si-do from wall to wall.

"I heard a good one today," Worthy said to Bum as they sat near the kitchen woodstove waiting for the fire to take off.

"I could use a good tale," Bum said. "I ain't up to my usual."

"What's ailing you?" Usually Bum was the most good-spirited man around Old Kane.

"It's my cousin Broom Hetzel over in Haypress. Dropped dead with no prior hint. I wouldn't think so much about it if he was ninety, but he's two years younger than me. It got me to thinking how I could go in the blink of an eye, just like cousin Broom. One thing about it, when I *do* go I don't want no fal-de-ral at the church, with the preacher talking about how I'm setting at God's right hand. I wouldn't feel right taking up God's time, being a nonbeliever like I am. What about you, Worthy? Are you expecting to go somewheres else when you pass on?"

"I ain't expecting anything, but I sure as hell won't turn down a chance at another go-round. I might be rich in the next life," Worthy added, chuckling. "But one thing I know for sure. Thinking on it won't stave it off, so you might as well set back and enjoy a game of rummy."

"The truth is, I ain't ready to go, Worthy," Bum said. "There's my girls to think about, and what would you do come Friday night if I wasn't around?"

"Jesus, Bum, all I know for sure is you're ruining *this* Friday night. Now do you want to hear what I've got to tell or not?"

"I can see there's no staving you off either." After seventy years of friendship, he was accustomed to Worthy's methodical setting of a scene before launching into a story. Bum propped his feet on the ash bucket and closed his eyes.

Worthy settled back in his chair and lit his pipe. "Here's how it went. This morning I walked into Finice Darr's Garage to set and talk awhile. It ain't the same as it used to be at Pick's Grocery Store, you know that, but any barn in a hailstorm. Anyway, there was a half dozen of us gathered around smoking or chewing. Finice was patching Dabs Terpening's flat, the right front one, and a couple of others was watching Finice work.

"Finice says, 'Guess what I seen last Saturday walking up and down Main Street in the broad light of day. A Negro man!'

"'It ain't against the law for a Negro man to stop off in Old Kane if he's of a mind,' I says.

"'Unless he tries to eat at Mundy's Cafe or stay the night,' Finice says back. 'There's strict rules against—'"

"I can't say as I ever talked to one," Bum interrupted. "What did he have to say?"

"Seems he was looking to find a relation."

"Did Finice tell him there wasn't any of his persuasion in the whole of Greene County?" Bum said.

"He did, but he said he picked his words careful so as not to sound spiteful."

"I wonder if he talked like Negroes in the moving pictures? They sure are funny." Bum laughed, recalling an old musical. "Did Finice say anything about that?"

"He said the man talked like you and me, maybe better, like he'd been to high school."

"Damn. I wish I'd been there to hear him in person, I'm never where I'd ought to be. But what about that relation he was looking for?"

"There's your mystery," Worthy said. "The man swore up and down his sister's growed daughter had moved to Old Kane. He said she wrote a letter about it, even mentioned Bank Night at the picture show, and buying gasoline at Finice's garage. Finice told him Dot Stringer was the closest to his shade around Old Kane, but she got that way from laying out in the sun overly long."

"What happened next with the Negro man?"

"Finice said he stayed upwards of an hour, and as he was leaving he said a peculiar thing under his breath, but not so low Finice couldn't hear it."

Bum leaned in closer, Cousin Broom forgotten. "What did he say, Worthy?"

"'She must be passing.' What in God's name do you reckon he meant by that? 'She must be passing.'"

Bum thought for a minute. "Likely he meant she was passing through Old Kane when it come to her there wasn't no other coloreds. Or maybe he meant she was merely passing on her whereabouts so her folks back home wouldn't worry." Bum suddenly remembered Cousin Broom. "Maybe he meant the poor girl had passed on."

"We'll never know," Worthy said, shaking his head. "Too bad he couldn't of stuck around for the minstrel show. It's coming up soon. I'd rather watch a real Negro man any day than Dabs Terpening dancing around onstage with stove black smeared on his ugly face."

"When was the last minstrel show, anyway?" Bum said. "I can't hardly call up my own name these days."

"All I know is it was back before the war," Worthy said. "It didn't seem right having fun while our boys was dying, and that's when they stopped the minstrels. But we'd better make the best of this show, they may get to be a thing of the past. Some colored folks is bent out of shape at us pretending to be them."

Bum stood up. "Well, time I was going home."

"But what about our game?" Worthy protested. "I was planning to bring up some cider—"

Bum looked at his pocket watch and sat back down. "Cousin Broom's past helping anyway. And I sure wouldn't want you to get lonesome, Worthy," he added.

Cappy was in the kitchen reading more of *The Naked and the Dead* when Bum arrived. He'd gotten to the part where Father Leary told Gallagher that his wife had died in childbirth, but the baby had lived. That could be the story of my birth, Cappy thought, except in my case there was no grieving husband. He tried to get back into the book but found himself listening to the story about the Negro. Laying his book aside, he began making notes. He felt like a teenager again, sitting behind the potbellied stove in Pick's Grocery Store eavesdropping as Worthy, Bum, and their cronies talked about the war that was lasting longer than anyone had thought, how daylight saving time was not God's time, and about loose girls joining the army.

With sudden insight, Cappy realized he was privy to a fading culture. Joe Bray had been right; he needed to pay close attention to what he saw and heard, and dig back in his memory for stories he had listened to as a boy. Maybe he should seriously consider writing that book about Old Kane. What better way to keep the past from disappearing along with Worthy and Bum and others of their aging generation? Cappy slipped upstairs and began to write.

The next morning Cappy returned Joe Bray's call. "I'll need a reliable typewriter."

"Go ahead and buy what you want and send me the bill," Joe said. "You can pay me back once the money starts rolling in." He laughed. Everything was funny to Joe Bray. Although Cappy had never met the editor in person, Cappy had picked up on some things about him from their frequent conversations. Joe believed that country people read only the *Farmers Almanac* and *Successful Farming*, and that their language was "quaint." If confronted, Joe Bray would probably have defended himself by saying that his beliefs were not prejudice but fact.

"And an extra hundred for a car that runs," Cappy said. "I can't expect my pa to let me wear out his old car."

"You're a hard man, McGee," Joe laughed again. "I hope I don't live to regret this bargain."

Me either, Cappy thought.

Cappy knew nothing about automobiles except that he needed one that was reliable but inexpensive. First thing Monday morning he went to see what Finice Darr had to offer in the way of a cheap, secondhand car.

"There's a couple out back that runs," Finice said. "The keys are inside. You can take 'em for a spin. Don't forget to pump the brakes if you expect to stop."

The two cars Finice had for sale—black Ford sedans built in the late thirties—had seen better days. Cappy got into the older one first, turned the key, pushed the starter button, and pumped the foot feed several times to get the gas flowing. The engine groaned but didn't start. He tried the second car, a year newer, which started on the first try. That makes the choice easy, he thought.

"Don't be fooled by that pretty one just because she started," someone behind him said.

Drayton Hunt was leaning against a light pole, smiling smugly. Dressed in faded overalls rolled up at the cuffs and a blue cap that advertised "Hawk's Laying Mash," Drayton was looking more and more like a farmer. "That first car you tried is a hundred times better than the second one," he said, "even if it's older and scratched and wouldn't start."

"Why would I buy a car that won't start? I'm not a moron!"

"I'm not saying you're a moron, you just don't have my know-how with motorcars. When it comes to cars, I'm a natural, picked it up on my own when I was a boy. If you'd grown up living with me, you'd know about cars."

"I won't buy a car that won't start."

"Oh, it'll start. You flooded it, is all. I could have it purring like a pussy in ten minutes. I may not be a genius at books, but I know my cars, and that car you favor is a piece of horseshit."

As much as Cappy disliked to admit it, he recognized Drayton's expertise with cars. Drayton's 1924 Moon was in perfect running condition. When Cappy worked at the *Democrat-Republican Patriot*, he had once been a reluctant passenger in the Moon. At Min Wollums's insistence, he had agreed to write an article about the unique car, and to make his writing more authentic he had accepted a ride. Drayton had purposely driven to the spot in the country where he had first tried to seduce Chastity Giberson, and when he made insulting remarks about the girl, Cappy had punched him in the nose and walked home through the rain. Like mother, like son, Drayton had thought at the time, recalling the rainy day Chastity had bloodied his nose.

In spite of Drayton Hunt's knowledge of cars, Cappy would not take advice from him. "I'm not buying a car that won't start," he snapped. He returned to the garage to make a deal with Finice.

As Cappy was turning Prough's Corner, not a mile from Darr's Garage, the car choked and sputtered to a stop. Swearing with each step, Cappy walked the half mile home and telephoned Finice to come pick up the car. He rode back to town with Finice and bought the other Ford, the one Drayton had recommended.

"The other day I overheard you two talking about the Negro man who was asking about a relative," Cappy said to Worthy and Bum, as they sat waiting for the television programs to begin. "I know what he meant by 'passing.' It's someone who's a Negro but doesn't look like one. Their skin is as white as a Caucasian's, and if they can pass for white their lives are easier."

"I never heard of such," Worthy said, shaking his head. "How'd you come to know this?"

"I had a Negro professor, and we discussed it in his class."

"It don't seem right," Bum said, "fooling people. You might not know better and invite 'em to your house for supper."

"Wait a damned minute," Worthy said. "Underneath all this, you're saying there's a woman amongst us who's doing this 'passing'?"

"It's possible," Cappy said.

"But who could it be?" Bum said. "Everybody I know was born and raised here." He thought for a minute. "Hold on, there's Audley Lomelino's intended. She's from down around Granite City or East St. Louis. Do you reckon it's her?"

Worthy laughed. "Audley's pa would keel over if that's true. But she's got yellow hair."

"According to Oleeta, most yellow hair comes out of a bottle," Bum said.

"What about that waitress at Mundy's, June Plummer?" Worthy said. "She's from somewhere else. She's got black hair, but it ain't curly."

"There's ways to take the curly out," Bum said. "Oleeta said that, too."

The next time Worthy and Bum went to Finice Darr's Garage for a cup of coffee, they passed on what Cappy had told them. It wasn't often that they had such big news. It sparked another argument among Finice Darr's customers.

"I say there's nothing wrong with it," Dabs Terpening said. "More power to her."

"And I say it's going against nature," Finice said. "What if us white people tried to pass ourselves off as Negroes? You can bet they wouldn't stand still for it."

"It can't be done anyhow," Worthy said. "Look at Al Jolson. He put black on his face and sang like a colored man, but he sure wasn't fooling anybody."

"I for one intend to keep my eyes open," Finice said.

"That's a good idea, Finice, or you're likely to fall flat on your face," Bum said.

SIXTEEN

"Not a fit day for man nor beast," Worthy said as he and Cappy were finishing breakfast at the height of a rare autumn thunderstorm. The kitchen was so dark Worthy had reluctantly pulled on the light above the table, going against his personal vow not to use electricity during daylight hours. Occasionally the lightbulb would flicker as the wind blew tree branches against the outside wires.

"I've been wanting to look around the attic for stories I wrote in high school," Cappy said. "Knowing Ma, she stashed them away as if Mark Twain himself wrote them. They'll make me cringe, but I want to make sure I haven't been wasting my time and money on school."

"Help yourself, I'm sure they're up there somewhere amongst the keepings," Worthy said. "I might just set here by the fire and read a spell. The new *Country Gentleman* come in the mail yesterday. I need to keep up with the latest us 'country gentlemen' is up to these days." He began thumbing through the pages.

Cappy climbed the steep, narrow stairs to the attic, the ideal place to be on a dark, drizzly day. His great-grandmother's dress form was still standing guard over the rest of the "keepings." When Cappy was very young, he was frightened of the form, made to duplicate the ample shape of Willa's mother. At first he believed it was the woman herself, but ominously without arms, legs, or head. Even after Willa explained its purpose, the four-year-old boy was careful not to touch it accidentally and risk being turned into a mere form of himself.

Hanging in an old wardrobe were clothes that had belonged to Chastity. As a child, Cappy always went there first. He knew each garment intimately: the blue plaid dress she wore to school, the white organza that was saved for Sunday school and parties, skirts and sweaters of every color—her favorite outfits to wear to the movies. Cappy would hold each garment up to his own small body to get a sense of her height and size when she was fourteen. Her final year.

Until Willa's stroke, she had continued washing Chastity's dresses every Monday morning and hanging them on the clothesline to dry in the fresh air. Tuesdays she carefully sprinkled and ironed the heavily starched dresses and hung them back in the wardrobe.

It was unfair that Chastity's clothes had outlived her by twenty-three years, Cappy thought. Today he didn't look at the dresses and sweaters.

Cappy opened an old trunk where Willa had stored, but never got around to trying, recipes clipped from the woman's page in the *Country Gentleman* and Chastity's, Tick's, and Cappy's school papers and report cards. His stories were not there, but he continued to look. Once a piece of paper entered the Giberson house, Cappy knew it was there to stay. ("If somebody goes to the trouble of putting words on paper," Willa had said, "it's not polite to throw those words in the trash.")

Cappy found his stories in the bottom drawer of a discarded bureau, tied with a piece of red yarn left over from a sweater Willa had knitted him. As he lifted the bundle from the drawer, he saw a smaller bundle, held together by a rubber band, that appeared to be letters. He was puzzled. Willa had never written or received letters. Everyone she knew lived in Greene County only a short distance away.

Cappy slipped the rubber band off and was surprised to see that the unopened envelopes were addressed to him, postmarked from the state penitentiary. He opened the envelope with the oldest postmark, which appeared to be singed along one edge, and began to read: *Dear Cappy, I am not good at writing letters but I hope you will take time to read this once or twice—*

One at a time Cappy tore open the envelopes and read each letter, none more than a page long: *Dear Cappy, I guess you are away at some fancy college getting smarter by the day, while I get dumber. Ha! When we both get out and come home to Old Kane, maybe we can have a cup of coffee together. I was joking about getting dumber every day. I have a new friend named Chaplain Davenport and he's teaching me all about the Bible. Maybe I'll end up like your brother. Preaching to sinners. Now wouldn't that be something—*

Cappy sat on top of the old trunk, thinking about the carefully written letters that told of the dangers of prison life, the awful food, and Drayton's hopes for the future— his own as well as Cappy's:

Dear Cappy, I hope you learn all you can about being a writer. You will end up making a lot of money, not like your old man who doesn't have two nickels to rub together.

Cappy didn't stop until he had read all of the letters—three years' worth. Apparently Worthy had kept the letters hidden but couldn't bring himself to throw them away. Cappy stretched the rubber band over the envelopes and returned them to the drawer. Although Cappy had a better understanding of the rough, uneducated man who claimed to be his father, he wasn't ready to accept Drayton into his life.

Cappy carried the collection of stories down to his room and spent the rest of the day reading his own essays on how to bring about world peace—written during World War II—and short stories about teenagers having wild sex in the backseat of a Packard parked in Jalappa Cemetery. He laughed at the youthful, pretentious writing. However, one of the stories gave him an idea for a series of articles to submit to the *Post-Dispatch.*

By evening, Cappy had decided to confront Worthy about the hidden letters. As they were finishing supper, Cappy said, "Guess what I found in the attic." His tone was accusatory, which slipped past Worthy.

"Well, I reckon you found them stories you was looking for."

"I found them, all right, and more besides."

"What are you getting at?" Worthy said. "You talk like a man with a fish bone stuck in his craw."

"The letters from Drayton Hunt, I found them. Why didn't you forward them to me? The envelopes had my name on them."

"Well, now Cap, I—" Worthy stammered, "I didn't want to upset you while you was studying so hard. I knew you couldn't tolerate the bastard, and them letters might have bothered you so much you'd of flunked a big test. I was only looking out for you."

"I'm a grown man. Whether I read a letter or throw it away unopened, I get to decide." He stormed out of the house, letting the door slam.

"That boy's got a temper to match Bum's girl," Worthy said. "A match made in heaven."

The following morning, Cappy stopped at Mundy's to eat lunch and make notes on a series of articles about how rural families were dealing with abundance after the war—from refrigerators and new automobiles to the return of coat pockets and cuffs on garments. He hadn't discussed his idea with Joe Bray, but he was pretty sure the editor would go for it. "Homey" is how Joe would describe such writing. Ten o'clock was early for lunch, but Cappy ordered a hamburger sandwich and a bottle of Coca-Cola. Chig grumbled at having to turn on the griddle so early in the day and made the hamburger half its usual size.

Sammy Postlewaite, Toby Vandersand, and Port Williams, town boys in their late teens, sat in a nearby booth discussing a surprise shivaree for Audley Lomelino and his bride-to-be, Betty Sue, the blond East St. Louis girl.

Cappy had never been to a shivaree, and he was curious to know what it was all about. Eavesdropping was easy, as the three boys were loud with their plans. He put aside his notes to listen.

"The wedding night whoopee will take place in that old cabin down by Macoupin Creek," Port was saying, "the one Audley's pa uses for fishing trips."

"The wedding's not till seven at night," Toby said, "so we'll have plenty of time to short-sheet the bed and hang rubbers on the doorknobs before the happy couple gets there."

"We'll give Audley time to get going good before we start ringing cowbells and shooting off firecrackers," Port said, laughing in expectation of the rowdy fun.

"Any chance we can peek through the window?" Sammy said. He was the only virgin among the three.

"I doubt we'd see anything," Toby said. "This being her first time, Betty Sue won't want Audley seeing her without her nightclothes on. She'll likely make him wait till the lights go out before she gives in."

"Let's meet at the cabin around six and get things set up," Port said. "I'll bring the cowbells and beer. Toby, you get plenty of firecrackers and a stink bomb if you can find one. And Sammy, you're in charge of rubbers. You can fill them with water after we get to the cabin."

By eight o'clock Saturday evening, Cappy was standing behind a catalpa tree near Lomelino's fishing cabin. The ground was covered with pods from the old tree, lying like parentheses under Cappy's feet. At sundown the temperature had plummeted to freezing, and a sharp wind from the north had kicked up. Shivering, he pulled his hat down over his ears and stuck his hands in his pockets. This better be good, he thought.

Toby, Port, and Sammy were hiding in the bushes when the newlyweds arrived. Audley parked his truck in front of the cabin, ready for a night of raucous fun. His only sexual experience had been with a waitress he met at the St. Louis Stockyards Cafe, and had cost him a week's pay and several visits to the doctor. Audley was tickling his bride, still in her wedding dress and veil. She giggled wildly. When Reverend Smith wasn't looking, Port had spiked the fruit punch with whiskey. Betty Sue was a big girl, and Audley was quickly out of breath from carrying her into the cabin. Once inside, he lit a lamp and resumed tickling her. Betty Sue giggled politely, but she had lost interest in the game. Dropping her wedding bouquet on the table, she walked resolutely toward the bedroom. Audley followed, giddy from punch and anticipation.

The three boys waited ten minutes, then began whooping, ringing cowbells, and setting off firecrackers under the bedroom window. Audley, naked, opened the front door. "Hello, fellas! Nice of you to drop by and be sociable! Come on in and set while I conclude my business!" He wagged his penis and guffawed.

The guests helped themselves to the beer and snickered at the grunts and squeals coming from the wedding bed.

Another ten minutes and Audley emerged from the bedroom, still naked, his mission obviously accomplished. "Damn, she's hot as a firecracker!" he said. He picked up a newspaper and fanned his crotch. "I might just have me another go-round after I get my wind back!" They all laughed and opened more beer.

As the boys were finishing their drinks, Betty Sue appeared at the bedroom door, a cigarette dangling from her moist red lips, as if she were Marlene Dietrich in a foreign film. Betty Sue's eyelashes were heavy with mascara, her face thick with pancake makeup and rouge. She was wearing a sheer, silky robe that showed her large pendulous breasts and prominent nipples. With one hand she expertly loosened the belt, and the robe fell all the way open. After a quick assessment of her bridegroom's friends, she pointed at Toby with her cigarette and said, "You in the green jacket, you can come in."

Toby looked at Audley, not sure he had understood the implication of Betty Sue's words.

"Shit, go on and give it a try," Audley said, not entirely with enthusiasm. "My pecker can use the rest."

"Well, I wouldn't want your bride thinking me rude," Toby said, as he followed Betty Sue into the bedroom—a look of pleasure and disbelief on his chubby face.

"Just save some for me!" Audley tried to joke. He opened another beer and sat on the sofa, his face glum.

To see better, Cappy had moved from behind the catalpa tree to the bedroom window. Although he was embarrassed at watching the couple have sex, he couldn't turn his eyes away. Even worse, seeing Betty Sue's voluptuous body, bent over Toby's crotch, had given him a healthy erection. Joe Bray wouldn't publish this story. "Too raunchy for *Post-Dispatch* readers," he'd say, "but keep it for that book you're going to write."

The book. It was never out of Cappy's thoughts. He was spending more and more time recalling events in his childhood or asking Worthy about something that had happened when he and Bum were boys—always with the book in mind. But would anyone want to read about the way life used to be in Old Kane?

By the time Cappy turned into the lane, Worthy was in bed and the house was dark. Still chilled from standing outside Lomelino's cabin, Cappy got out cocoa, sugar, vanilla, and milk, and fixed a pan of hot cocoa. He filled a mug with the steaming drink and dropped in two crusty marshmallows.

Sipping the hot drink, Cappy wrote a few notes about the unlikely shivaree. He laughed out loud as he recalled the bewildered look on the groom's face at Betty Sue's unexpected invitation to Toby. Cappy wondered whether

Port and Sammy benefited from the bride's generosity after he left.

One thing's for sure, Cappy thought, Betty Sue isn't the one who's "passing." She's a natural blond. But he would keep that information to himself. At times like this, Cappy missed Beany the most, wishing he could share the bizarre events of the evening with his late best friend.

Say, Old Bean! If you'd been there I bet Betty Sue would have called you in first!

I'm as bad as the old-timers, Cappy thought, living safely in the past where nothing unexpected can happen. He finished his cocoa and went to bed.

SEVENTEEN

D o you reckon Sorphus Peak will jump Jim Crow this year?" Bum said, as he and Worthy sat at Worthy's kitchen table discussing the upcoming minstrel show. No one now living had ever seen the original dance, but it was said to have been originated by a deformed man with a limp who was trying to walk without falling down.

"There's none better than Old Sorphus once he gets to going," Worthy said. "He can gyrate and jump Jim Crow better than anybody I ever seen."

Cappy, always after a good story, joined the two men.

"And you don't think there'll be any problems?" Cappy said. "Negroes are sensitive about how they're portrayed."

"How many of 'em will be setting in the Old Kane grade school come October 27?" Worthy said.

"The woman who's 'passing' might be there," Bum said.

"I hope you don't get picketed by a busload of Negroes from East St. Louis," Cappy said, thinking how naive Worthy and Bum were about the world outside Old Kane.

"You fret too much," Worthy said. "Since you come home from that highbrow school, you've forgot what's fun."

"Who's directing the show this year?" Bum interrupted. "I hope to hell he knows what he's doing."

"Sam Galloway, the new high school band teacher," Worthy said. "He'll likely try to change it around to suit hisself, that's usually how it goes."

As Worthy predicted, Sam Galloway brought his own ideas to the show. His first innovation was to dispense with blackface. He announced this to the players at rehearsal in the high school gym.

"Hell, it won't be a minstrel show if everybody's got a white face," Sorphus argued. "How would it look if white men was to shake tambourines and play bones? It ain't natural! And on top of that, it ain't funny!"

"Amen to that!" several men shouted. Twenty minutes of protest followed, voices raised, everyone talking at once.

In the end, Mr. Galloway gave in to tradition. His next attempt at change was to hold auditions for the singing and speaking parts, but everyone who came to the first meeting had already chosen the part he wanted and expected to perform.

"We're the Old Kane Banjo Band," Harry Post, the originator and leader said proudly. "Take us or leave us!" But when Mr. Galloway heard their performance of "Alabama Bound," he was pleasantly surprised at their professional sound, though not his taste in music.

Because of his authoritative voice and handlebar mustache, Mayor Dinghie Varble assumed the part of Interlocutor. The endmen, Tambo and Bones, would be performed by Worthy and Bum, whose reputations as storytellers assured them of those leading parts. For past shows, they'd already spent many hours practicing to make their voices sound like Negroes in the movies and rolling their eyes for dramatic accent.

At the first rehearsal, Mr. Galloway clapped his hands for silence. "All right, now, let's everybody get in the spirit of the show. We'll run through the endmen's dialogue first."

"Try not to mess up your lines," Worthy whispered to Bum.

"Just you worry about your own lines," Bum whispered back.

"Don't forget you're playing 'Bones,'" Worthy said.

"Hell, I ain't got hardening of the arteries!"

"All right, all right, everybody quiet down," Mr. Galloway said. "Go ahead, endmen, and put some life in it."

Worthy and Bum took their places at the front of the stage.

Bones: *Tambo, she's gone dead!* Bum rattled his pair of bones.

Tambo: *She's dead, Bones?* Worthy shook his head in disbelief.

Mr. Galloway wasn't satisfied. "Endmen, don't just stand there! Move around!"

Bum began again.

Bones: *Tambo, she's gone dead!* He rattled his bones and danced a jig.

"That's more like it," Mr. Galloway said.

Worthy and Bum finished practicing their routine and bowed. The rest of the cast applauded.

"Not bad," Mr. Galloway said, laughing in spite of himself.

After two weeks of nightly rehearsals, the show was ready to go on. Cappy was sad that Willa and Tick weren't there to share the evening. Willa, smelling of vanilla extract, would have been sitting in the front row so she wouldn't miss a word, and Tick, his hair slicked down with Brylcreem, would have been at Cappy's side.

Earlier that day, Oleeta had called and offered to save a seat for Cappy. "I have to be there early anyway to help Pa with his costume, so it's no trouble."

"That would be great," Cappy said. "Get seats up front."

When Cappy arrived at the high school gymnasium, most of the seats were taken. "Do you know how hard it is to save a seat?" Oleeta said. "Some people got really mad at me, and said seats were first come, first served."

"They're right," Cappy said, "but I'm glad you held your ground. These are great seats."

At eight o'clock the curtain, made of heavy oilcloth and advertising local places of business, rolled up like a window shade. Members of the Old Kane Banjo Band, comprising two banjos, one violin, a pair of bones, a tambourine, and a triangle, were dressed in trousers, vests, white shirts, and stovepipe hats. Except for white paint around their lips, their faces were burnt-cork black. They sat in front of the stage awaiting their cue.

With the entire cast of men standing in a semicircle on stage, the Interlocutor spoke in a booming voice and flourished a deep bow. "Gentlemen, be seated! We will commence with the overture!"

After a medley of songs, "Jenny Get Your Hotcake Done," "Dixie," "Walk Along, John," the troupe cakewalked to three choruses of "Alabama Bound." One at a time each man danced to the center of the stage and performed his specialty. Finice Darr got the most laughs. His act was removing his clothes, one garment at a time, until all twenty layers were on the floor at his feet and he was left wearing only a suit of long red underwear.

The Amoma Sunday School class was collectively shocked at the vulgar display. "Finice Darr, you'd ought to be ashamed!" Lydia Summer shouted when he finished his performance. "It's a good thing your poor mother's dead and can't see you parading around practically in your altogether!" As teacher of the Amomas, Lydia felt responsible for the spiritual guidance of her class. But since the ladies had paid for tickets, Lydia gave them permission to stay for the entire show and close their eyes when necessary.

During intermission, Cappy and Oleeta went to the refreshment table for a glass of strawberry punch. "The show's good," Cappy said, his voice low, "but watching it makes me uncomfortable."

"Why would it?"

"Because they're making fun of Negroes."

"You're too judgmental," she said. "I bet Negroes themselves would think the show's funny. Haven't you seen how they act in the movies?"

Cappy was surprised to find Oleeta so provincial. Doesn't she ever read a newspaper to see how the world's changing? he thought. "You've been stuck in the country too long," he said. "If that's being judgmental, so be it."

"Just because you went to school near Chicago, you think you're smarter than I am."

"I had a creative writing professor who was a Negro, and he said white people think of Negroes only as dancers or singers. Those are the only acting jobs they can get."

"I bet your professor could have danced if he'd wanted to."

"That's the dumbest remark I've heard!" Cappy said, raising his voice. How could I have a relationship with someone so bigoted? he thought, though at the same time he knew she was just seeing things the way she'd been brought up to.

The show resumed with Sorphus Peak, who jumped Jim Crow to the accompaniment of the chorus and the banjo band.

> *First on the heel tap, then on the toe,*
> *Every time I wheel about I jump Jim Crow.*
> *Wheel about and turn about and do just so*
> *And every time I wheel about I jump Jim Crow.*

Sorphus received so much applause, the entire number was repeated.

Sam Galloway cued the endmen. Worthy stood up and strutted to the center of the stage, with Bum limping alongside. They bowed dramatically to a scattering of applause.

Bones: *Tambo, she's gone dead!* Bum said, rattling his pair of bones and wiping away an imaginary tear.

Tambo: *She's dead, Bones?* Worthy shook his head in disbelief.

Bones: *Yes, Tambo. Three days after she died she sent for me.*

Tambo: *No, Bones, you mean three days previous to her decease.*

Bones: *No, she had no niece. She was an orphan.* He sobbed with despair.

Tambo: Worthy scratched his head. *What you mean is, she sent for you three days before she departed this earthly tenement.*

Bones: *Come again?*

Tambo: *Three days before she died. Are you deaf?* He pointed to his ears.

Bones: *Dead or alive, I went to see her anyhoo. She says real weak, her voice shaking like she was praying to Almighty God above, "I'm going to leave this world of care."*

Tambo: *And what did you reply?*

Bones: *I said I didn't care much. Then she sent me to the apothecary shop to see Dr. Night Bell.* Bum danced around Worthy.

Tambo: *That's the name of the bell on the door, Bones. The night bell. But I expect he was a pretty good physician?*

Bones: *No, he wasn't fishing, he was to home.* He pantomimed throwing out a fishing line. *Anyhoo he give me some pills for her to swallow.*

Tambo: *Was the medicine in any way efficious?*

Bones: *Now look here, Tambo!* He shook a finger in Worthy's face. *Be so kind as to address me in the English language!*

The show ended with the Interlocutor's stump speech. Instead of reciting the planned monologue from the play book, Mayor Varble took advantage of the opportunity to express his political views.

He took off his hat to show respect for his intended patriotic speech. "Now folks," he began, in his booming voice, "we've all had some good laughs tonight, but let me warn you! If Harry Truman beats Thomas Dewey in the upcoming election, this country won't be doing any more laughing. Before you can shake a stick we'll all be working in CCC camps again and standing in line for a bowl of thin soup. Us older folks know what we're talking about, so be sure to vote—"

When the audience started booing, the mayor quickly returned to his chair and signaled the banjo band to play something lively.

After the final curtain call, Cappy said to Oleeta, "Bum and Worthy's routine was the hit of the show."

"They were the funniest," she agreed, the argument with Cappy forgotten.

"Want to see if Mundy's Cafe is open?" Cappy said. "Hot cocoa sounds good. My car isn't the best in the world, but it runs."

"Sure. Wait here while I tell Pa that I won't be riding home with him."

Mundy's was overflowing with people who had come from the minstrel show, and there were no seats. "Let's go to my house," Oleeta offered. "I'll make the cocoa."

"You've made it before?" Cappy said skeptically.

"Of course I have."

"Then let's go." Cappy was surprised when Oleeta scooted next to him in the car. "Are you cold?"

"Not anymore." She snuggled closer.

Cappy wanted to touch her bare knee. "Too bad my car doesn't have a radio," he said.

"That's okay, I'm not in the mood for music. Are you in a hurry to get home?" she said.

"No. Is there someplace you want to go?"

"Maybe we could drive by Green Summit School. I heard it was being closed, maybe torn down. I had some good times there. Miss Coonrod was my favorite teacher. On Friday afternoons she polished all the girls' finger-nails."

"Sure, we can drive by and take a look at the old place," Cappy said. Five minutes later they were approaching Green Summit. He pulled into the driveway of the one-room school and drove around to the back. He switched off the engine and set the brake.

"Why'd you park way back here?" Oleeta asked.

"It's out of sight of the road," Cappy said. "I don't want any bushwhackers sneaking up on us. Want to get out and walk around to the front of the schoolhouse? I have a flashlight."

"Do you think the door might be unlocked?"

"We can see." Cappy took her hand, and led her over the uneven yard. They stepped onto the porch and Cappy tried the door. To his surprise, it opened. "How about that!" he said. They stepped inside and closed the door behind them.

"It still smells like chalk and dirty kids," Oleeta laughed. She walked toward the dust-covered desks, four rows of them. "Shine the light over here, Cappy. This was my very first desk. I can't believe I was ever small enough to fit in that little seat." She took the flashlight and continued exploring the room, seeming to have forgotten Cappy.

"It's cold in here," Cappy said, shivering. "Let's go back to the car."

"Maybe I'll come back here in the daylight," she said, following Cappy. "I'd like to buy that desk for a keepsake. Do you think the school board would sell it?"

"It wouldn't hurt to ask." He helped her into the car and walked around to the driver's side. She snuggled next to him again.

Sitting so close to Oleeta, Cappy felt nervous, not quite sure what to do next. With Min Wollums he hadn't concerned himself—she knew exactly how to excite him—and his quick response was enough to excite and amuse her. Presuming Oleeta was inexperienced, he would have to go slow. Cautiously he put his arm around her shoulder and lightly kissed her cheek. She smelled of Evening in Paris. Even at the newspaper office, Min always smelled of Chanel, an expensive perfume she bought from Paris.

Cappy hadn't been intimate with a woman since his last time in Min's bed, the night before he left for college. "Call it a going-away gift," she had said, as she climbed into bed beside him and drew him close to her voluptuous body.

Oleeta turned her face toward Cappy and kissed his mouth, touching his lips with the tip of her tongue. It tasted like a ripe strawberry. That was all the encouragement he needed. He now had a full erection. He kissed her hard, exploring her open mouth with his own tongue. He slipped his hand under her sweater and pushed her bra aside. Not as ample as Min, he thought. But nice. He leaned down and put his mouth on her erect nipple.

Oleeta moved her legs apart. Urged on, Cappy put his hand under her skirt. Then without warning, she shoved him away. She scooted to the far side of the seat and rearranged her bra. "Let's go!" she said angrily.

Cappy was puzzled. "Did I do something wrong? I thought you were sending a clear signal. You're not playing fair."

"I have limits to how far I'll go," she said.

"Is one kiss your limit?"

"I'm not Min Wollums!"

"You sure as hell aren't!"

"I'm ready to go home."

"I'm ready to take you."

"You can forget about the cocoa," she said.

"I already have!"

Cappy switched the ignition and jammed the car into reverse, then shifted through the forward gears. A perfect end to a perfect evening! he thought, as he roared down the road, loose gravel flying into the ditch. He felt embarrassed and betrayed at being led on and then unceremoniously rebuffed as if he were to blame. With Min, he always knew where he stood—she never played games with his feelings. Cappy wondered whether he would spend his life comparing every woman with Min Wollums.

EIGHTEEN

After a few days, Tick was settling down to farm life as if he had never left. Getting his hands dirty brought back his young years on the farm: helping Worthy repair sagging fences, scooping manure from the cow barn, readying the fields for planting corn and soybeans. But his stay with the Wehrlys would be short, two or three weeks at the most. Winter was quickly approaching and he needed to keep walking north before the blizzards and ice storms set in.

The next morning when the rooster crowed, Tick jumped out of bed and hurriedly dressed. He was hungry again. As he entered the kitchen a minute before 5:00 A.M., Mrs. Wehrly was frying sausage and eggs. Biscuits were rising in the hot oven, the door propped open a crack to make them taller, more delicate. She was wearing the same faded dress as yesterday—a shapeless print with long sleeves—but her hair was neatly combed. And she had powdered her face with pink powder, the color Willa wore on movie night or to a revival. Mrs. Wehrly smiled at

Tick as he sat down at the table. Her husband arrived a minute later. He nodded to Tick but didn't acknowledge his wife. She set plates of hot food in front of both men and joined them at the table with her own breakfast of hot oatmeal and thick top cream.

"I could use some help in the garden," she said to her husband. "Can you spare the boy this morning?"

"Dammit, Mother, gardening is woman's work! Besides, I thought the garden was done for."

"There's potatoes left in the ground. They're too deep for me to dig out myself."

"All right, he's yours till dinnertime. I've got to drive into Energy and pick up some feed anyway."

Tick followed the farmer's wife to the large garden.

"Your husband calls you 'Mother,'" Tick said. "Have you got a real first name?"

"Elsie's my given name, but nobody's called me that since I married. Mostly I'm called Mrs. Beal Wehrly, like Elsie doesn't exist anymore. It's the custom here in the country." She held a gunnysack open while Tick tossed in large russet potatoes, scattered throughout the garden. He was surprised at the number they found, buried deep, covered with rich, black earth. He was reminded of the times he had helped Willa dig potatoes and how—when she wasn't looking—he would brush away the dirt and eat one.

That evening as bedtime approached, Beal Wehrly followed Tick to the barn. "How's that cot for sleeping?" he asked.

"I sleep like a baby no matter where I'm at," Tick said, "but I didn't do enough work today to have such a fine cot."

"I won't run around the mulberry bush, boy. The truth is, I don't need no farm help, but I do need to engage you in other ways. The wife has took to reading them *Redbook* stories, and has got ideas that I can't pull off while I'm in the midst of getting the fall crops out. To keep myself from falling to temptation I've already moved into the spare room, like I do every busy season. In the meantime, she's getting more sour with each passing day. I seen how she was looking you over, even powdered her face, so I'll give you room and board and a little extra if you'll entertain the wife to her satisfaction."

"You've got a fine wife," Tick said, "but I'm on a journey home, and I have to be there before the snow flies. All I could stay is a couple of weeks."

"That should be enough," he said. "Just make sure you sound like you mean it when you say them pretty words. You know how women are."

The next morning, Elsie Wehrly put on red lipstick that she kept for a Saturday night movie or Easter Sunday worship. She smiled at Tick as she set his breakfast on the table. "I can use the boy's help today," she said to her husband.

Beal pretended anger. "Hell, woman, I thought I was the one needing a farmhand! But I reckon you can have him till noon." He winked at Tick.

"One of my barn cats is missing," Elsie said to Tick when they were alone in the kitchen. "Maybe she wandered into the woods."

"She's probably a goner," Tick said. "There's all kinds of woods varmints that feed on cats."

"I won't rest till I find out. She's my best mouser." Elsie led Tick down a narrow path through the dense woods until they came to a brook of clear water, swimming with a few hardy minnows left from summer.

"Let's rest here a spell," she said, brushing dry leaves and twigs from a spot on the mossy bank. She reached into her dress pocket and brought out two Jonathan apples, red as her full lips. She gave one to Tick and took a bite of hers. It was crisp, and the juice ran down her chin. Tick leaned over and licked away the juice. Opening her bodice, she pulled Tick to her breast as if she were his mother. Tick didn't believe this was what Beal Wehrly had in mind, but Elsie Wehrly had her own ideas. Tick was loath to return to his role of fancy man, and to make matters worse, she reminded him of Willa.

Afterward Tick wanted to take a nap, but Elsie was ready to return to the house. She was entertaining her missionary circle and she needed to put a cake in the oven.

"What about your pussy?" Tick asked.

"We'll look again tomorrow."

Tick and Elsie continued searching the woods for the missing barn cat, the search always ending on the mossy creek bank. Each day brought a deeper chill to the Illinois autumn.

One morning at breakfast, Tick looked at the calendar on the kitchen wall: October 27. It was time to move on.

Before daylight the next day, while the Wehrlys slept in their separate rooms, Tick quietly packed his bag and headed north. By the time the rooster crowed, he was a mile down the road. He walked faster. Working for the Wehrlys made him more eager than ever to reach his destination: to sleep in his old bed, to see Worthy again, to help with the farm chores—even scooping out the barn. He wondered whether Cappy would be there but decided he was probably living in a big city somewhere, maybe Paris, France, and already famous.

That evening about sundown, Tick walked into the town of Rice, about sixty miles from Old Kane. He saw a small white church ahead; cars lined the street, along with a couple of buckboards. He could hear singing. Though he had left Billy Dupré behind, Tick was drawn to the church. Changing ways ain't easy, he thought. He felt in both pants pockets. All he had for the offering plate was a nickel.

The sign out front of the church said, "Evening Worship at 7:00 p.m., Theopholus Lemen, Pastor. Welcome!" Tick climbed the wood steps and opened the front door just as "The Old Rugged Cross" ended. Brother Lemen was praying aloud. Unable to control himself, Tick closed his eyes and began waving his arms toward heaven. "Prroliss Crromist Erlidism." Everyone turned to look at him. A small boy clung to his mother and began to wail.

The pastor, a young man, addressed Tick from the pulpit. "Brother! Come on down and give us your testimony!"

Regretting his spontaneous outburst, Tick reluctantly made his way to the front of the sanctuary. He stood silently and looked at the congregation—some were whispering, others smiling in anticipation. But when he opened his mouth to speak, nothing came out. "Prroliss—" He tried again: "Prroliss—" Humiliated, he hurried back up the aisle and out the door. He grabbed his belongings, which he had left lying on the front steps, and walked away from Rice as fast as he could. "Well, that proves God's done with me," he said to the fenceposts as he hurried past. For weeks, Tick had suspected he had angered God by abandoning Billy Dupré in Round Knob. Now he was sure of it. I guess God wants me to plant corn in the ground instead of planting Jesus in men's hearts, he thought.

Tick was weary of his journey. A few more days, barring ice storms or a sprained ankle, he would be sleeping in his own bed. "I won't stop till I see Pa's mailbox," he said to a mother quail by the side of the road as she feigned a broken wing to protect her young. "I sure hope Pa's got some fresh side meat in a pan cooking."

NINETEEN

Cappy and Worthy, bundled up against the frigid, still evening, took their respective places on the stoop. The only sound was the occasional scream of a fox hoping to attract a willing mate.

"What's a 'back-fence' man?" Cappy said. "I've been hearing that term since I was a kid, but nobody ever told me what it meant." He had been encouraging Worthy to talk about the past at every opportunity.

"Is this fodder for your book?" Worthy said.

"It could be. I'll have to hear it first."

"Over the years I've known some fine back fencers, but they're a dying breed," Worthy said. "Old Buck Carmody was the most respected practitioner around Old Kane. When he was in his prime, he could scale a board or wire fence smoother than a yellow tomcat, and land on the other side without disturbing a single blade of grass."

"But what does a back-fence man *do?*" Cappy said.

"You want the whole story or something watered down?"

"Only the high points." Cappy knew how Worthy liked to prolong a story.

"Keep in mind I got most of the story straight from Buck Carmody, Junior, and that was years ago when I was only a boy. It's gospel so far as memory allows—his and mine." Worthy pulled up his coat collar and refilled his pipe with sweet tobacco, anticipating the pleasure of an audience.

Cappy settled back on the porch, ready to take mental notes. "Is this a folktale?"

"It's a tale told to folks by folks, so you be the judge. Now keep in mind I'll be guessing what was said, since I wasn't there to hear it myself."

"That's called 'poetic license,'" Cappy said.

"Call it what you want." Worthy took several puffs on his pipe as he was deciding where to begin. "Here goes.

"Buck Junior spent his growing-up years on the farm with his folks not too far from Coal Hollow. Summer evenings his daddy, Old Buck, would disappear along about twilight, the time of his leaving coinciding with how high the sun was in the sky. Buck Junior's mother, Odessa, she'd be busy on the front porch snapping beans or stringing peas, seeming not to notice her husband was gone, leastways she didn't raise a fuss the way wives do these days. On winter nights, with darkness coming early, Old Buck would drop out of sight about moonrise. While the north wind was blowing cold, Odessa contented herself by the woodstove with her quilting pieces in her lap, daydreaming about box socials when she was a girl and hay rides on a snowy night—"

"I still don't get a sense of what a back-fence man did," Cappy said.

"Don't rush me, you're worse than when you was a five-year-old. Anyhow, when Buck Junior was about fourteen, his curiosity got the best of him. So one summer's evening as the sun was about to set, he waylaid his father. He looked Old Buck in the eye and said, 'Where you off to, Pa?'

"Old Buck said, 'If you're old enough to pose the question, you're old enough to hear the answer. But first, I've got a question: Have you had any unusual goings-on with your privates?'

"According to Buck Junior, he was sorry he had brought the matter up, thinking he'd get a good whipping if he told the truth about his relationship with his privates. 'Never mind, Pa,' he said, 'I've changed my mind. I'll just stay home and help Ma stem strawberries.'

"Old Buck flew off the handle, like only Old Buck could do. Buck Junior peed his pants. 'Now hold on a goddamned minute,' Old Buck yelled. 'You brung it up! You'll see it through!' Buck Junior's face turned red just telling me the story. He said he knowed he was in a pickle, so he just come out with it. 'Sometimes my peter gets a little stiff,' he said, 'but I'm not letting no doctor get his hands on it.'"

Cappy laughed out loud.

"Old Buck toned down his voice some, probably recalling when he had went through them bodily changes hisself. 'The best doc in Greene County can't help what ails you, son. It's God's way of letting you know it's time to start pleasing the womenfolk. That's all I'll say on the matter now, I'm late as it is. If you promise to hang back I'll let you follow this once.'

"Buck Junior, a polite boy, wanted to tell his ma where he was going, but Old Buck put his foot down. 'A man don't discuss such as this with his mother or his wife. It ain't respectful.'

"So Buck Junior followed his daddy, staying in the shadows whenever possible. They walked through the back pasture, crossed the branch on slippery stones, and come to the first obstacle. Old Buck sailed over the six-foot-high board fence topped with a length of barbed wire, but Buck Junior caught his pants on a barb, tearing a large hole. He knew he'd catch the devil when his mother saw the tear. But Old Buck said, 'Hell, boy, your ma's sewed up as many barbed-wire tears over the years as there are ladybugs on a willow tree. It's part and parcel of being a wife.'"

Cappy interrupted. "If you had pulled such tricks, Ma would have packed your bags and sent you on your way."

"Sixty years ago, times was different, but I wasn't one to hop fences, never did, never wanted to," Worthy said. "So the two Carmodys kept on walking through the hills and hollows until they come to the Calvy farm, with Old Buck manipulating fences like he was a boy. The pair scaled the chicken yard fence, then the high picket fence around the house. 'Keep low to the ground,' Old Buck says. When they got as far as the root cellar, he whispered, 'Stay here and don't make a sound. I'll be back presently.'

"'But what if they've got a dog?' Buck Junior said he was worried for his daddy's safety.

"His daddy said, 'Me and him made our peace months back.'

"Buck Junior watched his father walk up to the two-story house and disappear through an open window as graceful as a deer. That was the last sight of him for the next hour.

"By then, Buck Junior claimed he was sorry he'd come. If he'd stayed home and helped his ma stem strawberries, at least he could have eaten a few. The entire evening was proving fruitless.

"When Old Buck finally returned, the boy was naturally curious. 'How come you didn't go in the door? What took you so long? Did you and Mr. Calvy play checkers?'"

"What did Mrs. Calvy look like?" Cappy interrupted, trying to picture the scene.

"I asked the same question. Turns out she was a big-boned woman with a tooth missing in the front."

Cappy wondered how Mrs. Calvy would have described Old Buck Carmody. "So what happened next?"

"'It just so happens the mister of the house was out.' Old Buck suspicioned that Mr. Calvy was a back-fence man hisself. There was a lot of 'em in those days," Worthy said. "In times past the backyards of Old Kane proper was a regular flurry of men crisscrossing through flower beds and over fences. But farmers need their sleep, especially at planting and harvesting seasons. I forgot to mention that back-fencing was generally a town preoccupation. Old Buck was the exception proving the rule, venturing through the countryside the way he done. So there you have it, back-fencing in a nutshell."

Cappy, recalling the night Worthy and Bum had taken him deep into Jones Woods to look for wampus cats and woods witches, viewed all of Worthy's stories with a grain of salty skepticism. "And is this back-fencing still going on?"

"Not that I know of. With the onset of television, most men are content to set and watch somebody else acting foolish."

"My professors said if you're going to write a far-fetched story it has to sound like it could be true under the right circumstances," Cappy said, "like science fiction."

"There ain't much science to what I told you, but it sure as hell ain't fiction."

"So this is an absolutely true story?" Cappy was not convinced. He knew that each storyteller added something from his imagination until finally it was impossible to separate fact from folklore.

"It may have gained some momentum over the years."

"I'll see what I can do with it," Cappy said. "I may have to embellish it some myself."

"Well, that's it for me, I'm heading indoors," Worthy said, as he pulled himself up using the porch rail.

"Maybe I'll give Oleeta a call before I go upstairs, just to let her know I haven't forgotten her," Cappy said. He had been surprisingly titillated by the idea of back-fencing and wanted to hear her voice. But when he picked up the receiver he heard voices already using the line—the Widow Bandy and Miss Shackelford.

After twenty minutes of listening to a discussion of Miss Shackelford's bunions and the Widow Bandy's dropped bladder, Cappy hung up. By the time they cover their entire bodies, it'll be too late to call, he thought. He would try again tomorrow night. He typed a few sentences about back-fencing and fell into bed. Maybe he would invite Oleeta over to watch television.

TWENTY

Whether it was his years in prison, where he'd had time to consider his mistakes, or his association with Reverend Marcus Smith, Drayton Hunt was feeling remorse. It was an unfamiliar experience, and he was worried. "Hell, I'm getting as soft as Worthy Giberson," he said to his dog. "That girl of his didn't exactly clamp her legs together in the barn that morning, so I'm only taking partial blame for that. But I never married her, that's the rub. Maybe if I had, Cappy would of been eating at my table instead of Worthy Giberson's." It suddenly occurred to him that he was no better than his own father, who had not bothered to marry Mae Hunt.

The dog jumped up and licked Drayton's beard, to show she was on her master's side.

"Jesus, this is a sorry state of affairs, talking to a god-damned dog." Drayton patted his best friend's head and handed her a pork bone. Maybe he would talk to Marcus about his disturbing feelings.

Friday afternoon, Drayton eased into his usual chair in Reverend Marcus Smith's study and opened his Bible. Unless he squinted, he was unable to read the small print. It was time to forget his pride and buy some reading glasses at the five-and-dime store.

"You can put the Bible away, Mr. Hunt," Marcus said. "Today we're discussing something different."

"That's all right by me," Drayton said. "I didn't think much of Deuteronomy. Too many laws and rules for my liking."

"There's something worth learning in every Old Testament book, otherwise God would not have inspired all thirty-nine of them. But here's what I want to talk to you about. At one of our early Friday sessions, you expressed a desire to preach the Word of God. Is that still your goal?"

"It is."

"Then it's time to see what you can do."

"What are you getting at?"

"It's time for you to stand in the pulpit and preach."

"But I'm not ready!" Drayton relaxed his grip on his Bible and it slid to the floor. He quickly picked it up. Neither the American flag nor the Bible should ever touch the floor, Chaplain Davenport had said.

"Nonsense. You claim you were called to preach, and if that's true, God will supply the words. I've arranged for you to accompany me to the Haypress Baptist Church for this week's Sunday night worship. There won't be anyone there who knows you. Your first sermon will be like an extended testimony."

"Son of a bitch."

"Please don't blaspheme in my presence, Mr. Hunt. Anyway, that's all for today. I'll pick you up Sunday evening about six. It shouldn't take more than an hour to drive to Haypress."

"But why do you want me to preach when I know I'm not ready? Are you wanting to sit back and watch me make a fool of myself?"

"Not at all. The longer you wait, the harder it will be. It's like jumping into a pond of icy water. That water's never going to warm up so you might as well take the plunge."

Drayton had no appetite the rest of the day, and he spent a sleepless night tumbling around in his bed. That's what I get for blowing off about myself, he thought. He wanted a shot of whiskey, but he hadn't had a drink since coming home.

Still awake at 4:00 A.M., he got out of bed and opened the damper on the kitchen cookstove. He stirred the embers and added a log, put a pot of coffee on to boil, and settled down at the kitchen table with a tablet and pencil. I ain't about to stand up in front of all them people on the chance God will put words in my mouth, he thought. I sure got myself in deep shit this time.

Sunday evening on the road to the Haypress Baptist Church, Drayton, to calm his nerves, provoked an argument with Marcus Smith about the Scriptures. "The Bible says God told Jesus to go into the wilderness for the purpose of being tempted by Satan," Drayton said. "Jesus wasn't using the brains God gave him. If God told me to jump in the ocean for the purpose of drowning, I wouldn't be dumb enough to jump."

"Mr. Hunt, you missed the whole point, which is that we all have to face our own private demons, no matter what form they take. We'll continue the discussion later, we're almost at Haypress. And please be careful tonight when you give your testimony. What's said from the pulpit carries more weight than what's said in everyday conversation."

As they approached the small white church, it looked as if the entire town of Haypress had shown up. Cars lined the country road, and families were filing into the church. Drayton had not felt so apprehensive since he was facing a three-year prison sentence. And on top of everything else, tonight was Halloween, a night he preferred to stay home with the shades drawn.

Marcus led the way inside the church. Drayton lagged behind, his Bible clutched in his hand. As the organist played "Sweet Hour of Prayer," the two men took their places at the front of the church. Drayton wiped his sweating hands on his pants.

When the prelude ended, Reverend Marcus Smith stood up and said, "Good evening, friends. I'm happy I could fill in for your pastor so he could enjoy a Sunday away from the pulpit, but we all know he's doing God's work wherever he is. There's no vacation from God!" A few people laughed. "Let's begin with hymn number fourteen, 'Brighten the Corner,' and we'll sing all six verses. Not too fast," he said to the organist.

Drayton tried to sing along, but he had never heard the hymn before, and he couldn't read music. He moved his lips so no one would think he couldn't read words either.

After the Scripture and offertory, Marcus said, "Now is the time for anyone who wants to speak of their sin and salvation to stand and be heard."

With a walker for support, an old woman slowly made her way to the front of the church. In emotional words, she told how she was saved as a young girl. "It took several tries before salvation took hold, the devil was inside me real deep," she said, "but I haven't sinned for the last ten years, except in my mind. Of course we can't control what our mind does. When my turn comes to discard this earthly shell, I know Jesus will gather me to his bosom and take me up in the sky. Amen." She shuffled back to her seat.

Drayton listened carefully to every word the old woman said. He understood what she meant, that it's impossible to control what your mind wants to think. Lately he had been thinking about his old life, and how in those days he wasn't burdened with the fear of offending God.

"Thank you for those heartfelt words," Marcus said to the elderly woman. "Is there anyone else?"

A teenage boy, yanked out of his seat by his mother, ambled toward the front with his head lowered and confessed his sin of smoking cigarettes on Sunday. As far as Drayton knew, the Bible didn't name smoking as a sin. He had given up the habit because he preferred to spend his money on food and gasoline for his Moon.

"I trust you two sinners have truly repented," Marcus said. "I wouldn't be able to rest if I thought you were on your way to Hell's fiery furnace."

"Amen to that, brother," everyone said.

"Now, if there's no one else who has been seduced by Satan and saved by Jesus, then I have a special treat for you members. I've brought along Mr. Drayton R. Hunt, an admitted sinner and ex-convict. He will tell you of his long journey from a lonely prison cell to God's pulpit."

Drayton stood up and made his way to the pulpit; the congregation applauded as if he were Billy Sunday. The welcome was exhilarating, like a shot of strong coffee. With sudden confidence, Drayton raised his Bible over his head. "Does everybody see this book?"

"Yes, brother!"

"This book can solve all your problems, it sure as shit solved mine."

A murmur went through the crowd at the expletive, a word they sometimes used, but never in church.

"That was Satan himself who put that sinful word in my mouth," Drayton said. "Thank God, Jesus yanked it out! You can leave here tonight telling how you saw proof of God and proof of Satan at the same church meeting!"

Loud applause filled the small church.

"One night when I was alone in my prison cell, I started thinking about what was wrong in my life. All at once this little white rat appeared, and it could talk as good as a human being. It stood on its hind legs and said, 'Sinner Hunt, change your ungodly ways or you'll go straight to Hell when you die.' Friends, I may not be a college professor, but I was smart enough not to choose Hell for my home in eternity. So that very night I got down on my knees on that hard concrete floor and gave my heart to Jesus. That's why me and Brother Smith are here tonight. To keep you sinners from winding up in a prison cell. We all know that white rat was Jesus in disguise."

By then Drayton was sweating. He wiped his face with a handkerchief and whispered to Marcus, "Is that enough?"

"Another fifteen minutes should do it."

Drayton went on to describe his years in prison and his relationship with Chaplain Davenport. He told how the chaplain had introduced him to reading, and the influence that Mark Twain's orphaned characters had on his life, especially because they didn't let hardships keep them from succeeding. "And one more thing before the benediction," Drayton said. "Even Jesus was tempted forty days and forty nights, but he fought Satan and won. But I think Jesus wasn't using good sense by going into the wilderness in the first place and—"

Marcus glared at Drayton.

"Anyway, that's my message to you good people."

After the service, the Mary and Martha Sunday school class served coffee and pie in the basement. All of the men shook Drayton's hand and wished him luck, and women crowded around him—smiling and saying they hoped he would come back soon.

On their way out of the church, Marcus said, "Well, Mr. Hunt, how does it feel to be a celebrity?"

"It was good, especially the part where the ladies crowded in close. I never had that many tits pressed against me at one time!" Drayton laughed loudly—several people looked his direction.

"What a disgusting thing to say!" Marcus said. "Even if you still think vulgar thoughts, they can't be spoken in the house of God. Maybe you should consider another line of work." He started to walk away.

Drayton grabbed his arm. "I'm sorry as hell that I can't think and talk like you, but I'm new at this game. And like that old woman who testified said, 'There's no way to keep your brain from thinking what it wants to!'"

"Apparently your brain is still in the cesspool!" They drove home in silence.

TWENTY-ONE

Cappy was coming out of Sorphus Peak's grocery store with bread and minced ham for lunch when he bumped into Oleeta on her way in. "Sorry, my fault," Cappy said, stepping aside. He and Oleeta hadn't talked since the night they parked behind Green Summit School. He thought she looked especially pretty with her hair in a tight ponytail, but he didn't tell her.

Oleeta wasn't smiling. "Cappy Giberson. I thought you must have left town again since I haven't heard from you or anything. Not since the minstrel show."

"I've been busy."

"Does that mean you've found a job?" Still no smile.

"Not yet." She isn't happy unless she's provoking an argument, Cappy thought.

"It doesn't matter, I'm too busy to go out with you anyway. The winter semester will be starting soon."

"Then you've made up your mind about a major?"

"I've narrowed my choices down to a couple, sociology or world history." She reached up and tightened her ponytail even more.

"What kind of work do you expect to find with those lame degrees?"

"What does it matter to you? Maybe I'll teach."

"But you said you didn't want to be a teacher. What changed your mind?"

"People change their mind," she said, getting angrier by the minute. "And you shouldn't talk. Your fancy degree hasn't helped you get a job."

He hesitated. "You're right, I don't have any right to criticize your choice. Sorry."

"I was out of line, too," she said. But she was still red-faced.

After an awkward silence, Cappy said, "I guess you'll be coming home on weekends? Blackburn College isn't that far."

"Why would I want to come home? Weekends at school there's always something going on. Parties, dances, basketball games. In Old Kane there's nothing to do but movies and church. I can do those things when I'm an old lady walking with a cane."

"Then I guess there's nothing more to say." She thinks only of herself, Cappy thought, walking away.

"I guess you're right." He's totally self-centered, Oleeta thought. She handed her grocery list to Sorphus.

Though Worthy continued to urge Cappy to find a friend, he preferred being alone with a good novel or sitting in Jalappa Cemetery. Any change was unlikely, and unwanted. His only close friend his entire life had been Beany Ozbun, and there was no one who could take his place. The only other Old Kane man Cappy's age and still single was Shag Kallal, and Shag chose the company of his pigs over humans.

"Pigs is smarter than human beings," Shag professed to a group of men one day at Finice Darr's Garage.

"If pigs is so damned smart, how come they end up on my supper plate keeping my eggs company?" Finice said. Everyone laughed.

But Shag didn't see anything funny. He found the idea of eating bacon as repugnant as eating his tabby cat.

"It ain't healthy being alone," Worthy said to Cappy the day of his run-in with Oleeta. "Either you're setting by yourself pecking on that typewriter or you're setting in Jalappa Cemetery thinking about what might of been."

"But what about yourself?" Cappy said defensively. "If you aren't pitching horseshoes or fishing for bluegills, you're sitting on the front stoop thinking about what *used* to be."

"Why don't you get yourself a girl? Oleeta Hetzel is ready and willing. I guarantee she can fill a place even Beany couldn't of."

"I'm doing just fine without friends, especially girls," he snapped at Worthy. "Now I've got some writing to do!" Cappy stormed up to his room as if he were an angry teenager.

Worthy shook his head. How many times had he seen Chastity storm up those same stairs?

Cappy had, in fact, been thinking constantly about Oleeta, but he wouldn't give Worthy the satisfaction.

Hungry and cold, Tick hurried past Lively Grove, around Bunker Hill, then into the outskirts of Jerseyville, cutting across fences and through woods to avoid the busy highway. Home was only a few hours away, if the weather held.

He began to imagine the taste of home-cooked food, and the feel of his own featherbed warming his body. But most of all he longed to have his family close, at least what was left of it. This would be his first time home since Willa died. He wondered how it would feel to eat in her kitchen without her being there to pass the food.

But what would Cappy say? Tick wondered. Cappy had made fun of his preaching, especially his speaking in tongues. Would Cappy walk out when he arrived home? What if Worthy had turned his old room into a junk room? And would he be allowed to eat at the kitchen table?

On November 1, as the first snowflake of the season fell on his bare head, Tick was turning onto the blacktop road leading from Route 67 into Old Kane. He now had a full beard, and his dyed-blond hair from his Billy Dupré days was showing its dark roots. He passed Kid Corner and continued walking down the wide streets—past the Baptist Church, the train depot, the schoolhouse. He looked neither right nor left until he reached the gravel road at the edge of town. It would soon be dark. He walked faster.

By the time he glimpsed the Giberson farmhouse, he was covered with heavy wet snow, and his eyes stung from the blustery north wind. Coal smoke poured from the chimney of the two-story red-tile house. Seeing the warm glow of lights inside, he began to run. But when he reached the back door, the family entrance, he stopped short. Was he still family? He tapped lightly.

"Come on in, she's open!" Worthy called out.

Timidly, Tick pushed the door open and stepped inside the steamy kitchen. A pot of chicken stew simmered on the back of the range, and Worthy was opening a box of saltines.

Tick's stomach growled. He hadn't eaten since yesterday. "I'm back, Pa," he said.

Worthy turned slowly, afraid to trust his hearing. For a moment he just stared at Tick. After so many weeks on the road, he looked like a hobo—long hair, unshaven, the smell of road dust and sweat on his body. "Well, I'll be damned. I never thought I'd live to see this day! Come on in, boy, and warm yourself. Christ! You look like a snowman!" He dropped the crackers on the table and hugged his son.

Tick was overwhelmed. He had no reason to expect this enthusiastic welcome. He hesitated, hot tears beginning in the corners of his eyes.

Worthy stepped back for a better look at Tick. "That jacket's too light for winter, boy. You can go through the closets after supper and see if there's an old coat that fits you."

For weeks, Tick had been dreading his next question of Worthy, but it had to be asked. "I'm done with preaching, I've saved as many souls as a preacher could. Now I want to go back to farming. Can I stay and help farm, Pa?" He held his breath, an expectant look on his youthful face.

"This'll come as a surprise, but I've give up farming. St. Peters and his boys rent the land and I set back watching them sweat while I collect my share of the crops. If you're bent on farming there's a chance they could use some help. As for you staying, your old room's just the way you left it. After you took off with that fool traveling preacher, Willa kept your room swept and dusted like you was sleeping in it every night. Remember how she counted heads on pillows every night? She never stopped counting yours. So you're welcome to your room. Now, let's eat, we can finish our talk later. I've got nine years' worth saved up. I expect you've got some stories yourself. Set the table while I dish up this old hen. To celebrate your homecoming, you can have the gizzard."

With a contented feeling he hadn't experienced in years, Worthy watched his thirty-three-year-old son tackle the childhood chore, lining up the spoons evenly with the top of the bowl, placing a paper napkin at the side, just as Willa had taught him when he was too short to reach the tabletop without standing on tiptoes. Now Tick was tall like himself, with a boyish look and manner that he might never lose. That's all right by me, Worthy thought, feeling he had been granted a reprieve from loneliness.

Willa, old girl, I reckon it's up to me to finish the job you and me started, Worthy thought. He passed a bowl brimming with chicken and egg noodles. "Dig in, boy. Cappy will be glad to see you. He's forever bringing up your name, wondering where you're at."

"Will he be here for supper? I'm sure lonesome for the sight of him."

"He'll be rolling in any minute but we won't wait for him. You must be about starved." Worthy stirred the stew and filled two bowls.

"I wish I was good at storytelling like you and Cappy," Tick said, his mouth full. "I've saw a lot of the world outside of Old Kane, leastways in Illinois. Me and Reverend Art even seen a little of Missouri. It wasn't nothing special."

"Cappy's in the midst of writing a book about Old Kane," Worthy said. "Maybe he can write down your stories, if they're not too churchy."

"Church is about all I know, that and—" Tick stopped, realizing his activities in bed were not for public consumption. He took a slice of bread, dipped it in stew gravy, and put the whole piece in his mouth.

"I hope you ain't planning to keep that beard," Worthy said, looking at his son critically. "Drayton Hunt's back in town, and he's sporting one. He's set beards back fifty years."

"On the road, there wasn't no way of shaving it off," Tick said, "but it kept my face warm. Can I have some more stew?"

"Eat all you can hold, there's no shortage of stewing chickens. I've got a chicken yard full of old hens that's too lazy to lay an egg. Their days is numbered."

"I was sorry about not fighting in the war," Tick said, "but Reverend Art said God needed me for a higher calling. I reckon Cappy was in the fighting?"

"Jesus, you've missed out on a lot around Old Kane. I'll start catching you up tomorrow. But in the meanwhile, it would greatly please me if you'd not bring up that damned preacher's name again," Worthy said. "Now, if you're full, we'll leave the dishes on the table and see what's showing on the television set."

"You've got a television set?" Tick said, a look of disbelief on his face. "Reverend Art said they're tools of the devil."

"Devil or not, I plan to watch. And what did I tell you about bringing up that fool preacher's name!"

"He wasn't all bad, he had a good heart, but I've about quit believing most of what he preached," Tick said as he followed Worthy into the dark front room.

The *Philco Television Playhouse* was beginning when Cappy walked in the back door. He grabbed a bottle from the icebox and poured a glass of sweet, cold milk. He started into the front room, but stopped in the doorway when he realized Worthy wasn't alone. Funny, he hadn't noticed a strange car in the lane. "I didn't know we had company," he said.

"Shit, I ain't company," Tick said, standing up, his face a wide grin. "I figured it was time I come home and give you some more lessons."

It took a few seconds for Cappy's eyes to adjust to the dark, the only light coming from the dim television screen. Cappy set his glass down and looked over at the man he'd always considered his brother, though he was in reality his uncle. Awkwardly, they embraced. "It's about time you came home and did your share of the work!" Cappy teased. "Are you staying long?"

"From now on. Pa said I could."

"But what about Reverend Art? Won't he throw a fit when he finds out?"

"He's throwed his last fit," Tick said, "unless he don't like where St. Peter puts him or the hymns they play up there." He pointed toward the ceiling.

"You mean he's dead?" Worthy said.

"A jealous deacon bashed his head in," Tick said.

"I don't wish harm on any man, but that deacon done the world a favor," Worthy said. "I never could abide the man, especially when he lured you away. It broke Willa's heart."

"I feel awful bad about Ma," Tick said, "but I went with Reverend Art because I got the call to preach."

"We can't do anything to change the past," Cappy said. "Let's put it behind us and start living for now."

"That's a good one, coming from you," Worthy said. "You're more tied up with the past than Tick and me put together. But let's quit gabbing and watch the rest of the program, half of it's already played. We've got from here on out to rehash the past."

TWENTY-TWO

Since his sermon in Haypress two weeks before, Drayton had been invited to other country churches to speak about his sinful life and miraculous salvation. "At the end of each service the collection plate will be passed and half of the money will go to you," was the promise. But in spite of his fledgling success, Drayton was beginning to question his new life, which amounted to studying the Scriptures with Reverend Marcus Smith and practicing his preaching technique. His doubts came from the Baptist religion itself, which was dedicated to physical restraint and a solemn countenance. Everything Drayton enjoyed was suddenly a sin. "There'll be dark times when you wonder whether you've made the right choice," Chaplain Davenport had warned him, "but salvation doesn't come all at once. You'll face peaks and gulleys on your journey to total redemption."

Drayton was losing patience with God's methods.

His job at Linder's Funeral Parlor was proving a big disappointment. Instead of gaining the respect he had hoped for, he was relegated to the secret, dirty work that took place in the moldy basement, unseen (and unimagined) by the public, while Bert, dressed in a black suit and tie, paraded around the visitation room, shaking hands with the bereaved and looking appropriately sympathetic.

Only in the presence of Reverend Marcus Smith did Drayton feel good about himself. For the first time in his life, he was beginning to trust someone besides himself. There was not another man or woman he could ever say that about. As a boy, he hadn't entirely trusted his mother, who sometimes went an entire day without speaking except to warn him to stay out of sight while she was "working."

"There's got to be a better way to earn money than this," Drayton said to Cyrus Pembrook's naked corpse, as he placed a wood block under the old man's bald head. Lately Drayton had allowed himself to consider robbery as a way of adding to his paltry funeral home pay. "But if I go back to robbing, I'd be undoing everything I've worked for since I got out of jail," he said to Cyrus. Drayton quickly put the thought out of his mind and covered Cyrus Pembrook with a warm blanket.

Friday afternoon during Drayton's Scripture study, Marcus Smith abruptly put his Bible aside and began to speak affectionately of his roommate in seminary, a young man who wrote poetry. His name was John Roley. Marcus told how he and John had spent hours sitting on the floor of their small dormitory room—John reciting, Marcus listening. As Marcus spoke of the beauty of John Roley's poetry, he began to quietly weep. Drayton had never seen another grown man cry; he didn't know how to react. Embarrassed, Drayton twisted in his chair and wound his pocket watch.

"John was a beautiful man," Marcus went on, drying his eyes, "filled with beautiful words and the love of God." He sat staring into space, as if remembering a special poem or moment he wouldn't share.

"What happened to this Roley guy?" Drayton said after a few minutes. Marcus spoke as if he were dead.

"After graduation we kept in touch for a few months, but then his letters stopped coming. I finally gave in and telephoned him late one night. A man answered. Not John. And that was when I knew we were no longer friends."

"I don't get your drift."

"It's simple. John had found another friend, so he no longer needed me."

"Why didn't you get yourself a new friend?" Drayton thought Marcus was making too much of the issue.

"Forget everything I said, I never should have brought the matter up! You obviously aren't capable of understanding!" Marcus opened his Bible, nearly tearing a page. "Let's get to this week's Scriptures."

Sensing he had let Marcus down by not understanding his melancholy, Drayton drove back into town that evening to make amends. He didn't want to spoil their growing friendship. As he approached the parsonage, he could see a single light in the kitchen, but the rest of the house was dark. He went around to the side door and knocked. He waited a minute, then knocked again, louder. Hell, I know he's in there, Drayton thought. He opened the door and let himself in.

As he walked through the kitchen, he heard a noise—like a dog whimpering—that seemed to be coming from the front of the house. He stepped inside the dark living room and pulled on a light. Drayton froze. A man he didn't recognize was lying spread-eagled on the sofa with the Reverend Marcus Smith's head buried between his skinny legs. As if he sensed Drayton's presence, Marcus pulled away and wiped his mouth on his sleeve.

"Mr. Hunt, I guess—I guess I didn't hear you knock," Marcus stammered, as he pulled up his pants and tucked in his shirttail. His partner grabbed his clothes and disappeared into another room.

There was no mistaking what was going on. In prison, Drayton had watched guards hold down a new inmate while old-timers raped him until their cocks were raw. But even worse, the act Drayton had just walked in on was consensual.

Drayton lashed out. He picked up a chair and threw it against the wall; a leg flew off. "Now I get the picture, you lying son of a bitch, why you was crying like a goddamned baby wanting his sugar tittie! Only it wasn't a tittie you was wanting to suck. You make me puke! You'd better hope God's looking the other way. The last I heard, He's against men laying with men!" Drayton's feelings about Beany Ozbun returned in a flash, and his fear, years before, that Cappy might have been coerced to do the unspeakable.

Feeling nauseated, Drayton ran out of the parsonage and drove to Oettle's Tavern. A beer this once won't ruin my new image, he thought, as he checked his pockets for money. Even Jesus drank wine. The owner of the tavern was ready to close, but knowing Drayton Hunt's temperament, he didn't refuse to serve him.

As Drayton downed his beer, he thought about the scene he had witnessed, akin to finding your wife with her legs wrapped around your best friend. But there was more to it than merely a matter of jealousy. A trust between two men had been broken, which Drayton believed was more important than a trust between a man and woman. How could I have been fooled by his high-sounding words? Drayton asked himself. And why does it matter so damned much? Disillusioned that Marcus Smith, his teacher and friend, had "feet of clay," Drayton ordered another beer.

A week later, Drayton was getting ready for bed when a car turned into the lane, its headlights off. His dog barked wildly at the slowly approaching vehicle. Ordinarily, Drayton didn't have callers, day or night. From his bedroom window, he watched two men climb out and walk around the house to the back door. Swearing under his breath, Drayton put on his pants. He opened the kitchen door a crack. "What the hell do you want?" he said. "It damned well better be important."

"You can start by asking us inside," said the taller of the two strangers, his voice friendly, a broad smile on his rugged face.

Drayton determined they looked harmless. "Come on in, but make your business quick." He stepped aside.

Without being invited, they sat down at the kitchen table. Drayton remained standing.

"I go by Charlie, and this here's Peanuts," said the spokesman. "It so happens we met up with a couple of old friends of yours, the Woosley twins. They said you're the best around Old Kane at sizing up prospects when it comes to earning a few extra bucks." He winked at Drayton. "On the quietus."

Drayton's heart began to pound at the thought of extra money, now that his bootlegging profits were in his sister's pocketbook. "So what did you boys have in mind?" Were they thinking big, or were they on the Woosley twins' level? Charlie's next remark settled any doubt.

"We was thinking about busting into the Old Kane Bank," Charlie said. He grinned in expectation of Drayton's enthusiastic response.

Instead, Drayton laughed out loud. "Jesus, I'll say this for you, your timing ain't the best in the world. The Old Kane Bank went broke on its own twenty years ago! Where you boys from anyway?"

"Across the river in Calhoun County," said Charlie. "Me and Peanuts come here in good faith. We sure as hell wasn't looking to be laughed at."

"It appears the twins were playing a trick on you," Drayton said. "If there's nothing else on your mind—"

"The twins said something about a man by the name of Worthy Giberson, how he's got a house full of valuables ripe for the picking. Do you know the man?"

Drayton laughed again. "You might say that. I spent three years in jail for having one of those 'valuables' in my car." Drayton had not realized the Woosley twins had a sense of humor.

Abruptly Charlie and Peanuts stood up in unison, as if conjoined. "It appears we've been made the butt of a joke. Sorry we wasted our time. But since we're here, the twins said to ask for 'Mae' and that she'd show us a good time practically free. They said if we talked real nice she'd even pay *us* for a romp."

Drayton's face turned red. He walked to the door and yanked it open. "Get your asses out of here while you've still got 'em! And you can tell them twin fools it ain't too late for me to have a talk with the sheriff. They'll know what I mean."

It's harder to escape from the past than from Alcatraz, Drayton thought, as he locked the door and turned out the light.

TWENTY-THREE

Worthy was in the cellar elbow-deep in hot, soapy water and dirty work shirts when he heard someone knocking at the back door. "Who the hell can that be on wash day?" he grumbled. "I ain't up for company."

Laundry represented the worst of being the woman of the house. By the end of the day Worthy's hands would be as wrinkled as an old crone's, and his eyes would sting from bleach fumes. He could never get the right amount of blueing in the white clothes. He wiped his hands on his overalls and climbed the basement steps to find Drayton Hunt standing on the porch.

"Jesus, can this day get any worse?" he mumbled under his breath. The last time Drayton Hunt had knocked at his door was on Cappy's seventh birthday, when he had tried once again to persuade Worthy to let him raise Cappy. Worthy gave Drayton a quick once-over. Dressed in a white shirt and black trousers, his beard neatly trimmed, he could have been a successful businessman. In the old days, he was usually decked out in an outlandish zoot suit.

Maybe that Baptist preacher's working a bona fide miracle, Worthy thought. "What do you want, Hunt?"

"I'm here to see your boy," Drayton said.

"Cappy ain't here."

"I'm here to see your own boy, not mine."

"I ain't up to arguing that fine point. What in the name of God do you want with Tick?"

"I come to talk to him about his preaching," Drayton said, "and maybe get some pointers on being an evangelist. Brother Smith says the right words, but you can fall asleep listening to him." Drayton recalled the fiery, threatening sermons he'd heard at the Holy Roller revivals. Sinners hearing *those* sermons were afraid not to walk down the aisle and accept Jesus.

"Tick's give up that foolishness," Worthy said, "so you may as well be on your way."

Just then Tick walked up carrying a small rooster. He didn't acknowledge Drayton. "Pa, there's something wrong with this chicken." He set it on the ground. "See? It can't stand up, let alone walk. What d'you reckon's wrong with it?" The rooster spread his wings and tried to balance itself but staggered and fell forward on its bill.

"It's got the drunken disease, that's what I always called it," Worthy said. "It happens sometimes with late-summer chickens, especially if they come from an old hen's egg. It's the same with women. An old woman's offspring is more likely to be a mite off-center."

"I'm thinking I'll take it to my room until it gets well." As a boy, Tick was the one who'd nursed the sick animals back to health, sometimes sitting all night in the barn with a sick calf's head on his lap until it recovered or died.

"Keep it in a box in your room, if you want, but don't get your hopes up about it getting well." Tick held the frightened rooster close to his body to calm its fears.

"Your pa's right, you might as well put that poor chicken out of his misery. That's what some humans do when their loved ones get sick." Drayton Hunt knew how to raise Worthy's hackles.

"If you wasn't such a no-good bastard, Hunt, you'd have been here when your own ma passed. She could of used a helping hand. Mae Hunt had nobody but her children, and they wasn't nowhere to be seen."

Drayton immediately backed off. "Everything you said is true. I was a poor excuse for a son, but I'm doing my level best to change." He addressed Tick. "In case you don't remember me, I'm Drayton Hunt. In a roundabout way you might say I'm almost a part of this family."

Worthy's face turned crimson. "You know, Hunt, I'd just as soon kill you as look at you on wash day. There's no room for you in this family. Now get your sorry ass off my land. Unless you're claiming my land, too."

"My business is with your boy, it's got nothing to do with you or Cappy. So, Tick, how about you and me having a little talk? I've got some questions on preaching."

Tick looked at Worthy.

"Go ahead and answer, Tick. You're a growed man, you don't need to ask your daddy when to pee."

"I know who you are," Tick said, responding to Drayton's earlier remark. "You went to jail for smothering Ma." His voice expressed no anger.

"That *is* why I went to jail, but your daddy knows I wasn't nowhere near your ma when she passed. Isn't that right, Worthy?"

"Is he right, Pa?"

"The man's right, Tick."

"Then who done it?"

"Let's just say it was her time to pass and let it go at that." Worthy would never tell Tick what had really happened. "Now I've got to run some overalls through the wringer." He disappeared down the basement steps.

"Worthy never could stand still when I was around," Drayton said as he and Tick sat on the back stoop. "I've tried to tell him I'm a changed man from what I used to be, back when me and your sister laid together in the hay-mow, but he closes his ears."

"He don't much like you," Tick said. The rooster lay still in Tick's arms.

"You probably know I got out of prison a while back, the big one down south," Drayton said. "At first I thought I'd go crazy being penned up like a sheep, but then I found my calling. The new Baptist preacher here in town has been helping me study the Bible, but we've had a falling out—I won't go into that. I've been walking the narrow Baptist line, but Old Kane won't take me serious. Have you got any words of wisdom from the Bible?"

Tick was dumbfounded. No one had ever asked his opinion. He tried to recall some of Reverend Art's favorite Bible quotes. "Don't hide your light under a bushel. Ask and it shall be given. Walk upright in the way of the Lord." But none of those quotes answered Drayton's question.

Hoping to draw Tick out, Drayton said, "It appears you've give up preaching just as I'm starting. Chaplain Davenport would say I was called to fill your place, like a newborn baby fills the place of somebody who's croaked."

"I guess." Tick was not comfortable discussing why things happen.

"Maybe you can teach me to speak in tongues," Drayton said. "People will come from miles around to hear a preacher with that gift."

"If God wants you to speak in tongues, He'll teach you Hisself," Tick said. "Anyhow, the last time I tried, the words wouldn't come out, like I was tongue-tied. I figured God had took my gift and give it to somebody else."

"Maybe that'll be me," Drayton laughed, but Tick didn't catch the humor. "How about the two of us meeting at Mundy's Cafe in the morning around ten o'clock? I'll buy you a cup of coffee and we can talk some more."

Tick was reluctant to agree, knowing Worthy wouldn't approve, but hadn't Worthy just told him to start making his own decisions? "I'll be there, unless my chicken takes a turn for the worse." He walked away, comforting the chicken. "Now don't you worry, I've saved lots of animals worse off than you—"

Worthy struggled up the basement steps carrying clothes for the line. "Christ, I thought for sure you'd be gone, Hunt."

"One thing more, Worthy, and then I will be. You'll get a kick out of this. With Tick and me both wearing beards, he looks more like me than Cappy does."

"Jesus Christ, but you know how to gall me." Grumbling to himself, Worthy hung a work shirt on the line to dry.

The next morning, Cappy walked into Mundy's and saw Tick sitting at the counter with Drayton Hunt. "Now what scheme are you up to!" he shouted at Drayton, feeling the heat of anger on his red face. "You're bound and determined to interfere with me and my family!"

"We're just drinking coffee," Tick said, "and then I'm going to tell him what I know about preaching."

"Jesus, the blind leading the blind," Cappy scoffed.

"I don't know a lot of things like you do, Cappy, but I do know about preaching," Tick said quietly. "More than you know even."

Cappy was immediately sorry he had spoken in haste. Drayton Hunt brought out the worst in him. "I didn't mean to hurt your feelings, Tick, but nothing you say will make a preacher out of this man. Come on, I'll drive you home and we can talk about it."

"I ain't ready to go." Tick took another sip of his coffee.

"I won't do harm to your brother," Drayton said. "If you'd set here for five minutes and hold a conversation, you'd find out I'm not the man I used to be."

"There won't be any conversation between us," Cappy said defiantly. "Are you coming, Tick?"

"I said I ain't ready."

"Well that's just great!" Cappy stomped out.

"Cappy don't much like you," Tick said. "Reverend Art used to say people got sick from having hate in their hearts. I sure wouldn't want Pa or Cappy to get sick from hating you."

"If you get them two to say a decent word to me, you'll be working a miracle," Drayton said. "Now, tell me about speaking in tongues. Is your tongue like everybody else's?"

Tick stuck it out. "It's the very same."

"So how'd you get started?"

"When I first tried preaching, Reverend Art said I'd never make a good preacher because I couldn't think of what to say, and if I did think of something it was wrong. So he come up with the idea of me speaking in tongues. That way, people listening wouldn't know if I made a mistake or not."

"The Baptist preacher's been taking me around to churches on Sunday nights to give testimonials," Drayton said. "Why don't you come along and speak in tongues and maybe I'll get the hang of it?" Although he still felt betrayed by Marcus Smith, the Bible said to be forgiving. And no one knew better than Drayton Hunt how easily a man could be tempted to sin.

"I've give up preaching, mainly because even I didn't know what I was saying," Tick said. "Besides, I throwed away my white suit and white Bible, I reckon God ain't about to forget that. I'm going home now and look after my sick rooster."

When Tick walked into his bedroom, the rooster wasn't in its box. He looked under the bed and in the closet. He ran downstairs. "Pa, my chicken's gone!"

"I was setting here reading the paper and it come waltzing down the stairs and over to the back door. I let it out, and it's strutting around with the rest of the chickens. I've never before knowed a chicken to get over the drunken disease. I guess you cured it."

"But how could that be? All I did was talk to it and keep it warm."

"I reckon some ills can be cured with the right words. Leastways that's what I've heard. I'll tell you what, the next time I come down with a bellyache you can cure me with some of them pretty words!" He laughed, and patted Tick's head affectionately.

But Tick was serious. He went to his room and sat on the side of the bed thinking. The rooster's recovery was no small matter to him. But what did it mean? Reverend

Art said everything happens for a reason. Was God trying to lure him back into preaching by giving him a second gift? Healing to replace speaking in tongues? Tick hoped not. If the story got around Old Kane that he could heal with words, he'd be talking the rest of his life.

He went back downstairs. "Pa, don't tell nobody about me curing that rooster. I don't want people around town getting word of it, else they'll be lined up on the front porch wanting me to cure their hives or hiccups."

"The only person I mentioned it to was Bum on the telephone just now, but he won't say nothing. He don't believe it anyhow."

Tick returned to his room and tried to remember the exact words he had spoken to the rooster. There must have been one special word that had worked the miracle, he thought. Maybe that miracle word could bring about a reconciliation between Cappy and Drayton Hunt.

TWENTY-FOUR

For several nights after Charlie and Peanuts knocked on his door, Drayton couldn't sleep. He wasn't tempted to join an ill-conceived venture with friends of the Woosley twins, but he desperately needed money. Though he didn't want to revert to his old ways, a man has to keep his head above water or sink to the bottom like an anvil, he thought. And doesn't the Bible say the Lord helps those who help themselves?

Drayton believed he had no choice but to plan one more robbery.

When the Old Kane Bank failed in 1930, store owners began carrying their money home every night and tying it up in a pillowcase for safekeeping. But Drayton would not break into someone's house in the middle of the night and risk stepping on a cat's tail or bumping into the man of the house on his way to relieve an urgent bladder. In his young adventuresome days he would not have hesitated to pilfer a house with the owner asleep in the next room, but he was older and wiser. Caution was now a virtue. And though he didn't like to admit it, at age forty-seven he moved a little slower.

There was Dinghie Varble's movie theater, but with the growing competition from television, people were choosing to sit in their own front room and watch the grainy black-and-white picture. The Old Kane Picture Show would not be worth burglarizing.

Sorphus Peak's Grocery Store and Finice Darr's Garage were profitable, but since Drayton did business with both places, some of the money he would be stealing might be his own. He scratched those two possibilities off his list.

After carefully considering each place of business, Drayton settled on the United States Post Office. With the holidays approaching, families would be picking up their Sears Christmas catalogs, making lists, checking them twice, and then returning to purchase money orders and stamps. The post office, in preparation for increased business, would have more money on hand than at any other time of the year.

But Drayton suddenly found himself facing a hurdle he had never encountered. A conscience. How could he justify stealing another man's hard-earned money and still consider himself a changed man? But any obstacle can be reasoned around if you put your mind to it, he thought, as he set about dealing with his emerging conscience. The solution suddenly became clear. Once a customer handed money to the postmistress for postal cards or stamps, that money then belonged to the government, not to the poor workingman. Everyone knew the government had money to throw away and did so every day on one useless thing after another. So if he were to steal from Uncle Sam, who wasn't a real man anyway, robbing the post office would not be abandoning his new way of life. Hell, I'll give 10 percent of what's in the safe to the

Baptist Church, he decided. Surely that will cause God to look the other way this once.

"Damned if I don't sound like the Woosley twins," he said to his dog that night as they were drifting off to sleep. This idea is about as ignorant as when those two gave up robbing the rich and went to robbing the poor. Drayton pulled the heavy wool blanket over his head, the bedroom nearly as cold as outdoors. After the post office job, maybe he could afford storm windows.

Drayton's first step was to learn the layout of the post office building, which had originally housed the defunct Old Kane Bank. He would begin by becoming friendly with Pearl Owens, the postmistress.

Pearl had worked at the post office since she was a high school girl, first as clerk, finally as postmistress for the past twenty years. Now, approaching retirement age, she knew all the tricks and wouldn't be easy to fool. More than once customers had tried to pay for stamps with counterfeit bills. If a bill slipped past her, she was required to reimburse the government. She quickly became an expert at spotting a counterfeit ten-dollar bill, even if the person passing the bill was a white-haired grandmother wearing a flowered hat.

Old Kane widows were notorious for hiding a letter inside a package without bothering to purchase the required stamp. Another form of robbery, in Pearl's judgment. So she began charging first class postage for every package, based on the probability that there was a letter inside looking for a free ride. Pearl would not allow anyone to cheat the post office which was, in her opinion, tantamount to being unpatriotic.

Hoping he hadn't lost his touch, Drayton sauntered up to the post office window and grinned. He took off his cap and ran his hands through his hair. "Hello there, Miss Pearl. You're looking handsome this morning."

"It's 'Mrs.,'" she said curtly. Even though she had been a widow for two years, she refused to think of herself as single. She continued to wear her "widow's weeds" to validate her place in the community. Contrasting with her dark conservative dress, her short, permanent-waved hair was silver.

"Pardon my mistake," Drayton said, "but you look young enough to be a 'Miss.'"

"That line won't get you anyplace, Mr. Hunt," she snapped. "The last thing I want is another man."

Drayton hadn't expected hostility.

"Do you need stamps?" Pearl concentrated on sorting the mail.

"I'll need a couple as it gets closer to Christmas. How much are they going for?"

"Same as always, three cents a stamp."

"I guess you keep a big supply on hand in case a rash of people want to send Christmas cards. Any chance you'll run out?"

"Mr. Hunt, rest assured the post office will not run out of stamps. The safe is full of stamps, money orders, what have you."

"You're lucky to have that bank safe setting there in the corner, a real old-timer she looks to be. I reckon it's called a 'safe' for a good reason," he laughed. "Those stamps, money orders, and what have you are safe as an unborn calf till you work the lock every morning." He hoped his lighthearted manner would coax Pearl to relax her guard.

"Oh, we don't use that old safe, never have since I've been working here," she explained. Few people took an interest in the post office. Pearl was eager to answer Drayton's questions. "Years ago when the bank president passed on, he took the combination with him, well, not literally," she smiled briefly. She was not accustomed to smiling during working hours. "So when the bank was taken over by the government, it was decided that buying another safe would be easier than finding someone who could figure out the combination to the old one. The new safe's inside that closet over there." She gestured toward an open door at the back of the room. During the day, Pearl left the safe door open as well. Lately she had been forgetting the combination.

"But what's to keep a couple of husky thieves from carrying the safe away in a pickup truck?" Drayton said.

"Oh, no, Mr. Hunt, that wouldn't be possible. It weighs four thousand pounds! It was made back in 1910 by the Hall's Safe Company in Cincinnati, and they built it to stay put." Pearl was as proud of her safe as if she had built it. "Now, Mr. Hunt, if you want to buy some stamps, please say so and let me get back to my work. The rural carrier is grouchy as Ebenezer Scrooge when he has to wait on me to get the mail put up."

"I'll take a stamp, then." Drayton reached in his pocket and found a nickel. "Keep the change," he said.

"I'm not allowed to accept gratuities." She handed back two pennies. "Here's your stamp. Make sure it doesn't get wet or it won't stick to your envelope."

Drayton strolled around the post office, as if admiring it. Pearl didn't take her eyes off of him. He had been asking an unusual number of questions about the safe and what it contained. She would have to be cautious dealing with this man. She knew his reputation.

"The old bank makes a fine post office," he said. "I was thinking, Miss Pearl, since you don't have any help, what about hiring me to keep the floors swept and scrubbed, and the windows washed? Not that you aren't doing a good job," he added. "I could even take care of raising and lowering the flag." Working for Pearl would allow him to be inside the post office without raising suspicion.

Drayton's offer sounded legitimate, but she would take her time before giving an answer. She wasn't sure that she could trust him. Of course she would have to pay him out of her own pocket, but it would be nice to have help again. After her husband had retired, he helped her with those chores. "I'll think about hiring you to help with the cleaning," she said, "but the sacred American flag can only be raised and lowered by a sworn employee of the United States government."

As Drayton drove home, he made a list of tools he might need to open the safe. "This will be a onetime detour to get me on my feet," Drayton promised himself and God, "and then it's back to the pulpit for Drayton R. Hunt." That was his sincere intention. But as preachers of the day often said, "The road to hell is paved with good intentions."

Drayton's first challenge would be getting inside the post office after hours. Since the building was formerly a bank, it had two heavy doors, front and back. He was not skilled with locks, and he couldn't blow the doors open with dynamite because of the noise and smoke. He went back to see the postmistress.

"I was wondering, Miss Pearl, have you give my offer any thought yet?"

"Yes, I have, Mr. Hunt. I can't pay much, but it would be a great help if you could come in late Friday afternoons and do the floor. My back isn't what it used to be. But you can't wash the windows because they're barred."

"How about if I was to take the bars off?"

Pearl's guard went up again. "Oh, I don't know about removing the bars, Mr. Hunt," she said, pursing her thin lips, as if she were seriously considering his offer. "They're to keep people from breaking in."

"Now, why would anybody want to break into a post office, cheap as stamps are?"

"Nevertheless, the bars must stay where they are."

"You know best, Miss Pearl. I'll be here Friday afternoon."

"But what about your job at the undertaking parlor?"

"I'll keep my fingers crossed that no one keels over on Friday."

Though he hadn't seen the safe up close, Drayton knew there would be no easy way to break into it. And whatever he chose to do would have to be done quickly. He was lucky that the safe door was left open during business hours. Perhaps while Pearl was taking down the flag or visiting the outhouse in the alley, he could wedge something in the door so it wouldn't close all the way. Or maybe he could disable the lock, making it accessible when he returned in the middle of the night. He knew next to nothing about safes. But almost anything can be broken into with a good screwdriver and a steady hand, he thought. He had considered stealing Pearl's door key, but she wore it on a chain around her neck.

At home that evening, Drayton sat by the stove, his dog at his feet, remembering some of his previous burglaries.

He was most proud of the night back in 1940 when he and the Woosley twins had broken into Turk Mowrey's feed store across the street from the movie theater. It had been early one Saturday night while everyone in town, including Turk, was watching *Jesse James*. There was no money in the cash drawer, but they carried a dozen sacks of laying mash out the front door, practically under Old Kane's nose. The next morning, Turk reported the theft to the sheriff but nothing came from it.

And there was the time he and the twins broke into Macel Scroggins's shack and stole a picture of her dead fiancé, lost in the Spanish-American War. When Drayton was in his prime, stealing had been a challenge, not for the value of what he stole but for the excitement of taking something of value to the victim and not getting caught.

Drayton didn't want to go back to his old life, but here he was, planning to do just that. "This venture's a long shot," he said to his dog, his palms beginning to sweat. "I'm too old for this shit."

TWENTY-FIVE

At four o'clock on Thursday afternoon, Mundy's Cafe was crowded with teenagers horsing around and retired men shooting pool. Drayton Hunt was having his hamburger at the counter when Harda Prill shoved her way up next to him and ordered a chocolate ice-cream cone. She was a pretty girl with long, black hair and green eyes. She reached in her jacket pocket to make sure she still had the nickel she had taken from her mother's purse. Although she'd been told to come straight home after school, she was willing to risk her mother's anger. I'm old enough now to do what I want, she thought. Today was her thirteenth birthday, and last week she had become a woman. The bleeding had stopped, but she continued to wear the elastic sanitary belt and soft pad because she liked the way they felt touching her body.

"That ice-cream cone looks good enough to eat," Drayton said to her.

Harda didn't answer. All men and boys were morons. She licked around the edge of the double cone where the ice cream had begun to melt.

On her way to Mundy's, Benny Mourning and Jimmy Day, two fifteen-year-old boys who couldn't get past the eighth-grade promotion test, had caught up with her. She pushed them off the sidewalk. "I'll let you know if you can walk with me, you dummies!" she said to the horny boys.

Benny pulled a rumpled eight-pager from his pocket and shoved it in her face. "Me and Jimmy will do these nasty things to you if you don't watch out!"

She knocked the small book from Benny's hand, laughing as it fell into a ditch of muddy water.

"You'll be sorry, Miss Know-it-all," Benny said, as he retrieved the soggy book. It had cost a month's allowance and now it was ruined. He gave her the finger, and he and Jimmy raced away. Harda walked the rest of the way to Main Street alone.

"And what's your name, little lady?" Drayton tried again to talk to the girl next to him. He noticed she was wearing lipstick like the older girls.

"Harda Prill." She bit off the tip of the double cone, daring the ice cream to drip onto her new birthday dress.

"I don't recall ever hearing the name 'Harda' before. It's pretty, though."

"Mama thought it up. When I was born, all she could think of was how hard it was, so she named me 'Harda' so she wouldn't forget and go through the ordeal again."

Drayton laughed out loud. It had been a long time since he had enjoyed a good laugh. At least laughing was not a Baptist sin, unless it was in response to an off-color joke. He took the last bite of his sandwich and focused his gaze on the girl. "I guess you like school? I never cared much for it myself, but girls generally like school better than boys do."

"Not me. School's boring," Harda said, making a face as if she were a six-year-old taking her daily dose of castor oil. "Can I have a drink of your cola?"

Drayton was caught off guard by her forward manner. "Help yourself." He watched her put the glass to her red lips, feeling suddenly thirsty himself. A smear of lipstick remained on the glass.

"Thanks," she said, as she licked ice cream from her fingers. She smiled and offered Drayton her sticky hand; her mother had taught her to be polite to older people.

Touching Harda's small, soft hand awakened feelings Drayton thought he had lost. He wished he were twenty-three again, knowing what he knew now. Too bad I'm a reformed man, he thought with honest regret. Not since Chastity Giberson had he seen a girl as beautiful as Harda Prill, he thought, as he watched her walk out the door.

June offered him more coffee, but Drayton refused. These days coffee went directly to his kidneys. Besides, he was shaky enough without another jolt of caffeine. Tomorrow afternoon would be the first step in robbing the post office, and he needed steady hands and a cool head. He refused to consider the possibility of being caught and sent back to prison, afraid of jinxing the job. After Saturday night, if all went well, his immediate money problems would be solved, and he would go back to studying the Bible.

"Did you take in the minstrel show?" Drayton asked June. "I heard it was funny as hell, but I stayed home with my dog. I can't tolerate crowds anymore."

"I had to work, but I wouldn't have gone anyway. I don't think minstrel shows are the least bit funny." June was in a rare bad humor.

"You don't like the jokes?"

"I think they're dumb and mean-spirited. Are you sure you don't want a refill?"

"I'm about to float away as it is." On impulse, Drayton said, "How about you and me taking in a picture show? There's a good one playing tomorrow night down in Alton. *The Big Sleep* it's called. That Humphrey Bogart's some actor."

She didn't hesitate. "Sure, I'll go," she said, smiling broadly. A slight overbite made her face almost childlike.

"I'll pick you up in my Moon at six o'clock. That'll give us a good hour before the first show starts."

"Do you know where I live?"

"West of town in that silver trailer?" He had passed it often on his way to the Carrollton Library to pick up books.

It had been a year since June's last date. If only she had a new dress—and her hair was a mess. She wrote out a ticket for Drayton's sandwich and handed it to him, leaning close. "Yeah, that's my trailer. Coffee's on the house," she whispered.

Drayton dug into his pocket for a dime to leave as a tip, then changed his mind and left a quarter.

Humming, June dropped the coin in her apron pocket and cleared his cup and plate from the counter.

The next afternoon, Drayton arrived at the post office with a box of tools and cleaning supplies. He would sweep and dust, and when Pearl stepped out the back door to the privy, he would work on the safe. In the old days he would have felt excitement at the challenge, but robbing the Old Kane post office was merely a means of putting food on his table and gasoline in his Moon.

At least there was the evening to look forward to—a good picture show and a sack of hot buttered popcorn. And June Plummer looks like she's hard up as me for a good fuck, he thought. I sure as hell hope my pecker don't let me down.

Drayton went about his work, with Pearl keeping close watch to make sure he didn't miss any dirt or steal a stamp. She hadn't forgotten her initial suspicion of him. Hoping to leave early—guests were coming for supper—she put the money drawer and stamps in the safe to get that end-of-the-day chore out of the way.

When Drayton finished sweeping, he turned his attention to the windows. It took only an instant to realize the bars were there to stay, a fact he should have recognized from the first. "Shit, there goes that!" he said to himself. The only alternative was to bring a crowbar and pry open the back door. Even with a full moon, the alley would be dark.

"It looks like the windows will have to stay dirty," he told Pearl. "Those bars won't come out."

"I've got along this many years without clean windows. I expect I can tolerate them until I retire next spring."

After what seemed an eternity, Pearl finally went to the toilet, leaving Drayton alone. Quickly he studied the formidable black safe. A picture of an eagle poised for flight decorated the center of the door, indicating that the safe had been built especially by the U.S. Treasury for use in a government office.

"Well, here goes nothing," he muttered to himself. Using his screwdriver, he pried off a rectangular metal plate on the inside of the door, exposing the maze of inner workings. Taking a chance, he unscrewed a large bolt. With a little luck, he thought, that bolt has something to do with how the lock works. Stands to reason that if the bolt's gone, the lock will be out of commission. If this don't do the trick, I'm fresh out of ideas. By now, he was sweating like it was the middle of August. He pulled a bandanna from his pocket and wiped his face.

"Well, that's all the damage I can do." Hurriedly he replaced the metal plate. He closed the door and finished dusting the outside of the safe just as Pearl walked in the back door.

"You can look and see if there's any dirt I missed," Drayton said pleasantly. "Since you're having back trouble, I went ahead and closed that heavy door on the safe and give the lock a turn."

"Why, how nice," she said. Drayton Hunt had turned out to be a thoughtful man, nothing like the awful stories she had heard about him. But in case she was mistaken, Pearl had left a ten-dollar bill near the cash box, as if she had forgotten to put it with the rest of the money from the day's business. Drayton couldn't miss seeing it. Would he return it to her or slip it in his pocket?

After a quick inspection of Drayton's work, Pearl handed him two dollars. "You did a fine job," she said. "I'll expect you next Friday."

"I'll be here." He started out the door. "I near forgot, Miss Pearl, I found this ten-dollar bill on the counter. I guess you must of dropped it."

"Why, thank you, Mr. Hunt, I must be getting careless in my old age."

Drayton drove home to get ready for his date with June. His stomach cramped as if he had eaten a basket of green apples. He hoped the movie would take his mind off the post office and that damned safe.

After Drayton left, Pearl finished tying up the day's mail slated to go out, affixed a padlock to the large canvas bag, and left it by the back door for the mail truck to pick up.

Gathering up her own mail, she took one last look around the office and activated the recently installed burglar alarm.

Drayton spent extra time getting ready for the evening, choosing a white shirt and dark brown trousers, and he made sure his hair and beard were clean and combed. June was fond of his beard; once she had asked to touch it. By the time Drayton parked in front of her trailer, his stomach had settled.

June answered the door wearing a bright red dress, its fitted bodice accentuating her small waist. Her hair was in a French roll, held in place by a rhinestone comb. She had splurged on a bottle of Tabu.

"Come on in," June said, amused at the look of pleasure on his face. "I made a pot of chili. We have time for a bowl, unless you think we need to leave right now."

Drayton hadn't thought about supper, but he was hungry. "We're in no big hurry—chili's one of my favorite things to eat," he said, climbing up into the trailer. "My mama used to make it every Sunday night." He followed June into the tiny kitchen. The chrome-edged table was set with bowls and soup spoons, saltines, dill pickles, grated cheddar, and tall glasses of iced tea.

Drayton and June talked through the meal and were still talking as she served thick slices of a Newlywed cake roll and strong coffee.

"We'll have to watch Humphrey Bogart another time," Drayton said, when he suddenly realized it was after eight.

"This is better than any old movie," June said. She reached across the table and put her hand on Drayton's. "I'll find some music on the radio."

Drayton was unaccustomed to such special treatment. Throughout his life, he had been the aggressor.

Early on, the two had discovered how much they had in common—both children of absent fathers and unmarried mothers who made a living with their bodies.

"My mother was a dancer," June said. "Before she was saddled with me, she had dreams of being in the movies or on the Broadway stage, but she wasn't good enough, or else she didn't know the right people. And some people thought that her skin wasn't pretty enough. She had to powder it to make it look pale and perfect. Anyway, she ended up dancing on the stage of the Grand Theater in St. Louis, taking off her clothes behind a giant fan made of feathers. She was known as Fannie the Fan Dancer."

June made another pot of coffee and served more cake. When the clock struck one, Drayton said, "I didn't know how late it was. I'd better go or you'll start charging me rent. Maybe we can do this again?" In spite of his desire, he had given up the idea of sleeping with her. He was afraid he might disappoint her.

But June had her own desires. "You don't have to leave," she said. "There's no curfew." She took his hand and led him into her bedroom. The lamp was low, and the covers were already turned down. Who could resist?

"Sit here on the bed with me," June said. "Before we get any cozier, there's something you should know about me—"

TWENTY-SIX

Friday evening Shug Combrink, the elderly janitor at the Old Kane grade school, was finishing his duties for the week. When he stepped outside to empty a dustpan, he noticed something lying on the ground near the swing set. The hunter's moon was just peeping over the treetops, lighting up the playground as if it were midday. "Some dumb kid's forgot his jacket," he mumbled, as he went to retrieve the garment.

"Criminently!" he said, as he reached the swings. It was a girl, her dress askew, and she was not wearing underpants. He leaned down and straightened her dress, careful not to touch her. In that brief look, he could see she was already a mature female. Shug recognized Harda Prill, Ed's girl. I better get some help with this, he thought, as he hobbled back inside the school to call her parents. In a few minutes the Prills arrived, Hannah in tears, Ed with a puzzled look on his face.

"This is just how I found her," Shug said. "I expect she'd ought to go to the hospital, but I didn't want to do nothing till you got here."

"Lord, what's happened to my little girl?" Hannah moaned, as she bent over Harda's unconscious body. She rubbed Harda's small, cold hands in an effort to revive her.

"By God, I'll kill whoever done this," Ed said, his fists doubled. Suddenly he lashed out at his wife. "This is all your fault, Hannah Prill. I tried to tell you the girl needed to be on a short leash! And the way you let her paint her mouth! And why wasn't she home listening to the radio in the first place?"

"She was staying the night with Margie Prough," Hannah said, drying her eyes. "They were going to the picture show."

"Them damned picture shows are the ruination of young girls, the way them female movie stars prance around half naked!" Ed Prill needed someone or something to blame.

"I'll call for the ambulance," Shug said, as he went back inside the school to use the telephone. He asked Central to ring Bert Linder, whose hearse doubled as an ambulance.

Dr. Ed Johnson, the emergency room physician who examined Harda, told the Prills that their daughter had been raped, and while he couldn't see anything seriously wrong, it was his opinion that her brain was blocking out what happened, thus causing her to remain unconscious. "Leave her here a few days and we'll keep a close watch over her," he said to the anxious parents.

"But what if she conceived?" Hannah cried, thinking ahead to the shame of raising an illegitimate child.

"This being her first time, it's not likely," the doctor reassured her.

Hannah Prill sobbed quietly but Ed paced the floor, his fists clenched, itching to confront the perpetrator. "The sheriff ought to pick up that goddamned Drayton Hunt!" he said. "Things like this was just waiting to happen with a convict living amongst us! Hunt's always had an eye for the young ones. Look what happened to Worthy Giberson's girl."

Early Saturday morning, the Boyd Memorial Hospital in Carrollton notified Sheriff Ridenour of the attack on Harda Prill. The aging lawman slammed down the telephone receiver, damning the messenger. "Jesus! And me stuck in bed with the goddamned lumbago!"

Other than a petty theft now and then, or an outhouse turned end over end on Halloween, there were few crimes in Greene County that a lawman could put all his efforts into and take pride in solving. And now, with what appeared to be a major crime in Old Kane's midst, there was no way Sheriff Ridenour could do the investigation that needed to be done. Unlike the previous sheriff, Amos Ridenour loved his work.

Chief Deputy Specs Kirbach had lost his heart for the job after the Cleo Clendenny tragedy and resigned. So the sheriff sent for Royal Whiteside, local game warden. Royal had no police work experience, but because he was accustomed to dealing with men who broke animal laws, Sheriff Ridenour reasoned he could easily make the transition to human laws. And Royal already knew how to carry a gun and wear a badge.

When word reached Royal that the sheriff had a job for him, he was surprised, then suspicious. Ordinarily Sheriff Ridenour avoided him as if he had TB. Just what's that crafty old sheriff up to? he wondered, as he drove to the sheriff's house.

Under ideal conditions, Sheriff Ridenour was not an easy man to deal with, and because of his lumbago, Royal expected the encounter to be worse than usual. Mrs. Ridenour, exhausted from tending her demanding husband, escorted Royal to the sickroom and closed the door behind him. Taking advantage of a few minutes' respite, she dropped into a chair and took several swallows of whiskey straight from the pint she carried in her apron pocket.

Even though he was ill and off duty, Sheriff Ridenour was dressed in full uniform down to his gold-plated badge, which he had purchased himself. His shirt was stretched tight over his belly; several buttons were ready to pop off, hanging by a thread. He had propped himself up in the bed with pillows, and he was scowling.

"Don't bother setting down," he grumbled as Royal started toward a chair. "I'm not inclined to prolong this meeting, so pay heed to what I've got to say so I don't have to waste my breath repeating it. A girl from your neck of the woods was found laying on the ground unconscious in back of the Old Kane grade school. Some bastard raped her."

"What's that got to do with me?" Royal asked. He started to sit, then remembered the sheriff's warning not to.

"Specs Kirbach up and quit on me because of that Cleo Clendenny business, and I haven't got around to replacing him. The county budget only allows for one deputy at a time. This goddamned lumbago has me laid up indefinite, so I'm hereby appointing you acting chief deputy. Consider yourself deputized. Your job will be to do some nosing around, conduct questioning, and report anything you deem suspicious. Of course when the girl wakes up, she'll be able to tell who done the deed. By that time I'll take over, providing I'm out of this goddamned sickbed."

Royal Whiteside knew he was not qualified to handle an investigation of this scope. Even a man with eight grades of schooling under his belt would be hard-put to carry this off, he grumbled to himself. City detectives had sophisticated technology to work with, but a country lawman had to get by with his wits and gut feelings. Royal considered himself to be of average intelligence, average height, and average weight. He had medium brown hair and his facial features were average. Until now, he had lived his average life unnoticed, but he feared that was about to change. There was a knot the size of a hedge apple in his gut. "If word gets around I'm not doing my game warden's job, the poachers will go hog wild," Royal protested. "Before long there won't be a damned quail or rabbit that ain't already full of shot."

"Clem Doyle can fill in for you."

"But Clem's never did my kind of work and—"

"I agree the man's no ball buster, but how many brains does it take to check a man's pocket for a hunting license?"

"Hell, Sheriff, I don't know the first thing about investigating," Royal said, admitting the real source of his reluctance.

"Jesus, Royal, stop your bellyaching. Just do the best you can and try not to embarrass yourself or me. You might start with Drayton Hunt. I hear he's back in town. Young girls are right up his alley. Now get out of here and let me get some rest."

Word of the attack quickly spread throughout Greene County. By the time Royal arrived at the schoolyard around noon, it was as crowded as the annual American Legion fish fry. Townspeople had left their dinner tables to get a glimpse of the scene where the attack occurred and speculate about the identity of the man responsible.

Since leaving the sheriff's house, Royal had gone over in his mind who he would question and what questions he would ask. The logical person to begin with was Shug Combrink. With the attack happening in the school's backyard, the old janitor might be able to provide some helpful answers.

Shug was eager to help, but his knowledge of the crime was limited to having found the girl. "I was inside the school building the whole evening," he said, "mopping, sweeping, scraping chewing gum off desks, so I didn't see nothing out of the usual. Boys and girls that age is always coming to play on the swings after dark. From the looks of the rubbers laying on the ground, I doubt they're doing much swinging, though." He chuckled.

Royal decided to delay further questioning until he could spend some time at the Carrollton lending library studying proper investigative procedures. He didn't want to do something dumb and be the butt of jokes for the next ten years.

"Thank you kindly for your time, Shug. I'll be looking around the schoolyard in case the attacker left a clue. But first I have to buy a special tool from the hardware store. This ain't your ordinary case, you know."

According to a Sherlock Holmes novel Royal once read, a magnifying glass was an essential tool in every investigation. The clerk at Gardner's Hardware found one tucked away in the storeroom, covered with two decades of dust. "If you don't find a clue, bring it back," the clerk reassured him, carefully putting the glass in a paper sack and handing it to Royal.

Eager to test the magnifying glass's worth, Royal hurried back to the schoolyard. It was midafternoon when he parked his truck in front of the school. He hoped he would recognize a clue if he found one. With glass in hand, he got down on his knees and searched the ground beneath the swing sets—scuffed bare of grass by young, restless feet. He searched the sidewalks, the ground under the teeter-totters, the softball field, but the attacker had not left a scrap of evidence. At the very least, he had expected to find a used condom. He refrained from swearing until he left the school grounds.

While Royal searched the rest of the afternoon for clues, Old Kane party lines hummed with gossip. No one was without a theory about what had taken place the previous evening in the schoolyard. Royal knew he would have to be careful not to listen to whimsical theories, and consider only the facts he uncovered. Unfortunately, he would soon learn there were far more theories than facts.

Later that same afternoon, Drayton drove into Old Kane to pick up supplies for his pantry and gasoline for his Moon. Even though the day was chilly, his palms were sweating. Tonight was the big night. It couldn't come too soon. After paying for gasoline and groceries, he would be flat broke.

As he sat in the car waiting for Finice to fill his tank, he overheard two men discussing the assault on Harda Prill. "Goddammit," Drayton swore under his breath. Certain to be the first man suspected of any crime within a fifty-mile radius, from cattle rustling to jaywalking, he would have to take extra precautions not to be seen near the post office. The assault was a complication he didn't need. He'd known that girl was trouble as soon as she sat down next to him. He drove straight home, forgetting the groceries.

Although he had no appetite, he fried a soft egg for supper. He would need all his strength to get through the night. He sat near the woodstove gathering his thoughts, going over his plans for the hundredth time. At midnight he would drive into town and park in a dark alleyway several blocks from the post office. He hoped there would be clouds to hide that damned hunter's moon. All the stores on Main Street would be closed, and Old Kane would be sound asleep. The theft wouldn't be discovered until Monday morning when Pearl opened the empty safe. It sounded easy enough.

Drayton didn't believe in premonitions, but for the past two days he'd had a foreboding that followed him like a homeless kitten. What if I've lost my touch with break-ins? he thought. I sure ain't the man I used to be with the ladies. His date with June Plummer the night before had not turned out as either had hoped. June had done her part to arouse him, but he couldn't manage an erection. He hadn't been with a woman for over three years. Embarrassed, he wondered whether she would give him another chance.

Drayton tried reading the newspaper to pass the time until midnight, but he couldn't concentrate. He threw down the paper. "Hell, maybe I'll postpone robbing the post office till Old Kane cools off," Drayton said to his dog, stretched out on the hearth at his feet. "And after the job's done, maybe I'll sell this place and you and me can move south. I've had my fill of chopping wood for these damned heartless winters." The dog jumped up and licked Drayton's face, ready to follow him anywhere. Affectionately, Drayton rubbed her head. "Let's you and me go and saw some logs."

Lying in bed, Drayton questioned whether he would have gone through with his plan to break into the post office, even without the Harda Prill matter. From the beginning something had been holding him back, like that long-ago day his mother held him by his overall suspenders to keep him from falling into the cistern. Was there a God holding him back now, in place of his mother? No question, he'd lost his nerve. Was it fear of getting caught and being sent back to prison? Was he beginning to believe the Bible Scriptures, even the foolish ones?

Or was it Cappy? One more slip, and his son would be lost to him forever.

"For whatever reason, tonight wasn't supposed to be," Drayton said, as his dog happily jumped onto the bed. "But if I don't come up with some money right quick, you and me will have to give up eating."

TWENTY-SEVEN

M onday morning, Royal Whiteside spent several hours at the Carrollton library studying books on criminal investigations. One word that kept appearing in his reading was "surveillance." He looked it up in the dictionary (the librarian helped him find the difficult word), and was relieved to learn it meant nothing more than watching a suspect without the suspect's knowledge. I can handle that easy, Royal thought. He had spent many hours crouched down out of sight, patiently waiting for a hunter to shoot or trap an animal out of season. Nothing was more gratifying than slipping up on a couple of poachers as they were loading a feed sack full of out-of-season quail into their truck bed or skinning a mother mink and leaving her offspring to starve.

From reading dime mystery novels as a boy, Royal knew that the perpetrator of a crime often returned to the scene, either to watch the havoc the act caused and experience the pride that goes with a job well done or to make sure a clue wasn't left behind. So that afternoon, Royal hired little Roger Steinacher to sit under the buckeye tree across the street from the grade school and make note of anyone entering the school grounds. Since the attack on Harda Prill, school had been dismissed indefinitely. For his surveillance work, Roger was to receive ten pennies each day and all the buckeyes he could stuff in his pockets.

Cappy was asleep when the telephone rang. He glanced at the Baby Ben clock on his bedside table. Midnight. "Shit!" He grabbed his pants and hurried downstairs before the ringing woke Tick and Worthy.

"Cappy, Joe Bray. Did I interrupt anything?"

"Only the best dream I've had in weeks! What's going on?"

"I'm calling to ask *you.* I got word there's been a crime in Old Kane, and my star freelance reporter didn't let me in on it."

Cappy had assumed the big-city editor wouldn't be interested. "I'm sorry, Joe. What do you want to know?"

"Everything! My readers will want to know how such crimes are handled in a village like Old Kane. Usually a rape doesn't get written about, but with the victim a ten-year-old girl, that's news."

"She's thirteen."

"Still news. Who's in charge of the investigation?"

"Technically it's Sheriff Ridenour, but he's laid up with lumbago so he's turned it over to Royal Whiteside."

"I suppose this Whiteside is the chief deputy?"

"He's actually the game warden."

Joe Bray laughed. "Then here's what I want you to do. Start riding around with this game warden–turned–deputy and send me something every day, even if it's only a few lines. It'll be like a Saturday afternoon serial at the movies that leads up to the climax of finding the guilty man. What do you think?"

"If I get the sheriff's okay, I'll start tomorrow."

"That's great. I'll be waiting for your first installment."

Excited about this assignment, Cappy hurried through breakfast the next morning and drove to Sheriff Ridenour's home. But the sheriff, waiting impatiently for his first cup of coffee, refused to discuss Harda Prill. "Hell, do what you want. The whole thing's already blowed out of shape anyway. We're done talking."

When Cappy knocked on Royal's door and explained his reason for being there, Royal didn't object. "Two heads is better than one," he said politely, though he would have preferred to work alone. In the world of game wardens, the more men looking for poachers, the less chance of finding them. A half dozen men tromping through the woods couldn't sneak up on a dead man. Royal suspected it would be the same when searching for a rapist.

"I'll only be observing," Cappy assured Royal. "I promise not to butt in."

Royal hesitated. "I was wondering, will you be using my name in the newspaper?"

"Unless you don't want me to."

"The trouble is, I ain't schooled for this job. I don't want to come out looking like a dumb country boy."

"I'd never write anything to embarrass you," Cappy said. He touched Royal's shoulder and grinned. "I'm a country boy myself."

Sheriff Ridenour's office was in the Greene County Courthouse, but since there was no branch in Old Kane, Royal approached Turk Mowrey about using a back corner of his feed store for a temporary office to work from. Royal hoped people would stop in to pass the time of day and inadvertently mention something helpful they had seen the evening of the crime.

"Can I use the back corner or not?" Royal repeated to Turk.

"Hell, no, I'm not having rowdies coming in and out of my place of business."

"Who said anything about rowdies? It's my thinking that men might drop by to soak up some heat from your wood-stove and let something slip about who they seen hanging around the schoolyard. And maybe they'll buy an extra bag of manure while they're at it," he added as inducement.

"I don't know." Turk rubbed his three-day growth of whiskers as he considered the possibility of increased business. "I guess it won't hurt nothing, so long as you only let in one rowdy at a time."

Wednesday morning, with Cappy trying to stay out of the way, Royal carried in a large crate to use as a desk, a barrel to sit on, and an extra barrel for whoever stopped to talk. In the store window he placed a sign announcing the hours he would be available.

He had just finished putting the sign in place when Lydia Summers, respected Sunday school teacher, entered the front door. Since it was not customary for ladies to make purchases at the feed store, he correctly assumed she was there to see him.

"Just follow me, Miz Summers."

"Thank you, I will." Lydia nodded toward the several men who were watching her curiously.

"What can I be doing for you today, Miz Summers?"

She sat on the barrel across from Royal and cleared her throat, as if she were presenting a lesson on canning peaches at the Household Science Club—a group of women who shared recipes and poetry readings. She straightened the flowers on her hat. "I'm here with a message from my table."

Royal laughed. "For a minute I thought you said 'your table.'" But then he realized she was serious.

"That's what I said. When I heard you was in charge of the Harda Prill investigation, I figured you'd be needing all the help you could get, so I inquired of my table."

"What in God's name does a piece of furniture have to do with the problem at hand?"

"I'm about to tell you, Royal, if you'll hush up." She took a lace handkerchief from her sleeve and put it to her flushed face. She'd be glad when she was through the change of life; every day was like the middle of July.

"Whenever I or my neighbor has a problem, we set around my table. So last night I posed some questions about the town trouble. What we do, you see, is we set with our fingertips touching the top of the table and if the answer is 'yes,' one corner of the table—that's why you can't use a round table because there's no corners—one corner raises up and taps once for 'yes' and twice for 'no.' Now here's where you have to be watchful. There's some tables that tap the opposite, twice for 'yes' and once for 'no,' so you have to make sure which kind of table you've got before you can put any stock by the answer."

Royal began to fidget. "Miz Summers, I'm a man with a mountain of problems to climb over, and I'd take just about any leg up that's offered, but it beats me how a table could know the answer to questions when a human being don't. But I thank you for coming by." He stood up.

But Lydia Summers didn't move. "Now hold on, young man, you didn't ask what the answer was."

"Hell, ma'am, I don't even know what the *question* was."

"The question was, Did that awful Drayton Hunt attack that sweet little Harda Prill? And my table said, 'Yes, he did.'"

"There's others waiting to talk to me," Royal said, noticing a short line forming near the bags of chicken feed, "but I thank you for coming by, Miz Summers. And thank your table for all its trouble."

"A body has to do what's right," she said. She nodded pleasantly to the men as she left, proud that she and her table had done their part.

Although by the end of the day Royal had learned nothing useful regarding the crime, Turk Mowrey sold more manure than he had in months.

Joe Bray will like this, Cappy thought, as he typed up his account of the day's investigation and put it in an envelope to mail. A serious subject can always use some relief.

While Royal Whiteside was working to find the rapist, Harda's condition remained the same. She had been in a coma for four days and was being fed intravenously. Her parents took turns hovering over her, watching for an eyelid to blink, indicating that she was waking up.

With Cappy tagging along, notebook in hand, Royal questioned every family in and around Old Kane, focusing on families whose homes were on Mill Street near the school. Everyone had seen Harda Prill strolling to and from the school grounds all hours of the day and night, even when school was not in session. (Her parents weren't properly looking after her, were the whispers.) And those same people had seen Drayton Hunt driving to and from town in his fancy car, passing the school on his way to the Baptist Church or Sorphus Peak's grocery store. And the day before the assault, he had been seen sitting at the counter in Mundy's Cafe boldly talking to the girl, even laughing. Old Kane's imagination took over, making an assumption that soon became truth to them.

When Royal told Sheriff Ridenour what people were saying, the sheriff, having a particularly painful day, said, "Arrest the bastard!"

Cappy had not foreseen this awkward situation. "I don't feel comfortable sitting in while you question a suspect," he said to Royal. "Tomorrow you can go by yourself and tell me later what took place."

"But what if I don't recall everything?"

"I'll risk that," Cappy said, climbing into Royal's truck. "Just drop me at home now and I'll catch up with you tomorrow."

The next morning a little past nine, Royal drove alone to Drayton Hunt's house and parked in the driveway. The grass was mowed around the freshly painted house, and bronze mums—their fragile dried blossoms still colorful—lined the walkway. The next strong wind would scatter them over the yard. To the passerby, Mae Hunt could still have been alive, keeping her house inviting. Royal knocked timidly on the front door.

"I wondered how long it would take you to get here," Drayton said. He was carrying a cup of cold coffee left from breakfast. "Are you arresting me?"

"I ain't got no choice, Drayton." Royal felt like apologizing. "Sheriff Ridenour says I'm to take you in for questioning and lock you up. Have you got bail money?"

"None of my own, but there's somebody who might give me a hand. I'd like to point out you never even asked me if I did it, Royal."

"Either you done it or you didn't, that ain't my concern. I'm merely following orders like a foot soldier." Dealing with animals was easier than dealing with humans, Royal thought. Animals don't talk back or look you in the eye. Common sense told him Drayton was guilty, but Royal had a hunch that he was arresting the wrong man.

Soon after Drayton's arrest, Reverend Marcus Smith arrived at the courthouse and paid the fifty-dollar bail. They had not spoken since the incident in the parsonage.

"I didn't do it," Drayton said, as the two men walked out together and got into Marcus Smith's car. "I never once had to force a female to lay with me, and I ain't—I'm not about to start now."

"According to Deputy Whiteside, there's no evidence, just suspicion because of your past history with young girls."

"Hell, that don't give me no relief."

They rode in silence until they reached Mae Hunt's house. Drayton waited before getting out of the car. "I know I haven't been around since I walked in on you and your poet friend, but I was thinking maybe I need to clean up my own fence row before I fault you for yours."

"That's generous of you, Mr. Hunt," Marcus said, taking Drayton's words to be an apology. "I had no idea John Roley would come back into my life, though I'd thought of him often over the years. When he showed up at my door, Satan took over. Ministers can be sinners, too."

"Much obliged for helping me out at the jail," Drayton said. "I'll get you paid back."

"No hurry. Have a good night, Mr. Hunt." He touched Drayton's arm with affection. "I've missed our Scripture study."

Word quickly circulated that Drayton Hunt had been jailed and subsequently bailed out by the Baptist minister, all within the course of an hour.

Outraged, as if it were a personal affront, Cappy drove to the church and burst into Marcus Smith's study. "Do you really think Drayton Hunt is not responsible for attacking Harda Prill?" he shouted, his face contorted in anger. "Take the blinders off!"

"All I can say is this, young man. I've worked closely with Mr. Hunt since he came home to Old Kane, and I believe he's sincere. He has a strong motive for changing. He wants you to stop being ashamed that he's your father."

"That day won't come," Cappy said.

"It's clear you're filled with hatred. Maybe you should back off and give the man some slack. He didn't grow up in a home like yours with two loving parents. We all make mistakes, Cappy, and he's trying to atone for his."

Marcus Smith's quiet words had a calming effect on Cappy. He knew the minister was right. He had heard the same words from Worthy and Tick. But giving up twenty-three years of hating Drayton Hunt wasn't easy. "Anyway, we'll know the truth when Harda Prill wakes up from her coma," Cappy said.

"*If* she wakes up."

While Harda lay in a coma, Royal Whiteside was searching day and night for the man responsible. The hours at the library had been worthwhile, but a man can learn only so much from books, Royal thought. Since Bert Linder had picked up Harda Prill and transported her to the hospital, maybe he knew something. Royal found the surly undertaker in the dank basement of the funeral parlor poking around the cold body of Miss Letty Lawson, spinster schoolteacher. As the door squeaked open, Bert glanced up from his work.

"Don't just stand there like a ninny," he grumbled, grouchy as an old man though he was only thirty. "Come on in and don't take too long."

Looking at Miss Letty's frail, naked body on the table seemed disrespectful to Royal, as if he were looking at his own skinny grandmother. "I'll talk from here," Royal said, just inside the door.

"Suit yourself."

Royal glanced around the room, dark except for the bright light over the embalming table. "You doing all the work yourself these days?"

"I had to let Hunt go, he was driving away business," Bert said. "This is my first body in a month. What do you want?"

"You know the sheriff's got me looking into the Harda Prill business," Royal said, as he pulled a notebook from his pocket and licked his pencil lead. "When you picked her up, did you notice anything peculiar?"

"Nothing's more pitiful to lay your eyes on than a sixty-year-old spinster," Bert said, as if he hadn't heard Royal's question. "Look at this, would you? Except for a few scraggly gray hairs between her legs, she's bare as a baby."

Royal began to sweat. "I was asking about the Prill girl."

"I heard you. One thing I can say, her hairdo wasn't even mussed up. I figure once the rape started, she laid back and enjoyed it. That's how them things usually go. Look here, Royal. This may be your first and only chance to see what an old virgin's privates looks like—"

But before Bert could finish his sentence, Royal was out the door, wishing he were deep in Jones Woods following a trail of rabbit blood.

With the rest of Old Kane speculating about the Harda Prill mystery, Tick was caring for whatever sick animal he could find. "Reverend Art used to say everything happens for a reason," Tick said to the small rabbit he had found struggling to free itself from a steel trap. He massaged its mangled foot and applied some iodine to the wound. The rabbit barely flinched at Tick's gentle touch. "If Reverend Art hadn't been killed by that jealous deacon, I never would have walked home. I guess once you're a preacher, God ain't about to let you out of the deal. It appears He still has need of me." Tick determined that he was being recalled by God to cure hurt animals and settle the rift between Cappy and Drayton Hunt.

So next time Cappy and Tick were walking alongside the trickling branch in the south pasture, Tick brought up again the subject of reconciliation. "You'll feel like a new man if you and Drayton get to be friends," Tick said. "It probably says so in the Bible if I knew where to look."

Cappy laughed and walked more quickly. Tick followed, still talking.

"Nothing happens by accident," Tick said, "not even accidents. That's what Reverend Art said."

"You know what I think of Art Gimmy and his kind," Cappy said, practically running now. "And I thought you'd given up that religious drivel. And what do 'accidents' have to do with anything?"

"I'm saying that Drayton Hunt being your daddy come about for a reason, that it wasn't an accident. Reverend Art said God causes everything."

Cappy stopped and faced Tick. "Are you saying God caused World War II, or caused Chastity to die giving birth to me? What kind of God is that?"

"The only kind of God there is, I reckon," Tick said. He wished he could think of a better answer. During his years with Reverend Art, he had not been allowed to ask questions that put God in a bad light. "Reverend Art said a person who hates another person can get sick from it. I don't want you getting sick, Cappy."

"If I get sick you can say your miracle words and I'll be cured," he said with sarcasm. "Listen, Tick, I'm not that same little kid who believed everything you told me. And most of what you told me was wrong anyway," he added, "like when you said if a man used a rubber during sex the woman would get pregnant. You should have heard the laughing when I passed that on at school. It took me months to live it down."

"But you ought to think about forgiving Drayton Hunt," Tick said. "Jesus even forgave the men who killed him and—"

"I'm not Jesus. Between you and Oleeta and Pa and the constant nagging, you're squeezing the breath out of me. Why don't you just tend to your sick chickens and crippled rabbits and leave me alone?"

TWENTY-EIGHT

On November 18, as the final maple leaf fluttered to the ground like a sparrow's feather, Harda Prill opened her eyes and looked around the sunny hospital room. She yawned and stretched, as if she were waking from a long afternoon nap instead of a thirteen-day coma.

A nurse making hourly rounds was the first to discover Harda awake. She ran to inform the head nurse, who told the doctor, who phoned Hannah and Ed Prill, who notified Sheriff Ridenour. The sheriff, still nursing his lumbago, sent for Royal Whiteside. Within an hour, Harda was surrounded by people with questions.

"I don't remember," Harda answered, trying out her hoarse voice and sipping juice through a hospital straw. Her face was thinner, with dark circles under her eyes, and her long black hair was matted against the pillow.

"But you surely know if he was a stranger or somebody you knowed," Royal said, his frustration growing. If only Sheriff Ridenour would recover.

"I don't remember," Harda repeated. "Maybe I'll just go back to sleep." She closed her eyes.

"No, dear, don't do that," Hannah Prill said, gently shaking her daughter. "It's time you came home." The hospital bill was putting a serious strain on the family budget.

Royal was puzzled by Harda's attitude. Most girls would have been eager to name their attacker and get even. "Do like your mama says, girlie, and after a day or two I'll stop by and you can tell me the man's name." He patted her head.

"I'll probably be asleep," Harda said. She yawned.

Two days later Royal knocked on the Prills' back door. Cappy was with him.

"I've come to talk to the girl again," Royal said to Hannah.

"You can come in, but it won't do you any good," Hannah said. "The doctor says she's still blotting out what happened."

"How about letting me give it a try? Cappy here will help me keep track of what she says."

"Suit yourself." Hannah led the way to the front room, where Harda was lying on the sofa listening to *Jack Armstrong, All American Boy* on the radio. Hearing her mother and the two men approach, she turned up the volume and closed her eyes.

Royal switched off the radio. "Hello, there, little lady." He raised the pitch of his voice an octave, as if speaking to a baby or a puppy. "I've come to see if you remember what happened in the schoolyard yet."

"I remember," she said, her eyes still tightly closed. "I fell off the top of the swing set and bumped my head on a rock."

"She's still mixed up from the coma," Royal whispered to Hannah and Cappy. "Let's try again, girlie. Do you remember who it was that hurt you?"

"I told you. It was the rock that hurt me when I fell off the swing set."

"Then what happened to your underpants?"

"I'll have no more questions like that, Royal Whiteside!" Hannah Prill said. "You'd better leave!"

"Damned stubborn girl," Royal said as he and Cappy got in the car to leave. "I may be new at this police work, but my guess is she's protecting somebody."

"But why would she do that?"

"Who can know a teenage female?"

That evening when Cappy sat down at his typewriter, he realized he couldn't write everything he heard during the course of the investigation. If there were a trial, the case could be compromised. He might have to invent something that would keep Joe Bray and the *Post-Dispatch* readers interested. Poetic license, Cappy thought, as he began to type:

This is a warning to the man responsible for the rape of Harda Prill. You are being relentlessly pursued by Royal Whiteside, a man equal to Sherlock Holmes in his ability to ferret out criminals. Although not formally trained for the job of investigator, Mr. Whiteside is taking his experience as game warden and making the leap to chief deputy.

It's always possible that a new suspect will be arrested at any time. You will read it first in the St. Louis Post-Dispatch. Cap Giberson, reporter.

Like everyone else, Royal had assumed that when Harda awoke from her coma she would tell the name of her attacker and that would be that. But she stubbornly insisted that she had fallen and hit her head. Royal could no longer delay moving ahead with the investigation.

He longed to stroll through Jones Woods for old times' sake. He might find a stand of fall mushrooms to fry for tonight's supper. But instead of a detour into the woods, Royal drove directly to Mae Hunt's. Drayton was in the shed changing the oil in his Moon.

"That motorcar is sure something to see," Royal said, approaching the car. He touched the shiny nickel door handles.

Drayton ignored Royal's attempt at small talk. "I know this ain't a social call. If it was, you'd be the first." Drayton was as lonely as when he was a boy. Because of the Prill tragedy, he now stayed away from Mundy's Cafe and June Plummer. Even though Reverend Marcus Smith had provided Drayton's bail, their friendship continued to be fragile, their Scripture study suspended. Cappy, his flesh-and-blood son, would have nothing to do with him. And who knows whose bed his sister was keeping warm?

"I'm only doing the sheriff's work with this questioning," Royal said. "Now, let's get to it. Did you see Harda Prill the day she was accosted?"

"No, but I saw her the day before. I was setting in Mundy's Cafe when she come in for an ice-cream cone and set down next to me. A right pretty little thing. Her scent was warm and musky, like all young girls."

"What were you doing that Friday evening?"

Drayton thought for a minute; he didn't want to bring June Plummer into the picture. "I had my Bible reading to do, and then I listened to *Duffy's Tavern* on the radio till bedtime," he lied.

"Any proof of that?"

"Not unless you'll take my dog's word for it, she never left my side. But why don't you ask the little girl herself who it was who done the act?"

Royal was tired of being judged inept. "I've asked her till I was blue in the face. The doc says she's blotting out the real happening."

"I didn't do a damned thing to that girl," Drayton said. "I learned my lesson years back, so do your looking somewhere else. Now I'm going inside and open a can of beans." He turned to leave.

"Hold up, Hunt," Royal said. "The sheriff says for me to officially arrest you. And this time there won't be no bail."

Stunned, Drayton turned to face Royal. "You've got evidence against me?"

"Sheriff Ridenour got a tip claiming your Moon was parked in front of the schoolhouse that Friday night."

"Who the hell told that bare-ass lie? Let him say it to me direct!" Drayton's face was red with anger, his fists clenched.

"Calm down, Hunt. I'll tell you—it ain't like it's a secret. It was Hubert Bent."

Drayton laughed out loud. "Hubert Bent! I might of known. Poor old Hubert's still carrying a grudge against me for bedding his bride back when we was all in our twenties. He swore to get even, and now, by God, he's done it."

"Grudge or not, it's enough to take you in. So round up your belongings, I've got other things to do besides hauling you back and forth to jail."

"I can't leave my dog to starve."

"I'll see to your dog."

Drayton touched the hood of his Moon, sensing it would be a long time before he returned home. "Who else is a suspect?"

"Only you."

When Drayton heard the familiar sound of the cell door locking, something went out of him, like an old man's final breath. He lay on the cot considering his bleak future. He wasn't guilty of the charge, but with his luck, that wouldn't make an iota of difference. He knew the routine. There would be a trial of sorts, then sentencing, and then that long train ride south. What would Chaplain Davenport have to say about his protégé's apparent fall from grace? In Old Kane, the only person who supported him was Marcus Smith, and he probably had doubts he wouldn't own up to.

As he sat in the small cell that was barely large enough to turn around in, he thought about his coming home to Old Kane. It hadn't turned out the way he had hoped, which fit the pattern of his life. Only in the quiet of the night did he acknowledge to himself that he wasn't the man he had always presented to Old Kane, that he had taken the stance of a bully to cover his shortcomings.

It was easy to be a "big man" with his little sister or Chastity Giberson, and the Woosley twins treated him like a king. But in dealing with Cappy, his bravado turned to mush. All he had to show for his life was an old car and a broken-down house. What son could be proud of such a father? Drayton thought. He might as well resign himself to going back to prison, where his greatest challenge would be to make it through the night without becoming some burly thug's lady.

TWENTY-NINE

E nergized by the prospect of the trial, Sheriff Ridenour made a sudden recovery, thus allowing Royal
Whiteside to return to his beloved woods. "No use putting
it off," the sheriff said, as he hurried forward with plans.
"It costs the county to keep a prisoner setting in jail. The
sooner this trial is over, the sooner the state can start feeding and housing Drayton Hunt." No one enjoyed the excitement of a trial more than Sheriff Amos Ridenour.

On November 29, the courtroom was full, as it had
been the previous time Drayton R. Hunt was on trial.
Cappy found a seat in the front row and prepared to take
notes. This would be the final installment for Joe Bray and
his *Post-Dispatch* readers. Each submission, sometimes as
short as a single line, was written in the style of a Saturday
matinee serial, building suspense with every carefully chosen word, and the serial would end when the accused was
found guilty or innocent.

*While Harda Prill sits at home recovering from her attack, the
trial of Drayton R. Hunt, the accused assailant, moves forward*

256

toward its predictable or surprising conclusion. Which will it be? Will Hunt testify in his own behalf? Will Harda testify? We'll know the answers tomorrow. Cap Giberson, reporter.

The six men chosen for the jury filed in. To a man, they believed this trial was "much cry and little wool," a fact the jury foreman would be quick to point out during deliberation. Females were always crying "rape," and men, guilty or innocent, were made to pay.

When Drayton Hunt was ushered into the packed courtroom, a murmur went through the crowd. He appeared to be an old man—his face drawn, his eyes dull, his beard untrimmed though he had only been in jail a week.

In Drayton Hunt's first trial, he had laughed throughout the ridiculous testimonies of the witnesses, amused at the irony of his situation, but this time he wasn't laughing. Old Judge Jurnikan had been lenient, sentencing him to only three years because the evidence against him was circumstantial, but Drayton knew he wouldn't be so fortunate with Judge Jones on the bench. Known for his harsh sentences, this judge would see that Drayton served every day of the maximum sentence. Drayton recalled a solemn Jesus, His picture hanging on Chaplain Davenport's wall. Another man resigned to his fate.

Judge Jones pounded his gavel for quiet. "Let's get started with the prosecution's opening remarks."

Benjamin Hawk, a soft-spoken, white-haired man who looked like someone's grandpa, spoke eloquently on the likelihood that Drayton R. Hunt had committed the unspeakable assault on the helpless little girl. "Even though there's no tangible evidence," he said, "you gentlemen of the jury should act on your instincts, your gut feelings. Consider the past history of the accused, and go from there. Make no mistake about it, Drayton Hunt is guilty of this crime." He smiled and sat down.

Patrick Michael, a young man who had never defended anyone before, sat nervously shuffling through his notes, recognizing that a real trial barely resembled the mock trials in law school. Summoning his composure, he stood and faced the jury. In spite of his jitters, he spoke with authority.

"Unless it's proven otherwise, Drayton R. Hunt is an innocent man. Every bit of evidence has to be considered before he can be found guilty. Unfortunately, in this case there isn't any hard evidence that you can pick up and examine, or hold under a microscope. Instead, you will be dealing with rumors and innuendoes and half-truths and out-and-out lies. While it's true my client has served time, past offenses cannot be considered during this trial. As far as you, the jury, are concerned, Drayton Hunt has a clean slate. The defense will prove that he's innocent of the assault on Harda Prill, and that he's a victim of false accusations." He sat down at the table next to Drayton.

"Call your first witness," Judge Jones said to the prosecutor.

"I call Shug Combrink," the prosecutor said.

The bailiff administered the oath. "State your name and occupation."

Shug sat up straight in the witness chair, feeling like a man of importance. "Shug Combrink, janitor at the Old Kane grade school."

"On the evening of November 5, please describe what you found. Take your time and make sure you don't leave out any important details."

"Well, sir, I had just finished cleaning the kindergarten room and I stepped outside the door to empty a dustpan when I seen something laying under the swing set. I figured some kid had left his jacket there, they're forever leaving something behind, so I went to pick it up. And then I seen it was Harda Prill."

"Then what did you do?"

"First off, I pulled her skirt down—she was naked underneath—and then I went and called Ed and Hannah Prill, her folks."

"Did you see anything suspicious at the scene of the assault?"

"Nothing out of the ordinary."

"Does the defense have any questions of this witness?" Judge Jones said.

"Yes." Patrick Michael stood and faced Shug. "Mr. Combrink, when you saw Harda Prill lying beneath the swing set, what was your first thought?"

"I figured she had been hit over the head and raped."

"And why did you think she'd been raped?"

"She was laying there half naked, what else was I to think?"

"I have no more questions."

As the trial moved forward, Cappy realized how easily any man could be charged and convicted with only circumstantial evidence, or in this case no evidence at all. If Reverend Marcus Smith was right about Drayton's being a changed man, this would be the second time he was tried, convicted, and sentenced for something he hadn't done.

"Call your next witness," Judge Jones said.

"The prosecution calls Dr. Ed Johnson."

"Thank you for taking time away from all those sick folks, Dr. Johnson." Prosecutor Hawk had a perpetual smile on his face.

"Just doing my duty," the elderly doctor said. He considered testifying at this trial a waste of his valuable time.

"Let's go back to the morning Harda Prill was found. When she was brought into the hospital, what were your initial findings?"

"She was a thirteen-year-old unconscious female with no visible signs of trauma, except a small contusion to her head."

"And what was your diagnosis?"

"As I just said, contusion to the head, which accounted for her being unconscious, and rape."

"What treatment did you advise?"

"That she should remain in the hospital for observation. Of course, I fully expected her to regain consciousness in a couple of hours, not remain in a coma for thirteen days."

Judge Jones said, "Does the defense want to question this witness?"

"Yes, I have a question. Doctor, what did you base your diagnosis on?"

"Observation and examination, son," he said. "I don't know of any other way since the medical board took away my crystal ball."

Everyone laughed. "Order!" said the judge, pounding his gavel. "I won't tolerate a sideshow!"

"And what did the girl's parents say when they brought her to the hospital?" Patrick Michael said.

"The mother did most of the talking, and she was near hysterics. She said, 'My daughter's been raped! What if she's conceived!' over and over. And Mr. Prill mentioned the name of Drayton Hunt as a suspect."

The next witness was Chig Mundy.

"Mr. Mundy, tell us what you observed in your cafe the afternoon of November 4."

"There was a lot going on, there always is that time of day."

"Which was what time?"

"Near to four o'clock."

"Go on."

"Harda Prill come bouncing in like she owned the place and sat on a stool. She ordered an ice-cream cone, chocolate I think, and she sat there licking it."

"Who was sitting next to her?"

"Some high school kid on one side, Drayton Hunt on the other."

"Do you recall anything special?"

"Only that Hunt couldn't keep his eyes off her, and he was in a jolly mood, laughing and going on."

"When you heard about the assault on Harda Prill, what was the first thing that came to mind?"

"That Drayton Hunt done it, no question. He had that look in his eye—"

"The prosecution rests," Benjamin Hawk said.

"Proceed with your defense," Judge Jones said to Patrick Michael.

"I call as my first witness Reverend Marcus Smith. Please state your name and occupation for the records."

"The Reverend Marcus Smith, pastor of the Old Kane Baptist Church."

"What is your relationship to the defendant, Drayton Hunt?"

"We became acquainted when he came to me asking for help with the Bible."

"So you would describe your relationship to be teacher and pupil?"

"At first, but now we're friends." Marcus smiled at Drayton.

"Since you first met Drayton Hunt, would you say he's changed?"

"Oh, my, yes. He's determined to become an evangelist, and is an astute student of the Scriptures. He believes his own past sins make him able to relate to the ordinary sinner. He knows firsthand how difficult it is to maintain a spiritual countenance. And Mr. Hunt has a gift for speaking in the pulpit."

"Reverend Smith, could Drayton Hunt have raped Harda Prill?"

"Absolutely not. I'd stake my career on it."

"Any more defense witnesses?" the judge said.

"Yes," Patrick Michael said. "I call Drayton R. Hunt to the stand."

A murmur went through the room as Drayton slowly made his way to the front of the room. He slouched in the witness chair.

"State your name and occupation."

"Drayton R. Hunt, recently let go from my job at the undertaking parlor."

"Why were you let go?" the defense attorney asked.

"Bert said people had stopped dying since I came to work for him."

There were a few laughs among the audience.

"Mr. Hunt, are you *acquainted* with Harda Prill?"

"I wouldn't exactly say I'm acquainted with her," Drayton said, "but the day before she was hurt she sat next to me at Mundy's Cafe. We exchanged a few words."

"What did you think of her?" Patrick Michael said.

"Objection!" said Benjamin Hawk. "Harda Prill's not on trial here!"

"I want to establish her demeanor that day."

"I'll allow the question," the judge said.

"I thought she was a pretty little thing," Drayton said, "and bold for her age. That's about all I thought. I had other things on my mind."

"Your witness," Judge Jones said to the prosecutor.

"Mr. Hunt, where were you the evening Harda Prill was raped?" Benjamin Hawk said.

"I was . . . with a friend."

"And will that friend substantiate your whereabouts?"

"Maybe, but I won't say my friend's name."

Benjamin Hawk walked toward Drayton Hunt and leaned forward, nearly in his face. "Mr. Hunt, it's a well-known fact that you have a liking for very young girls, thirteen-year-old girls, in fact—"

"Objection!" Patrick Michael was on his feet. "What's in the defendant's past isn't relevant!"

"You're right," the judge said, "but let's hear the answer anyway."

"I don't deny my reputation, but I was a young buck in those days, not the forty-seven-year-old man I am now. As God is my witness, I never hurt Harda Prill."

"Mr. Hunt, you can't use God as a witness," Judge Jones said. "Anyone else, Mr. Michael?"

"I'd like to call Harda Prill."

"She isn't in the courthouse, and as I told you before, because of the delicacy of the crime it would not be proper for her to sit in the witness chair and be stared at. Now, if there are no more witnesses—"

"Defense has one more witness, your honor," Patrick Michael said. "I'd like to call June Plummer to the stand."

Drayton's heart sank. By providing his alibi, she was ruining her own reputation.

As June made her way to the witness chair, whispers went through the crowd. She was wearing her waitress uniform, planning to return to Mundy's Cafe when she finished testifying. She crossed her legs, waiting nervously for the first question. She glanced at Drayton and smiled.

"Miss Plummer," Patrick Michael began, "tell us in your own words what you did the evening of November 5."

"After work I went home to get ready for a date."

"Who was the date with?"

"Drayton Hunt."

"And where did you and Mr. Hunt go on your date?"

"We had planned to go to the movie in Alton but ended up eating supper at my place. And . . . talking."

"How long did Mr. Hunt stay?"

June hesitated. "He spent the night. He left after breakfast."

The men in the audience chuckled, the women raised their eyebrows.

"I have no more questions," the defense attorney said.

"Your turn, Mr. Hawk," Judge Jones said.

"Now, then, Miss Plummer, you say the defendant spent the night with you. Are you and Mr. Hunt engaged to be married?"

"No."

"How long have the two of you been going together?"

"This was our first date."

"So you're saying you allowed a man you barely knew to spend the night with you?"

She paused. "Yes."

"How do we know you aren't making up a story to save your newest boyfriend?"

"Because I don't lie," June said emphatically.

"Miss Plummer, we know you're a *floozie,* so perhaps you're also a *liar.*" He emphasized the judgmental words.

"I object!" Patrick Michael said, jumping to his feet. "Miss Plummer has sworn to tell the truth and—"

"Disregard the last question."

"Then get on with your summations, gentlemen," the judge said impatiently, "and make them concise."

In a dramatic voice, as if he were a stage actor, Prosecutor Hawk reiterated to the jury members how they should keep the defendant's past in mind when making their decision, and to view Miss June Plummer's testimony with extreme skepticism.

In his defense summation, Patrick Michael pointed out that Drayton Hunt was now a religious man, incapable of harming Harda Prill, and according to June Plummer's testimony, he was with her at the time the rape occurred.

Drayton was deeply moved by June's willingness to substantiate his alibi, knowing she had risked her future in Old Kane. No one had ever made such a sacrifice for him.

During the testimonies and summations, the six men who composed the jury had heard only what they wanted to hear. The entire town wanted Drayton Hunt to be guilty, and the jury complied.

Found guilty on the first vote, Drayton was sentenced by the judge to ten years, more than the usual sentence for rape. "When you get out, Drayton R. Hunt," Judge Jones said in a self-righteous voice, "you'll be too old to hurt little girls."

Hell, I'm too old now, Drayton thought, recalling his embarrassing failure in June Plummer's bed.

THIRTY

Cappy gathered up his notes and left the courtroom, angered at what had passed for a fair trial. He honestly didn't know if Drayton was guilty, but something had to be done or no one would be safe from this kind of shoddy treatment in the courts. But there was something more. No matter how much Cappy wanted to deny it, he was Drayton Hunt's son. Without his realizing it, Cappy's feelings had begun to change that day in the attic when he read Drayton's letters from prison.

That night after supper, Cappy was still pondering what he could do. The fire in the kitchen woodstove had died down to a few glowing embers. Worthy opened the door and added several small pieces of sassafras. The fire took off, the wood popping and crackling. The three Giberson men sat quietly for a few minutes, each with his own thoughts. The evening was too cold to sit outside.

"That trial was a damned circus," Worthy said, "and Judge Jones was the head clown. There'd ought to be somebody higher up who can make sure a judge stays in line. Yesterday in the courtroom I kept thinking that could just as well of been me up there facing bogus charges."

"He wouldn't have gotten away with that farce in a big city court," Cappy said.

"And that jury was deaf to Drayton's alibi," Worthy said. "Something tells me that little waitress was saying the truth."

"Maybe God's got a reason for him going to prison that we don't know about," Tick said. Neither Cappy nor Worthy responded. They knew they couldn't persuade Tick to change his belief, any more than they could change their own nonbelief.

Finally Worthy said, "Cap, you'd better go see Hunt and get this damned thing between you two settled once and for all."

"You don't know what you're asking," Cappy said.

"Like hell, I don't. This grudge has been gnawing at me since you was born and your mama died. I've spent twenty-three years full of hatred for Drayton Hunt. It's hurt me more than him."

"That's just what Reverend Art always said," Tick said.

"Jesus, Tick, can't you get through a day without bringing up that man's name?"

"So you're asking me to forgive all the hurt he caused?" Cappy said.

"At least put it on the back burner and give the fire a chance to go out," Worthy said. "Drayton and Chastity gave in to their natural urges that morning in the haymow, and you're the outcome. Maybe it's time we looked at Drayton Hunt in that light."

Tick didn't mention that earlier that afternoon, he had taken the two o'clock passenger train to Carrollton to see Drayton Hunt. Sheriff Ridenour, enjoying a fairly good day, was at his desk when Tick walked in. Someone was required to be on duty at all times in case of a fire, and to make sure the prisoners had three meals a day.

"I come to see Drayton Hunt," Tick said.

"You're Worthy's boy, ain't you, the one who speaks in tongues? It beats me why Drayton Hunt's so damned popular. First that Baptist preacher was here and now you. Next the governor will be showing up. What's your business with Hunt?"

"It's between me and him."

"To each his own."

Tick followed the sheriff into the back of the jail where the cells were located. The only light came from a small barred window near the ceiling. Drayton was in the first cell, and another prisoner was in the adjoining cell sleeping off too much Ripple—the cheapest wine Oettle's Tavern sold.

"Hunt! You've got more company," the sheriff said. He unlocked the door and Tick stepped into the small cage-like room. It was the first time he had been inside a jail cell. It reminded him of the roadside cabins he had shared with Reverend Art Gimmy. Drayton was stretched out on the narrow cot. He was wearing the clothes he had on at the trial, now wrinkled and smelling of sweat.

"Yell out when you're done," Sheriff Ridenour said as he left the two men alone.

Before Drayton could ask, Tick launched into his reason for being there. "Me and Pa and Cappy was at your trial yesterday," Tick began.

"Is that why you're here? To talk about how I was hung out to dry?"

"No, that ain't why. As near as I can figure, God wants me to help fix what's bad between you and Cappy. There's things I'd a whole lot rather do, but knowing God, He won't let me alone till you and Cappy stop hating each other."

"You're talking to the wrong man. Cappy's the one holding out. I've tried for the past twenty-three years to settle what's between us."

Tick sighed. "I guess it's up to me, then. God's got a bad habit of telling a person to do something and then not telling how to do it. I'll try talking to Cappy again."

"Much obliged for coming by," Drayton said. "It looks like my preaching days are over before they got started."

"There's plenty of sinners in jail you can preach to," Tick said, in an effort to comfort him. "Maybe that's why God made you lose the trial. God's a great one for playing tricks on people."

When he'd visited earlier in the day, Reverend Marcus Smith had said much the same as Tick, but in a more articulate way. "If you expect God to smile on your work, you've got to reconcile with your son. Do you pray about it?"

"I can't get the hang of praying," Drayton said. "There's something about it that doesn't sit well. Like leftover turkey."

"You're going at it in the wrong way," Marcus said. "Instead of praying for yourself, focus on Cappy. Pray that he'll accept you as his father, and leave yourself out of the prayer."

"If I was going to pray, I'd start by asking God to get me out of this goddamned jail."

The evening before Drayton was to be transported to the state penitentiary, Cappy asked Sheriff Ridenour if he could speak to the prisoner.

"I don't know why you'd want to," the sheriff said. "Unless you're planning to write something for the newspaper?"

"Yes, that's the reason," Cappy lied. He followed Sheriff Ridenour to Drayton's cell.

"You've got more company, Hunt." The sheriff unlocked the door and handed Cappy the key. "Lock up when you're done."

Drayton was lying on the cot. When he saw Cappy, he stood up and faced his son. "What's this about?" he said, his voice tired. "Have you come to gloat over your old man?"

Cappy stood awkwardly in the middle of the tiny cell. "I've come for that talk."

Drayton laughed. "Don't you think it's a little late for that?"

"Worthy says it's time to settle what's between us."

"Worthy Giberson said that? Now I know I'm dreaming!"

"I don't know where to start but—"

"That ain't so hard. What's between you and me started with your mama. As I recall, this very cell is where I told you about her and me, back before I went to jail the first time."

Cappy would never forget that revelation, and how he had asked Worthy whether Drayton Hunt was telling the truth.

Worthy had said, "I'll be real honest with you, Cap, I don't know. In spite of Hunt's claim, I figure your real daddy was a stranger passing through the countryside and just let it go at that. Some would say me and Willa stuck our heads in the sand. Then when you was born and your real ma passed, taking the secret with her, there didn't seem to be no use in worrying the issue."

Drayton's voice jarred Cappy back to the present.

". . . a pretty little thing, long gold hair the color of yours, and hard to turn away from. When I come across her in the barn that morning, she was ripe as a summer peach and ready to know a man—"

"You're talking about my *mother*," Cappy interrupted, "not a common street girl." Although he had never known Chastity Giberson, Cappy was repulsed to hear her described in this intimate way.

Drayton, looking defeated, sat down on the cot. Cappy remained standing. Drayton went on: "My regret is that I didn't marry your mama, but at twenty-three I was full of myself and not ready to settle down with a wife and squalling baby. After she died, I done my best to persuade Worthy that you was mine to raise, but he wouldn't hold still for it. Every year on your birthday I went to his house to claim you, but Worthy wouldn't budge. I got tired of butting my head against a stone wall, so I finally give up getting you. But I never give up wanting you."

Worthy had not told him about the birthday visits. "Go on," Cappy said.

"About Beany Ozbun—I was fearful he was leading you down that queer road he was on. That night when I seen you and him setting in the car outside the schoolhouse after the March of Dimes dance, I went off like a sky rocket. I waited till you drove away and then I called him to account. We got into a little tussle, and he ended up in a snow pile, out cold. Me and the Woosley idiots drove him out to Chief's Gulley, and I made the mistake of leaving him there. I thought he was only knocked out and would wake up with a sore head and have a cold walk home. I never meant for him to die. Now you know the whole story."

"Beany wasn't a queer," Cappy said, reliving the pain of that night. "His mother kept him practicing the piano so much he didn't have time for girls, that's all."

"It don't matter now," Drayton said. "There's one more thing. Willa Giberson. I sure as hell never smothered her, and I've got a strong hunch you already know that. I suspect Worthy done the deed to put her out of her misery. He always was soft. But here's the puzzle. I know why Worthy hated my guts, but I never could figure out why you had it in for me."

"You were a bootlegger and thief, an embarrassment when I was growing up," Cappy said. "And now, I can't forget what happened to my real mother and Beany."

"Like I said, I never meant for them things to turn out so bad. As for Harda Prill, I wasn't even close to that little tart except once in Mundy's Cafe."

Cappy was quiet as he considered Drayton's words. He believed Drayton's accounts of what happened with Chastity and Beany, and he knew he was telling the truth about Willa. And though he couldn't prove it, he believed Drayton was not guilty of raping Harda Prill.

"I'm glad you come by, this being our last chance to talk," Drayton said, standing up again. "This time when I get out of the big jail, I sure as hell won't be coming back to Old Kane to stay. But there's one more thing, a favor."

Cappy's body tensed, afraid to hear what Drayton wanted.

"Would you look after my dog while I'm gone?" Drayton said. "Royal Whiteside's been stopping by to feed her every day, but I'll feel better if she's with family. She'll be lonesome with me gone. A dog needs more than food."

"A dog?" Cappy knew how Worthy felt about dogs.

"She's a stray I took in, a good dog, won't jump up on you. Will you keep her? It would mean something to me."

"Worthy hates dogs," Cappy said. "You sure Royal can't do it?"

"Royal isn't who I want keeping her."

"I'll have to see what Pa says."

"Hell, he won't help me out."

"Have you forgotten he's the one who told me to come here and talk to you?"

"So will you keep my dog?" Drayton said.

"I'll work it out."

"Much obliged." Drayton looked down at the floor and then looked at Cappy expectantly. "Is it time we shook hands and call what went on between us settled?"

Cappy hesitated, then gave his hand to the man he had spent a lifetime despising. As they shook, Cappy felt he had been released from his own prison.

Cappy couldn't allow Drayton to go to the penitentiary again. If he had to, he would invent a story to clear the man, with no qualms. On his way out, Cappy knocked on Sheriff Ridenour's office door to return the key. The sheriff was playing Solitaire, the cards spread out across his cluttered desk. He was losing.

"Sheriff, I want you to hold off taking Drayton Hunt to the big jail."

"Now why in Christ's name would I do that?" He rubbed his aching muscles, sensing his lumbago was about to flare up.

"I've got new evidence that says he's not guilty."

"What kind of new evidence?" He concentrated on his cards, looking for a place to put the jack of diamonds.

"I'd rather not say yet, but give me a couple of days."

"I'm curious, why would you want to help a man like Hunt?" Sheriff Ridenour said, finally looking up from the cards.

"Because I think it's wrong for an innocent man to go to prison, that's all," Cappy said.

"I think there's more to it than you're letting on, but I'll give you two days and then he's out of here." The ailing sheriff didn't feel up to the long train trip anyway. Maybe he would feel better in a couple of days.

"Thanks, Sheriff," Cappy said.

"Shut the door on your way out," the sheriff said, as he peeked to see which card was under the king of hearts.

"You done what?" Worthy said to Cappy. Surely he heard wrong.

"I promised Drayton I'd look after his dog while he's in prison."

"Just where is this dog going to be while you're looking after it?"

"She'll have to be here." Cappy had known this wouldn't be easy.

"Jesus, you know how I feel about dogs. I've never owned one and I don't want one here on a visit. They're noisy and cost a fortune to feed. What was you thinking?"

"Maybe it's a way of easing my conscience," Cappy said, "but whatever the reason, the dog is moving in. In fact, she's sitting in the car right now."

"I won't have one of them little yipping dogs underfoot," he protested. "What kind of dog are we talking about?"

"She's a shepherd mix, a medium-size dog, mostly brown."

"But what about a doghouse? I guess I could build one if—"

"Drayton said she's a house dog."

"Jesus Christ. Not only will I have Drayton Hunt's dog on my property, she'll be living inside my house!"

"Can she sleep in my room?" Tick said, excited as a child.

Worthy thought about it, mumbling to himself. "Hell, you might as well go bring her in," he said finally. "She might be getting cold."

When Cappy brought the dog in the house, she jumped on Worthy and licked his face, her tail wagging furiously. "What's her damned name?" Worthy said, wiping his face with his sleeve.

"Drayton didn't give her one," Cappy said.

"That don't surprise me. Well, she's as big as two dogs, so how about 'Dog Dog'?" When Worthy woke up the next morning, Dog Dog was sound asleep next to him, with her head on Willa's pillow.

THIRTY-ONE

The morning after his visit with Drayton, Cappy stopped at Mundy's Cafe for coffee and a glazed doughnut. He found a quiet booth and spread his notes from the trial across the table. He had only two days to present his "evidence" of Drayton's innocence. This wasn't the first time Cappy's exaggeration had put him in a bind.

Carefully he went over the notes. He thought a higher court should review the trial, but he knew that wouldn't happen without strong new evidence or documented irregularities in the trial itself.

"More coffee?" June asked Cappy. She was wearing a short pink uniform. The top two buttons were undone, showing a fair amount of cleavage (good for extra tips). When she was sixteen, wearing a secondhand blue taffeta formal, her black hair in an upsweep, she had been voted queen of the St. Clair County Fair. Although still pretty at age forty, her hard life showed on her face.

"Sure, I'll have coffee, and another doughnut," Cappy said.

June filled his cup and brought him a fresh doughnut on a napkin. "I wish I could've helped Drayton more," she said. "He's not the bad person most people think he is. I was surprised at how the trial turned out."

"But my question is, Why didn't you tell the sheriff before the trial?" Cappy asked.

"I did. I called him right off, but he said he had all the alibis and evidence he could use."

"That moron! But why didn't Drayton speak up as soon as he was arrested?"

"He didn't want my name sullied because of him being in my bed. It's not like we're married, you know." June blushed. "Drayton said I'd be ruined forever if that juicy tidbit got around town. I wanted to tell you about it. With you being a reporter I thought you'd know who to talk to, but Drayton said to leave you alone."

"But couldn't you have—" Cappy started.

"Then I went to see Drayton's lawyer, but Drayton made him promise only to call me to the witness stand as a last resort."

"June! You've got other customers!" Chig called.

"Sorry, Cappy, I have to get busy," she said.

Cappy sipped his coffee, watching June at work clearing away dishes and picking up the nickel and dime tips. She had a fairly dark complexion, looking like she had a suntan, which was strange at this time of year. All at once it came to him. "June, we don't know each other very well, but can I ask you a personal question?" He would have to choose his words carefully.

"Depends on how personal it is." She stopped wiping the counter.

"You don't have to answer, but if you do, it will be between only the two of us." Cappy leaned over the counter so he could keep his voice down.

"Now you're scaring me," she said, an apprehensive look on her face.

"A few weeks ago a man passing through town stopped at Darr's Garage inquiring about a relative who supposedly lives here. As he was leaving, he suggested that his relative might be 'passing.' Does that mean anything to you?"

"Why should it?" But the look on her face answered Cappy's question. "I guess this scoop will end up in the *Post-Dispatch*," she said bitterly.

"Joe Bray at the *Post* would publish your story in a minute. But I respect your privacy."

"I heard what was going around town, men making bets on who the mystery woman could be. When Drayton came to my place I told him the truth about myself," June said. "It's what I always do on a first date, and usually there's no second. But Drayton laughed and said that none of us are what we seem on the outside. He was real classy about it."

"I won't give you away," Cappy said, "but I think Old Kane would welcome you and your secret."

She laughed. "I've thought that before in other towns, but if my identity came out Chig would find a reason to let me go, and no one else in town would be needing help."

"For God's sake, June, them hamburgers is burnt to a crisp!" Chig shouted.

"Give my best to Drayton when you see him," she said.

If it wasn't Drayton, who was it? Cappy began reading through the trial notes again. One major flaw in the trial was Judge Jones's refusal to allow Harda Prill to take the stand. Cappy didn't believe her version of what had happened, that she had fallen off the swing set and bumped her head on a rock. He was convinced she knew who her attacker was but wanted to enjoy the celebrity as long as possible.

As a last resort, Cappy called on Judge Jones. "This better not be about the Harda Prill trial. I'm on my way out the door," the judge said. He had spent a long week in court and wanted only to put his feet up and have a highball.

"I respectfully want to protest what happened," Cappy said, "more specifically what *didn't* happen. Harda should have been put on the witness stand and made to tell who assaulted her. In fact, the whole case could have been settled out of court, right here in your chambers, Judge."

"As for my not allowing Harda to testify, I was under pressure from Ed and Hannah Prill," Judge Jones said. "They said they'd rather the guilty man went free than to further expose their daughter to gossip."

"But I thought they wanted the attacker to pay for what he did."

"After giving it more thought, they decided it would be better for Harda if the affair could be forgotten as soon as possible."

"What about Drayton Hunt's alibi for the evening of the assault?"

"That waitress should have come forward before the trial. It looks fishy that she just popped up in the courtroom."

"But she told Sheriff Ridenour and he ignored the alibi."

"Well, there you have it," Judge Jones said. "The court system is only as good as its lowest denominator. Sheriff

Ridenour was a good sheriff in his day, but with that lumbago he's no longer up to the job. We're finished here, Cappy. You're beating a dead horse."

The next morning, Cappy was on his second cup of coffee at Mundy's Cafe, his papers stacked in a neat pile. No need to look at them again—he knew them by heart. This was the day he had promised to present new evidence of Drayton's innocence.

All at once loud laughter erupted from a booth near the front door. Benny Mourning and Jimmy Day were playing keep-away with a group of other teenage boys. One of the boys grabbed the sought-after article from Benny and tossed it high in the air. Another boy caught it and started to run out the door, but he was no match for Benny, six feet tall, already shaving once a week. He caught the smaller boy by the collar and dragged him back to the booth.

Cappy walked closer to see what the fracas was about. And then he saw the object of the game—a girl's white underpants looking the worse for wear. For three weeks, Benny and Jimmy had been taking turns carrying the garment in their pockets, occasionally sniffing the crotch to catch the girl's tantalizing scent.

Cappy phoned Sheriff Ridenour. "Looks like them boys was having a little harmless sport!" the sheriff said, laughing as if it had all been a joke. "I'll send Royal over. I've had another damned setback with my lumbago. Doctors these days don't know shit from Shinola."

Cappy rode with Royal to the Mourning home on Railroad Street. Lonnie Mourning, Benny's father, was raking the last of the fall leaves into a large pile for a Saturday night bonfire and wiener roast. "What can I do for you gents?" Lonnie asked. He took a bandanna from his pocket and wiped his red face and neck.

"I suppose you heard about what happened to Harda Prill?" Royal said.

Lonnie gave a mirthless laugh. "I heard, but I wasn't surprised. Some lucky stiff got what she was advertising!"

"Maybe you won't think it's so funny when you find out your boy is carrying her underpants in his pocket," Royal said.

Lonnie wiped his face again. "If what you say is so, he'll wish to hell it wasn't. He knows better than to steal. Follow me around back of the house, and we'll see what he's got to say for himself."

Benny, who had hurried home from Mundy's Cafe, was splitting and stacking wood for winter, a chore he had been putting off.

"Benny, the game warden here's got some questions for you," Lonnie said, "and if you don't tell the truth you'll spend the next month inside your room counting fly specks on the ceiling. Go ahead, Royal, and ask your damned questions. I've got work to do."

"What do you know about the night Harda Prill was attacked?" Royal said to Benny.

Benny glanced at his father.

"Answer the man, goddammit!" Lonnie said. He clenched his fist, a gesture his son was well acquainted with.

Benny stuffed his hands in his pockets and stared at his sneakers. "I reckon I know something about it."

"Then spit it out!" Lonnie said.

"Me and Jimmy Day got tired of her all the time getting us worked up and then running off," Benny said. "We tried being nice to her, even showed her our eight-pager, and then she threw it in the ditch. We know how she goes to the schoolyard at night to hang around, so me and Jimmy decided to show her what for."

"What happened when you got there?" Royal said.

"It was starting to get dark, and she was setting on top the swing set, showing herself, and we told her to come on down, that we had something nice for her."

"Then what?" Royal said.

"Well, she climbs down off the swing set, and the next thing we know she starts hitting me and Jimmy with her fists. So we're wrestling around on the ground and she grabs hold of my wienie and squeezes hard, and that's when me and Jimmy pulls off her underpants. She must of hit her head on a rock or something. She was just laying there on the ground, not moving, so me and Jimmy, we took off running. We was afraid we'd get the blame if she was dead or something."

"You're saying you didn't rape her? Neither one of you boys?" Royal said.

"No, sir, we didn't," Benny said. "We just wanted to get out of there fast."

"That's about what I expected to hear," Lonnie said, slapping his son's back. "Hell, they was just having a little sport. Now if you gents will excuse me, I've got leaves to rake." He turned and walked away.

Royal grabbed Benny's shoulders and shook him until his cap flew off. "You and Jimmy Day caused a lot of trouble for a lot of folks by not coming forward. There's a man setting in jail right now because of you two. I'm on my way now to let him out. Have your daddy take you to the sheriff's office first thing tomorrow, and make sure Jimmy Day comes with you. We'll try to straighten out this mess. And hand over them unmentionables!"

Dr. Johnson, who had examined Harda initially, was not happy to see Cappy and Royal. "I have an emergency room full of patients waiting to be seen, so make this quick," he said, looking at his watch.

"We're here to ask about Harda Prill. A while back she was brought to the hospital unconscious. Do you remember her?" Royal said.

"Of course," the old doctor said. "I may be getting on in years, but my memory is flawless. She was partially undressed and had been raped."

"And you looked at her privates to make sure?" Royal said.

"Well now, Deputy, I couldn't do that. She was a young girl and I didn't want to embarrass her."

"But she was in a coma," Royal said. "She wouldn't have knowed what you was doing."

"Maybe not," Dr. Johnson said, "but when it comes to young women, I have my own ethics. It was clear to me, without invading her ah—privacy, that she had been the victim of rape. In my forty years as a physician, I've seen many such cases. This was a textbook example. The girl's dress was dirty and grass stained from struggling against her assailant, her hair had leaves in it, and her underpants were off. I could see no reason for an invasive examination. Now, I need to get to my patients." He walked away.

"Jesus Christ," Royal said to Cappy. "All this hoopla over a bump on the head."

THIRTY-TWO

B ecause of Drayton Hunt's trial and the days preceding it, Cappy had neglected his writing. His self-imposed deadline to complete one story for his book had come and gone. If he intended to put together a collection of Old Kane stories, he needed to write every day as if it were a full-time job with a paycheck on Friday.

With the Harda Prill mystery solved, Cappy was eager to get back to his typewriter. He walked into the house and found Worthy sitting alone in the dark kitchen, a cup of untasted coffee in front of him. The fire had gone out and the room was cold. "What's wrong? Are you sick?" Cappy pulled a light string.

"I ain't sick."

"Then what's wrong?"

"Bum's no longer amongst us." There was a desolation in his voice that Cappy hadn't heard since Willa's stroke.

"What are you saying?"

"Goddammit, what do you think I'm saying! Me and Bum was having our Saturday game of horseshoes this morning back of Mundy's, joking and laughing like we've did for seventy-odd years. Bum lets go with his first shoe and falls to the ground, the life gone out of him like a flat tire." Worthy wiped his eyes. "Just last night we was setting here watching Gorgeous George. Bum was eating cupcakes and drinking apple cider like nothing bad was about to happen. Christ, we never know when the reaper's coming with that goddamned sickle!"

Worthy could express his grief only through anger, as if Bum had died just to aggravate him.

"I'm sorry, Pa. I know about losing a best friend."

"You don't know a damned thing! Me and Bum was like brothers for seventy years."

Cappy wasn't offended by the harsh words. He reached over and patted Worthy's sagging shoulder.

"I set with Bum when his Imadean passed," Worthy said, "and he never left my side when Willa got sick. We never missed a Friday night together since Willa passed—let's see, that's fifty-two Friday nights times three years—that's more than 156 Friday nights of rummy, or television watching lately. On Willa's last night, Bum kept me from blurting out the truth of her passing. Sheriff Perdun would of took me straight to jail and I'd be setting there yet, molding like a brick of longhorn cheese." Worthy dipped water from the bucket and drank it in one gulp. He wiped his mouth on his sleeve. "Bum was the best pal a man could have. Jesus, what will I do come Friday nights?"

"I'm pretty good at rummy," Cappy said.

"You mean well, Cap, but you setting across the table wouldn't be the same as poor old Bum setting there."

"When's the funeral?"

"If Bum gets his way, there won't be one. But them girls of his will do their best to have it their way. I hate the thought of Bert Linder getting his slimy hands on poor old Bum."

"I'll talk to Oleeta," Cappy said. If she'll let me inside the house, he thought.

"Them poor little bluegills will wonder what's wrong, not being pulled out of the creek and throwed back every day. I'll have to put a line in now and then to keep 'em on their toes." Worthy blew his nose loudly and stuffed the wet handkerchief back in his pocket.

"Will you be okay while I drive over to Oleeta's?"

"Why the hell wouldn't I be? I don't need any help grieving, I've had practice enough. You go console little Oleeta. Besides, Tick will be coming in from the barn any minute now."

"I'll be back shortly." Cappy started toward the door but Worthy was still talking.

"You know, Bum had a dread of going the way his cousin Broom Hetzel done, in the flash of an eye, with no time to get ready for it and enjoy that final breath. And now it's come to pass. Bum died not knowing his last throw was a ringer. Son of a bitch!"

As Worthy sat alone in the cold kitchen, memories of good times when he and Bum were growing up rushed back: playing pitch and catch at Green Summit School, long hot summers bucking bales, slipping off to Macoupin Creek to fish or skinny-dip. Even as young boys, they competed to see who could tell the best stories. Occasionally they would get into a scuffle over the perceived theft of a favorite tale, wrestling on the ground until they were out of breath. But they always made up, as best friends do.

When they were seventeen, they had decided it was time to have a social life, which until then had been limited to Fourth of July picnics at Macoupin Creek and Roll Call Sunday at the Baptist Church—forced by their mothers to show up and be counted.

"How about if we was to try a play party?" Worthy said one Saturday afternoon. "There's one tonight at Fred Pope's. Anybody who wants to go is invited."

"I ain't much for playing games," Bum said.

"It ain't exactly 'games,'" Worthy said, "it's dancing, like the Virginia reel."

"Can you dance?" Bum looked skeptically at Worthy.

"No, but how hard can it be? You just hop around to the music and try not to step on some girl's foot."

"Is there refreshments?"

"How the hell would I know? I ain't been before either. Are we going or not?"

"All right, we'll go," Bum said, "but I ain't saying I'll dance."

When the boys arrived at Fred Pope's, the house was filled with laughing young people, and the rugs had been rolled back for dancing games. Music was being provided by the Crawford family—fiddle, banjo, and harmonica. They called themselves "The Crawdads." Fred Pope welcomed Worthy and Bum inside and hung up their coats. The first strenuous reel had just ended, and the dancers were making their way to the refreshment table to sample Mrs. Pope's sour cream cookies and cider punch.

Worthy and Bum joined the group at the table. Feeling like outsiders, the only boys wearing overalls, they were already wishing they hadn't come. They hadn't realized that play parties were dress-up occasions.

The next reel began and the floor quickly filled up, girls on one side, boys on the other. Worthy and Bum stood on the sidelines to watch and determine what the dancing entailed.

All of a sudden, Bum stopped patting his foot to the music, his gaze focused across the room. "I'd sure like to try my luck with that girl," he said. He nodded toward Imadean Perkins, the undertaker's daughter. She was a tall, somber girl with her dark brown hair styled in a severe bun. Her dress was also dark brown, with a high modest neckline. To Bum, she was the most beautiful girl in the room.

"Go on and get your feet wet," Worthy urged. Shyly, Bum walked across the floor, his hands in his pockets.

As Worthy watched the couples, a girl danced by with Junior Bent—a town boy whose father owned a stable of fine horses. The girl's long golden hair hung loose, and she wore a soft blue dress. By the time the reel ended, Worthy had decided she was the girl he wanted. When Junior walked away to get more punch, Worthy approached her.

"My name's Worthy Giberson," he said. At six feet, he towered above her.

She looked up at him and smiled. "I know who you are—I've seen you go by my house lots of times. Once I waved but you didn't wave back. My name's Willa Cope."

"I was wondering if you'll be dancing the next reel."

"I was planning to," she teased.

Worthy's face turned crimson. "I mean, will you dance the next reel with *me?*"

"Mama made me promise I'd only dance with Junior Bent since he brought me, but she won't find out."

A quick waltz began; Worthy and Willa touched hands and danced in among the others. Worthy was surprisingly light on his feet. Willa smiled up at him, wishing she had come to the party with him and glad she'd disregarded her promise to her mother.

Junior Bent, holding two full cups of punch, stood in the corner watching, his face glum.

By the time Worthy's dance with Willa ended, Bum had returned to the refreshment table for more cookies.

"Did you dance?" Worthy said.

"She don't like dancing."

"Then why'd she come?" Worthy said.

"I asked her that, and she said she don't like dancing with somebody short like me. I never thought of myself as short, Worthy. Would you call me short?"

At five feet, Bum *was* short. Worthy would have to choose his words carefully to avoid hurting his friend's feelings.

"First you have to decide what 'short' means," Worthy said. "You're shorter than me, but you're taller than a dog. You're shorter than a six-foot ladder, but you're taller than a footstool."

"But I *am* shorter than Imadean Perkins, and there's the rub."

"Forget about her and let's go. I'm tired of dancing." They got their coats and left, with Worthy still trying to console Bum. "And you're taller than a mailbox—"

"Give it up, Worthy. I'm tired of hearing your tongue wag."

Cappy knocked lightly on Oleeta's door. He was not good in these situations.

"Cappy. Come in," she said. Without thinking, he hugged her and they stayed that way for a few moments before she pulled back. Her eyes were red but she was composed. "Ogreeta and her husband are upstairs going through Pa's closet for burial clothes. He hasn't worn a suit since your ma died. We're keeping everything simple, just a graveside service, but Pa would still say we're making too much fuss. I guess this is one decision he doesn't get to make."

"Pa sent me to make sure you knew Bum's wishes about not wanting a big funeral at the church," Cappy said, "but I can see you have everything under control." He would have expected nothing else of Oleeta.

"Reverend Smith is in charge of the burial service, but we've asked him not to get too religious. He'll say a greeting and read the obituary and then he'll turn it over to Worthy for the eulogy. I know speaking won't be easy for Worthy."

Monday afternoon was cold, and a fall drizzle had begun. A drop of one degree in temperature, and the rain would have been snow. By two o'clock, family and friends were gathered around the grave site at Jalappa Cemetery. The women carried open umbrellas, the men wore caps. Reverend Marcus Smith read the creation story from Genesis, followed by the obituary of Bum's seventy-three-year life. Then he nodded at Worthy and stepped to the back of the group.

Worthy had never given a eulogy, but he would do his best for his old friend. With Bum's daughters and fifty or more friends waiting, Worthy cleared his throat a couple of times and took off his cap. The rain be damned!

"Bum would want everybody here to have a good laugh," Worthy said, trying to compose his voice, which was on the verge of breaking. "And he'd be mad as hell if he heard any sniffling." He blew his nose loudly. "Me and

Bum used to vie for storytelling honors. We've did it since we was boys. But even Bum would have to admit that I'm now the uncontested best storyteller in Greene County. So here goes with one of Bum's favorite stories, one the rascal stole from me."

He cleared his throat again. "It all started one October night when me and Bum was boys planning on hunting weasels to earn money for smoking tobacco. You see, back then weasel hides was in great demand by farmers, the hide being proof the weasels was no longer in need of the farmers' laying hens. And then the most god-awful racket started up . . ."

Cappy went home and began the first story for his book:

Bum Hetzel was no more than five feet tall, but he took advantage of every inch, keeping his back straight and his chin up like a bandmaster. A stranger might easily have mistaken him for a six-footer.

THIRTY-THREE

Drayton Hunt nailed a large sign to a tree in front of his house: FOR SALE. He put away the paint and tools and drove into town to pick up a few supplies for the pantry. If selling the house went well, he should be gone by the first of the year. As he was handing Sorphus his list, Cappy entered the store. There was an awkward silence.

"I hear your house is for sale," Cappy said finally.

"You hear right." The paint on his sign wasn't dry and already the news had reached Old Kane, Drayton thought with amusement.

"You're leaving town?" Cappy said.

"I don't have a choice. Even before the trial, Bert Perkins fired me from my job, such as it was. He claimed I was the cause of his business falling off, like I was keeping people from dying. I'd be a rich man if that was true."

"Where will you go?"

"Somewhere else. Old Kane has dried up. I told Tick he ought to limber up his tongue and come with me, but he's bent on nursing animals so I'll be going it alone. That's all right by me, I've been a loner all my life. It's too late to change."

There was another awkward silence. Cappy picked up a copy of last week's *Patriot*, glanced at the headlines, and put it back on the counter. "I can't call you 'Pa,'" Cappy said.

"Did I ask you to?"

"Worthy's still my father."

"Depends on what you mean by the word. I never even had one daddy, and here you've got two. It don't seem fair somehow." Drayton grinned to show he had put twenty-three years of hard feelings behind him. He paid Sorphus and picked up his groceries. Cappy followed him out and opened the back door of the Moon. Drayton set the groceries on the seat.

"Have you got a job to go to?" Cappy asked.

"I figured I'd try my hand at preaching. I've been going around to tent revivals with Brother Smith seeing how it's done, even gave a couple of testimonials that turned into sermons. There's no better revival draw than a bastard who's turned good, and I sure fit that bill. I'm not saying I'm entirely good, but close enough. Back in the state pen I lied to Chaplain Davenport about hearing the call from God to preach, but after thinking on it these past weeks, maybe I *was* called in a roundabout way. Right now preaching doesn't seem too bad a way to go. Don't worry, I'll be going as far from Old Kane as I can get. Maybe to Kingdom City over in Missouri. It's got a good ring to it for preaching, and nobody there will have heard of Drayton R. Hunt."

"What about your dog?" Cappy said.

"I haven't forgot her. I would've picked her up the day I got out of jail, but I knew she was in good hands, and I needed some time to get things in order at the house. I hope to hell she knows me."

"It hasn't been that long, she'll be all over you. I'm on my way home now if you want to pick her up."

"I have to stop by Mundy's Cafe, and then I'll be right behind you."

The cafe was empty except for June, who was drying cups and returning them to the shelf. She looked up when the front door opened, happy to see Drayton.

"Looks like I beat the crowd," Drayton said, approaching her. He noticed that her pink uniform suited her dark hair and eyes.

"They'll come rushing in before long, hungry as hogs." She dried the last cup and hung the dish towel on a nail.

"You're by your lonesome?" Drayton asked, looking around.

"Chig's on an errand," she said. "Grab a stool and I'll pour you some coffee. It just finished making."

"I could sure use some. And maybe one of those doughnuts."

She handed him a doughnut and filled a cup to the brim with strong, hot coffee. "Don't burn your tongue," she warned.

Drayton took a cautious sip and set the cup down.

"I'm sure grateful for what you did in court," he said.

"I only told the truth," she said simply.

"I guess you know I've put my house up for sale," he said. "As soon as it sells I'll be on my way out of Old Kane for good."

"Where will you go?" June asked, the smile falling from her face.

"Kingdom City, a little burg over in Missouri. Anyhow, I thought I'd drop in and say good-bye. Things will be getting hectic with selling the house and all."

"I'll be sorry to see you go," she said. "I was hoping we could make Friday night chili a regular habit."

Drayton was surprised. "You mean you'd give me another chance?" He was still embarrassed about that disappointing night in her bed.

"Sure I would." She reached across the counter and touched his hand. "We just need a little practice!" She smiled.

Drayton had never seen June look prettier. His next words surprised them both, spoken quickly before he lost his courage.

"Maybe you heard I'm planning to be a Baptist preacher," he said, "the grassroots kind that preaches by the seat of his pants. All I've got to my name is my dog and my Moon motorcar, and whatever cash I get from selling my mama's house." Drayton's palms were sweating. "I've never had a wife, but preachers generally have one. So what would you think of living in Kingdom City? Permanent."

June wanted to say yes to Drayton's unexpected proposal but accepting wasn't that simple. "There's a problem we have to talk about," she said. "What would happen if the people you preach to found out my secret? We wouldn't be your usual couple, you know."

"Then I'd say 'to hell with 'em' and we'd pack up the car and the dog and move to a different place. But times are changing. Before long nobody'll care anyhow. So will you come with me?"

This time she didn't hesitate. "I will." She leaned across the counter, threw her arms around Drayton's neck and kissed him.

Drayton pulled his Moon in behind Cappy's old Ford, parked in front of the Giberson house. Cappy, Worthy, and Tick were waiting by the gate. When Drayton stepped out of the Moon, his dog raced to him, jumping and licking, nearly knocking him over. "I see she's picked up some bad habits," Drayton said to Worthy, fending off the dog. "It'll take a year to get her back to normal after being around you." But there was no rancor in his words.

Worthy reached down and rubbed the dog's ears. "I never thought I'd hear myself say this, but she can stay here till you get settled, Hunt. For a dog, she ain't half bad."

Drayton was touched by the offer. "Thank you kindly, Worthy, but I'll be taking her along. I've been missing the old girl. I'd better be going, I've got a house to get sold." He moved toward his car, then stopped and looked back. "You know, Cap, if it wasn't for that pretty face of yours, you'd be the spitting image of your daddy."

Cappy watched as Drayton drove away in his Moon. A small cloud of dust followed, like his regrets.

In the week since Bum's funeral, Cappy had tried to get up nerve to see Oleeta. He could have telephoned, but he wanted to talk to her face-to-face. He wasn't sure what he'd say, but he hoped the right words would come to him. Now that his life was evening out, he wanted to make up for the past weeks of seeming to avoid her. Tentatively, he knocked on the back door.

Oleeta opened the door a crack. She had just finished washing and pin-curling her hair, the bobby pins held in place by a yellow scarf. "Come in out of the cold." She opened the door wide.

"The snow's really coming down, more like February than December," Cappy said, brushing off his cap. Oleeta moved aside. He stomped the wet snow from his boots and stepped into the warm kitchen. "I'm sorry I haven't come around sooner. It must be lonesome with your pa gone."

"I figured you had better things to do than coddle me," Oleeta said. Her voice was as icy as Jones Pond.

"Not better things, but I had to work out some problems with my past, and you know I've been trying to find a newspaper job. I couldn't ask you out when I didn't have any money. But Joe Bray, the editor at the *Post-Dispatch*, has a friend in the publishing business who's interested in my writing. Now all I have to do is come up with enough stories for a book. I was hoping to be farther along before I told you. In the meantime, Joe will pay me for any articles he publishes, which means I won't be rich, but I won't be flat broke."

"How wonderful for you," she said, without enthusiasm. "I have some news, too. I've sent my readmission papers to Blackburn. After the first of the year I'll be leaving."

"Oh—"

"Cappy Giberson! Is that all you can say? How is it you can write wonderful imaginative stories, but you can't put two words together when they really matter!"

"Well—"

"Well nothing! Either you want me to stay or you don't!"

Cappy wasn't expecting to have a say in her plans. "Of course I'd like for you to stay, but—"

"You know I can't stay. I've already put off finishing my degree longer than I should have. Now that Pa's gone, I'll be closing the house until I graduate, and then I'll probably sell it. I sure don't intend to stay and mildew in Old Kane."

Cappy was surprised. He couldn't picture her living anyplace else.

She cleared her few breakfast dishes from the table and carried them to the sink. "How long before you can finish your book?" she said, her anger subsiding.

"At least a year, and then there are revisions, and another year before it's published. *If* it gets published."

"Then here's what we'll do, I've given this a lot of thought. I'll go back to Blackburn, and you'll stay here and write your book." Oleeta knew what was best for both of them.

"But you know we can't be together five minutes without arguing—"

"We haven't argued *every* time we've been together," she interrupted, "or have you forgotten that night in your car after the minstrel show?"

"Of course I haven't forgotten, especially how you made me stop before—"

"You didn't believe me when I said I intended to wait until I'm married."

"I hoped I could change your mind."

"Before that night I thought you were shy or didn't like me. You weren't exactly tearing my clothes off."

"I'm not shy. But I haven't had any experience with girls like you."

"You mean with a virgin?"

"After that night in the car, you acted distant. I thought I'd ruined everything."

"I was distant because I didn't trust myself to say no the next time. And I'm serious about waiting for marriage." She reached up and hugged Cappy. "Then have we agreed to be engaged while I finish my degree and you write your book?"

He stepped back. "Who said anything about being engaged? Don't be putting words in my mouth, Oleeta.

What if you graduate from Blackburn and my book gets published, and one of us changes our mind? I think we should see how we both feel when we're more settled."

"Cap Giberson! You're the most aggravating man I've ever known. Maybe I'll flunk out of school, and maybe your book won't be any good. There aren't any guarantees. A farmer has no guarantees his crops will grow, but if he doesn't plant the seed, the guarantee is that there won't even be a crop!"

Cappy laughed. "I didn't know you were so good at metaphors. Maybe *you* should be the writer."

But Oleeta wasn't laughing. "This isn't going to work. You're determined not to listen to what's best for us. Go on home, Cappy, I've got a lot to do. Maybe I'll see you around town before I leave." She opened the door.

He pulled up the collar of his coat and stepped into the snowy morning. "I'm sorry," he said, turning to look at her.

"No you aren't." She closed the door before he could say anything else. Her eyes filled with angry tears. "Come back when you grow up, Cappy Giberson!" she shouted to the empty house. She finished addressing a large manila envelope to Blackburn College, Carlinville, Illinois, added two stamps, and carried her readmission application to the mailbox.

Now that the evenings were too cold to sit on the front stoop, the Giberson men huddled around the woodstove for their evening talks. Together they made up three generations. Father, son, grandson. Tick was his son by birth, with Cappy coming by accident, although Tick claimed there were no accidents. Cappy would be leaving once his book was finished, but Worthy suspected Tick was home for the long haul.

"I dropped in on Oleeta this morning," Cappy said to Worthy, warming his hands over the stove. "She suggested an engagement while she's at school and I'm writing my book. And then marriage. What do you think about that?"

"You're getting married?" Tick said. He had counted on the three of them living together, having meals together, watching television together.

Worthy didn't answer right away. "Marriage is a mighty big step in a fella's life. It's different with girls, they grow up dreaming about their wedding day. Their mamas see to that. But boys have a built-in suspicion when it comes to marriage, and rightly so, like an old hen has a built-in suspicion of a chicken hawk." Worthy stirred the coals and laid the poker back on the hearth. "But now that I think about it, maybe you and Oleeta getting married might be a good idea. If she'd forget about going back to school, you and her could get married right away. But you'd have to put off writing your book and get a real job with a regular paycheck. Would you be moving into Bum's house?"

Cappy hadn't expected Worthy to agree with Oleeta. "But I'm not ready to jump into marriage," Cappy protested. "Two years isn't long to wait while she finishes school, and who knows what will happen by then?"

"Of course you run the risk of her finding another fella," Worthy pointed out.

Cappy thought about that. He pictured Oleeta with the determined look on her face and her yellow head scarf and smiled to himself. "Maybe being engaged wouldn't be so bad."

"Women always have to run things," Tick said.

"Well, boys, what do you say I heat up this morning's coffee and we have us a cupcake apiece?" Worthy said. Obediently, as if they were children, Cappy and Tick left the warmth of the stove and followed Worthy to the kitchen table. He shook the coffeepot to make sure there was some coffee left, set the pot on the burner, and took three packages of Hostess cupcakes from the cupboard.

"I ran into Drayton this morning, before he picked up his dog," Cappy said. "He told me he's leaving town as soon as he can sell his mother's house."

"Jesus, if them walls could only talk, half of Old Kane would be red-faced," Worthy said. "Mae Hunt, she was quite the woman. Leastways that's what I heard," he added.

"He says he's going to try preaching," Cappy said.

"Won't that be something to hear!" Worthy said. "I may never stomach the man, but I don't wish bad luck on him. Now I'm for changing the tune. Say, Tick, how are you when it comes to bluegill fishing?"

"I'm good, Pa. Just thinking about fried bluegills makes my mouth water!"

Worthy winced. If only you was here to help out, Willa. I'm about wore out from being chief cook and housemaid.

The coffee finished perking. Cappy filled three cups, and Worthy handed each of his sons a package of two chocolate cupcakes.

Tick tore off the cellophane as if he were opening a Christmas gift. "What else but home is so good as this?" he said. He took a mouthful of cake and licked icing from his fingers. "It's just like old times."

"She's close," Worthy said, dipping his cupcake into his coffee. "But close only counts in horseshoes."